And Then She Came Back

A Detective Inspector Benedict Paige Novel: Book 1

Joshua Black

Rathbone Publishing

Joshua Black

Joshua Black is the pen name of Rupert Colley.

rupertcolley.com/joshua-black/

And Then She Came Back

R
Rathbone
Publishing

rupertcolley.com/joshua-black/

Prologue

Camden, North London, February 2023

Monday, eleven at night, and Antonio Cassese was worried – he was running late and he needed to get home as quickly as possible. He broke a red light on the high street, pressing his foot on the accelerator. Hopefully, Maria would be in bed by now, fast asleep and wouldn't hear him come in. But what if she wasn't? She'd demand to know why he was so late. Just a quick drink after work, he'd said. He'd be back by nine, he promised. Problem was she could spot a lie from a mile off; he'd never been able to lie to his wife; she always knew.

He took a right, taking the quieter back streets to home. Did he smell of her perfume? Maria would smell it on him. Damn, he should've been more careful but he'd got carried away, they both had. He was never going to get away with this; Maria was going to crush his balls once she found out.

He took a right onto Maynard Road, a tree-lined residential street with the sort of houses that Maria and he had always aspired to have. Not on their wages. It was never going

1

to happen.

He had to slow down to allow an old man walking his dog to cross at a pedestrian crossing. The man was taking an age. 'Hurry up, will you?' said Antonio, tapping his fingers on the steering wheel.

He sped off as soon as he could, putting his foot down. Almost home now.

A figure stepped out of nowhere. A girl, a young woman. He slammed on the brakes. Too late; he heard the sickening thud. He screamed as the car came to a screeching halt. He saw the girl on the ground via the rearview mirror. He swore. He needed to check but then in the mirror, he could see a second figure, someone running across the road. He was about to open the door and see whether the girl he hit was OK. He hesitated. The second person was a nurse, she was wearing the uniform. What to do? He had to get home but he'd hit someone. But if there was a nurse there, the girl would be OK; the nurse would look after her, do the right thing.

With his heart beating madly, Antonio gently pressed his foot on the accelerator and drew away.

He checked the mirror again and in doing so clipped his car against a parked car on the passenger side. He yanked the steering to the right. It was fine, it was fine, just a scrap. 'Christ, bloody hell,' he said aloud. One thing after another.

He should have stopped, he knew that, but it was already too late. He was committed now.

Five minutes later, Antonio drew up outside his house, still shaking. He just hoped the girl he hit was OK and, more importantly, he hoped Maria would be fast asleep by now.

Chapter 1: Benedict

Camden, North London, February 2023

Monday, eleven at night, Detective Inspector Benedict Paige was pleased to be driving home on what was a blustery but mild evening in late February. It'd been a long, rather tedious day of paperwork, writing reports and reading memos. He'd finished by eight and, after a hastily consumed sandwich, joined a couple of old colleagues turned friends for a drink. He never really relished remaining sober while those around him rapidly became inebriated. But he enjoyed their company as they reminisced on old cases and old faces, colleagues long gone, retired or dead, often bitter, invariably cynical but, if asked, wouldn't have changed a thing about their life's trajectory.

Now, driving slowly in his rather ancient Vauxhall Corsa through the residential streets of Camden Town, he switched on the radio and hummed along to the old Elton John and Kiki Dee hit, *Don't Go Breaking My Heart*. He was looking forward to getting home and seeing Sonia. Another busy day tomorrow and an important one – he was expecting his new Detective Sergeant, a woman he interviewed, transferring down from Manchester, young, keen and sharp as a pin.

He swung right onto Hatherley Avenue, a long, quiet street lined by trees. And up ahead he could see the flashing blue lights – both police and an ambulance. He considered reversing and heading down an alternative route but no, slowing down, he inched forward until a uniformed policewoman in a hi-vis jacket, standing in front of a blue and white police tape, ordered him to stop.

He stepped out of his car, buttoning up his coat.

'You'll need to turn around and find a different route, sir,' said the woman.

He flashed his ID card. 'Anything I can help with?'

'Oh, sir, sorry, didn't recognise you. Looks like a hit and run.'

He stepped under the tape and approached. One of the uniformed officers greeted him.

'You alright, constable? How's it going? Injury or…?'

'Yes, sir. Teenage girl. Not looking good though.'

Another uniform stood guard while two paramedics were carefully lifting the groaning girl onto a stretcher. The fact she was making a noise at all was probably a good thing. It was too dark and her face too obscured by her hair to see her face, beyond the fact that she was white, but he spied a pair of white earbuds loose around her head.

'How is she?' he asked.

'Not good,' said the male paramedic, as he and his colleague lifted the stretcher.

Benedict followed them as they hurried towards the open doors of the ambulance. 'Heavily concussed,' said the male medic. 'A couple of broken bones and some blood loss.'

'We reckon the driver was going far too fast,' said his female colleague. 'It's a twenty zone here. No way she was hit at twenty, not with these injuries.' They hoisted the stretcher into the ambulance.

'Good evening, sir,' said another police officer, Police Constable Stevens, snapping his notebook closed. 'Parents have been informed. They're on the way to the hospital as we speak.'

'St Cuthbert's?'

'Yes.'

'Do we know who she is?'

'Yes, she had the provisional on her.' PC Stevens consulted his notes. 'Zoe Wright, recently turned eighteen, lives three streets along. I reckon she was walking back from the Red Lion pub.'

The ambulance speeded off, its siren blaring.

'Witnesses?'

Stevens shook his head. 'Only the guy who found her. He was keen to help but he didn't witness the actual collision. I've taken a statement. Thirty-year-old walking home from his girlfriend's further down the street.'

'Was he the one who phoned 999?'

'No, sir, that's the thing. It seems it was Zoe herself.'

'She was able to phone 999, in her state?'

'That's the weird thing, sir, she didn't *call* 999, she texted it.'

'She *texted*? Sounds implausible, surely.'

'One would have thought so.'

Benedict paced around, focussing on the tarmac. 'Doesn't appear to be any skid marks or glass but we'll double check when it's light. I'm guessing there won't be CCTV on a street like this.'

'Nope, sadly not.'

'And looking at the size of these front gardens, I doubt any door cameras will reach far enough, and that's assuming there are any at this precise point. Still worth checking tomorrow though. Might get lucky.'

'That was the plan, sir.'

'Yes, of course. Well, let's hope the driver comes forward. They have twenty-four hours to report it otherwise…' He left the sentence hanging.

'I know, sir.'

'Right. Good.' He glanced at his watch. "Follow them to the hospital, would you?'

'Yes, sir.'

His phone pinged as he turned the ignition. 'You home soon? x'

'Ten minutes.' Then, for good measure, he added, 'Keep the bed warm!'

Sonia would smile at that!

Chapter 2: Benedict

Seven thirty, Tuesday morning, only just light. Benedict Paige was at the mirror in his bedroom's en suite bathroom, having a shave, while Sonia, his olive-skinned wife, got dressed in the bedroom. The radio news hummed quietly in the background while, not so quietly, his children were rampaging downstairs, arguing over breakfast.

'So, looking forward to meeting her?' asked Sonia.

'Hmm? Who?'

'Your new detective sergeant, obviously.'

'Oh her, yes, sure.'

'So, she's a woman?'

He patted his face dry. 'Yes. You know that.'

'Did you ask for a woman?'

He smiled at his reflection. 'Yes, I specifically asked for a tall, leggy, blonde. Why, you OK with that?'

She didn't answer for a moment and Benedict thought she might actually be taking him at his word. He walked through to the bedroom to find her sitting at the dresser, applying a layer of lipstick. 'It'll be a nice change from the usual short-arsed plump bloke I usually get.'

'Very funny,' she said, through puckered lips. 'Well, I hope she lives up to your expectations.'

'That's quite a low bar, to be honest,' he said, picking out a tie.

'As long as she knows how she stands.'

'Yes, my dear.'

'Why don't you wear your new suit in her honour?'

He'd quite forgotten that his wife had made him buy a new, dark blue suit recently at an eye-watering price. And he didn't even care much for it. 'Oh, I don't want to go overboard. Maybe next week. You got a busy day ahead?' he asked quickly.

She told him as he adjusted his tie above her. His wife worked as an architect for Camden council, but Benedict's mind soon drifted off, thinking instead of Zoe Wright, the poor girl lying in hospital, victim of a hit and run, her parents no doubt beside themselves with worry. He thought of Charlotte, buzzing around downstairs, making a fuss over who had hidden her school shoes. It didn't bear thinking about. Why didn't the driver stop? He couldn't, in all consciousness, drive off like that, leaving a person for dead, lying in the middle of a road, late at night. Why would someone text, not ring, 999 on *her* phone? It didn't make sense. By the time the paramedics had picked her up, she'd already lost a lot of blood. He only hoped the driver would wake up this morning, wracked with guilt and come to the rightful decision.

'Ben, have you been listening to me? Can you see what Charlotte wants? And make sure Harry's got his history book. He forgot it yesterday – again.'

'Yeah, yeah, sure.'

'And, erm, good luck today. Hope it goes well.'

'Thanks.' Placing his hand on her shoulder, he kissed her on the top of her head. She patted his hand and smiled. 'Thanks, love. I love you.'

'And I love you too.'

Sonia and Benedict had been married for fourteen years. It almost never happened, her parents, traditional Hindus, were not keen on their only daughter marrying outside the community but, eventually, Benedict's charm offensive slowly eroded their concerns and finally they consented. Just as well, because Sonia had made it clear – she would never have married him without her parents' blessing.

*

'Has she arrived yet?' asked Benedict of Detective Constable Jamie Kelly, an angular, fair-haired Scotsman, sitting at his desk.

'You mean Detective Sergeant Gardiner, sir? Aye, she's speaking to HR right now.'

A rake-thin man, DC Kelly was the sort who smiled a lot, an endearing feature even if it did, on occasion, seem a little inappropriate. At the desk next to him, Detective Constable Andrew Prowse, a London lad of colour, broad across the shoulders, a man who worked out; both of them, Kelly and Prowse, were in their mid-twenties, keen, good at their jobs, knowledgeable but strangely ignorant of the wider world beyond their work.

'HR, eh?' said Benedict. 'Well, if that doesn't send her scurrying back to Manchester, nothing will.'

'She'll be down in a minute.'

Benedict hoped she'd be happy here. Their first-floor office had recently benefited from a fresh lick of paint, three white walls and one 'feature' wall of bright green, bare apart from a large, framed portrait of King Charles. The office hummed with its usual activity, staff tapping on keyboards, hushed telephone conversations, the occasional ping on someone's mobile. On one side, three glass booths for the senior team, one of them belonging to Benedict's manager, Detective Chief Inspector George Lincoln. Benedict's desk was next to the window, and he'd always found the view over the city rather soothing, a London park always busy with dog walkers and joggers and beyond the treeline, reaching up, a church spire. Benedict tried it once – jogging. It almost killed him; he felt like a fraud, being overtaken by people twice his age, doubling over and wheezing after barely a few minutes. Never again.

Benedict kept his desk tidy, the only officer in the office whoever did. His colleagues accused him of having too much time on his hands if he had time to keep all his paperwork and reports tidy and organised. He had no framed photos of his children, and he kept an unopened pack of biscuits, namely chocolate digestives, in his bottom drawer there for 'emergencies'.

He logged onto his desktop computer. 'Any updates on last night's hit and run?'

'Yes,' said DC Prowse. 'The driver who hit her did some damage. The hospital hasn't released details except that she's in a coma and they're monitoring her progress. It's not looking too good, to be honest, boss.'

'That's a shame. What about her clothing?'

'Yeah, already on their way to the lab.'

'Any skid marks?'

Prowse shook his head.

'Glass?'

'No.'

'OK. Let me know if you hear anything.'

'Sir.'

Twenty minutes later, the new DS, Jessica Gardiner, made her first appearance. She nodded a hello at Kelly and Prowse, having obviously met them before.

Benedict introduced himself again, having met her at her interview, shaking her hand and welcoming her to the station.

'It's great to be here, sir,' she said, her Manchester accent breaking through. She had a short boy-cut hairstyle, dyed blonde, bright red lipstick and hazel penetrating eyes. Her handshake was reassuringly firm. Benedict put her in her early thirties – the perfect age for a detective, experienced enough to have been around the block a few times but without the inevitable cynicism that his older colleagues had absorbed. At forty, he was heading that way himself, he knew it, and however hard he fought it, he knew it was a losing battle. He pointed to a desk. 'This is yours, DS Gardiner. Make yourself at home. You've seen HR and survived.'

She chortled while placing her jacket over the back of her chair. 'Yes, sir.'

'Well, that was the hardest challenge you'll face for some time.' He sat at his desk. 'If you survive that, you'll be fine.'

Benedict checked whether she had her credentials for logging onto the network and made sure her email was working. He updated her on the hit-and-run. 'Uniform will be knocking on doors as we speak, but it was late, gone eleven, so we're not expecting much, if anything. Hatherley Avenue is a quiet residential street, very middle class, very respectable, you know the type.'

'Like where you live, sir?' asked Kelly with a grin.

'Yes, thanks for that, Kelly. Haven't you got something to be getting on with?'

'Any doorbell CCTV?' asked Jessica.

'We're hoping. Fingers crossed, eh? We're also checking the Automatic Number Plate Recognition–'

'The ANPR?'

'Yes. We're checking it for any dubious vehicles within a mile radius of the incident. I think it might be an idea if we pay a visit to St Cuthbert's hospital. If the parents aren't there, we'll go see them. I want them to see we're taking this seriously.'

He encouraged her to use her list of passwords to access the various databases and shared drives.

'Not much going on at the moment, but, being Camden, that won't last long so make the use of this time while you've got it. Get yourself frequented with as much as you can. Go see the guys in IT; they'll have your phone for you.'

'Sir.'

'Oh, and no doubt, the DCI will want to see you at some point. You'll remember him from your interview.'

'Oh yes, a lovely man.'

Paige smiled to himself. It was the first time he'd ever heard DCI Lincoln described as that. Poor woman; she'd soon learn.

Chapter 3: Benedict

Benedict and Jessica had finished talking to a doctor in the ward office and were about to go through the ward to see Zoe and speak to her parents. The doctor said that her injuries were consistent with being hit by a vehicle travelling at a speed not far off forty miles per hour. She also said that, given the extent of her injuries, there was no way she would have been in a fit state to text the emergency services. Yes, it had been her phone, but someone else must have used it.

Zoe Wright lay in her bed, a number of tubes monitoring her progress. Her parents sat on either side, her mother holding her hand. Benedict and Jessica hung back while a nurse took Zoe's blood pressure. Once finished, Benedict stepped forward, clearing his throat.

'Mr and Mrs Wright?' He showed them his ID and introduced Jessica and himself.

'It's Ms Johnstone, but it doesn't matter,' said the woman. 'Call me Tracey. This is my partner Phil.' She was white, her partner black. She had a pleasant smile, but, understandably, looked tired, her eyes drawn beneath the layer of mascara.

'Do you mind if we join you for a couple of minutes?' said Benedict.

'How is Zoe?' asked Jessica, while Benedict found two chairs.

'What do you think?' asked Phil. 'Look at her. Does she look well to you?'

'It's OK, Phil,' said Tracey in a gentle tone. 'She's only asking. The doctor says she's suffered from some internal bleeding and–'

'Some?' interrupted her partner. '*Extensive*, Trace. That was her word – extensive.'

'And head trauma.'

'She'll live,' said Phil. 'But we won't know how this might affect her, you know, long term. Head injuries…' He didn't finish the sentence.

'But whatever happens, we'll be here for her,' added Tracey.

'Of course,' said Jessica.

'Has anyone come forward yet?' asked Phil, sitting forward on his chair, the anger rising off him like steam.

'No, sir,' said Jessica. 'Unfortunately not.'

'There's a surprise, the cowardly bastard. I mean, yeah, it was probably an accident. We all drive too fast sometimes, especially late at night, but then not to stop, well, that takes some doing.'

'Sir, someone texted 999 from your daughter's phone,' said Benedict.

'Texted? Did you say text? I didn't know you could do that. Hang on, did you say from Zoe's phone?'

'Yes. Zoe couldn't have done it but someone, maybe the person who hit Zoe, did.'

'But they wouldn't have known the passcode.'

'You don't need the passcode to phone 999,' said Tracey.

14

'What we want to know,' said Benedict, 'is why didn't this person wait for the ambulance with Zoe, keeping her company and offering comfort?'

'Why didn't they use their own phone?' asked Phil, running his hand over his bald plate.

'It is a puzzle,' said Benedict.

'You'll catch them, won't you?' said Tracey, her hand tightening over her daughter's.

'We hope so, madam,' said Jessica. 'We'll be appealing for witnesses and checking to see whether anyone on the street has CCTV on their doorbells.'

'We've also sent her outer clothing for analysis,' added Benedict. 'We're looking for paint fragments, fibreglass or glass, although it looks like there were no broken headlamps.'

'Paint fragments? So what? You find it belongs to a Ford or something, that's not going to be helpful.'

'You'd be surprised, sir,' said Jessica. 'The paint from a vehicle can often be traced back to a specific make and even model.'

'Each car manufacturer will mix paints to a specific formula,' added Benedict. 'What we might think are two identical shades can actually have distinct compositions. We're feeling hopeful, sir.'

'Right.' The man didn't look convinced.

'Tracey,' said Jessica. 'Can you tell us about Zoe's movements last night?'

Tracey did the talking, telling Jessica about her daughter's night out – where she'd been, who with, and what time. She'd texted as she was leaving the pub, a seven-minute walk from home. When she hadn't returned after twenty minutes and wasn't responding to her mother's calls, they began to get concerned. After another ten minutes, two uniformed police officers appeared at their door.

'Right,' said Benedict. He glanced at Jessica. 'I think we've got everything.' He stood and handed Phil his card. 'Thanks for your time, and we wish Zoe a speedy recovery. We'll be in touch as soon as we get anything.'

Chapter 4: Mac

Five p.m. The block of flats loomed high in the London sky, dozens of lights twinkling. Mac tightened his scarf as he made his way towards Holbrook House, his shoes echoing on the dry pavement. He stopped to say hello to a little tabby cat slinking by. The flats were a 1960s urban block of flats in Kilburn, part of London's Camden borough, an ugly monstrosity of a building, a sort of place you wouldn't want to hang around outside late at night. It had a reputation for iniquitous activities, a magnet for drug dealers, petty crime and general nastiness. It was certainly considered a police no-go area. Nothing untoward had ever happened to him, yet each time, Mac felt as if he was running some sort of gauntlet by coming here.

Sure enough, he saw ahead of him, a group of young men, some white, some black, leaning against a car and a couple of mopeds, most of them wearing hoodies. They positively reeked of attitude. One of them had a massive dog straining on its lead, looking like he was sizing Mac up. He didn't know what type but it looked like one of those illegal breeds and looked mightily ferocious. The animal wasn't a pet; it was a bloody weapon.

He slipped his mobile into his back pocket, and kept his eyes down, aware of the total silence. No one was talking. He knew they were watching him. Mac was tall, broad-shouldered, but still, he was alone and acutely aware of his vulnerability. He walked quickly, aiming for the huge double doors fronting the block. One of the boys switched on the ignition to his moped and revved the engine. Mac quickened his pace. The boys giggled; they knew they'd spooked him. As long as it was all they wanted to do. He reached the door and sighed with relief as he entered the brightly lit interior.

It was a Tuesday night. Three or four times a week, straight after work, Mac visited his grandmother, making sure she was OK, that she was warm. He liked to check she'd eaten OK, something hot and nutritional. He always arrived with a couple more ready meals, not ideal, he knew that, but better than cheese on toast. Granny had little tolerance for anything too exotic, she liked her food traditional and plain – and preferably *English*. He did her washing, did a bit of housework and cleaned her toilet.

Granny lived on the eighth floor. What a place. The communal hallway was always being graffitied, the landing lights flickered and the lifts reeked of God-knows-what.

Truth was, however, Mac never truly relished these visits. His grandmother wasn't the easiest of people and while, on the whole, she was a silent person but when she did talk, she liked nothing more than to complain – about her neighbours, about their noisy children, the threatening youth, about the council, the politicians on the news, whatever it was, nothing was immune to her scorn. She lived alone. Mac had never met his grandfather who, apparently, buggered off decades ago.

Whether she appreciated Mac's frequent visits, he didn't know. She never said and certainly never thanked him or paid him for his purchases on her behalf.

He came out of the lift onto the eighth floor and, switching on the timed light, headed across the landing towards his grandmother's flat. He was about to insert his key when the neighbour's door opened, and there, wearing a floral frock, was Granny's neighbour, Mrs Angelopoulos, a name that Granny had never managed to pronounce properly, nor, out of some sort of misguided principle, had she wanted to.

'Mr Mac.' She always called him 'Mr Mac'. 'How are you? Hey, your grandmother had a visitor yesterday, very late.'

'My uncle?'

'No, a nurse.'

Now, he didn't expect that – apart from him and Uncle Geoff, Granny had never had a visitor since he'd started checking up on her. 'Really?'

'Seems very late to have a visitor – even a nurse. Is your grandmother poorly?' He caught the woman's gleeful tone.

'No. Well, she wasn't two days ago. Did they stay long, this nurse?'

Mrs Angelopoulos threw her hands in the air. 'I don't know. I saw her leave. I didn't see her arrive. I have better things to do than stare at your grandmother's door.'

'Yes, of course. Well, thanks for letting me know. I'd better go in and check how she is,' he said, holding up the key.

'You must send her our regards. We like your grandmother.' He'd met Mrs Angelopoulos several times but hadn't, to this day, set eyes on Mr Angelopoulos. She smiled and withdrew to her flat.

Funny that, thought Mac, for his grandmother had nothing but scorn for her Greek neighbours.

Mac entered the flat, expecting to see Granny sitting in her usual place in front of the TV, usually scoffing her way through a box of chocolates from the table next to her. But she wasn't there. He called out her name. She must've nipped to the toilet. But something felt off-kilter, something that made him alert, conscious of the flat's silence. He noticed, as he always did, the large wooden crucifix hanging from the wall above the fireplace – not that his grandmother ever mentioned religion.

The door to the bathroom was ajar, the light off – she wasn't there. Tiptoeing across the laminate floor, he called her name again. She wasn't in the tiny kitchen. His grandmother was forever making herself cups of tea but the kettle was cold to the touch. A dirty plate lay in the sink, submerged in slimy, cold water.

It left only the bedroom. He knocked and, in receiving no reply, eased the door open. She was in bed. But his relief lasted but a moment. She looked odd, lying on her back but with her head arched back on the pillow. Her arms rested on top of the duvet. He knew she was not asleep, not in that position. He rushed over. 'Granny, what's the matter? Granny?'

Her eyes were open but vacant, her mouth wide open, a spiel of saliva drooling but… was that really saliva? Oh Christ, that was not saliva; what the fuck was that? He leaned over, trying to fathom what it was. His hand flew to his mouth. Was that…? Christ, that couldn't be… The bile rushed up his throat. He ran out of the bedroom and into the bathroom, flinging himself in front of the toilet, and threw up. It kept coming, a torrent of vomit, unending. Finally, once he'd puked up everything he had, he wiped his eyes. He couldn't control his breathing. He must've imagined it; it couldn't be real. He had to check. No, he couldn't; it was too disgusting. No way he was going back in there. But, yes, slowly, he crept back into the bedroom, his eyes half closed. How silent everything seemed. He approached the bed on quiet feet. He opened his eyes. Fuck, yes, it was still there; he hadn't imagined it: poking out from his grandmother's mouth, a long pink tail, the tail of a mouse, a white mouse.

Chapter 5: Mac

Mac could hear the siren of an ambulance fast approaching. He paced the living room, still feeling sick. He couldn't get the vision out of his head; it was too revolting for words; it was beyond comprehension; his mind couldn't cope with what he'd seen. Eight minutes later, he opened the flat door to two paramedics, both of them rather overweight, a man and a woman.

'You alright?' said the man. 'You say your grandmother's passed?'

He couldn't speak.

'You alright, sir? You look…'

'There's a… a…' He couldn't bring himself to say the words. He pointed at the bedroom. They went through while Mac hovered at the door, unable to look at his grandmother again.

'Oh, shit,' said the woman.

'Christ, what is that?' said the man.

'You're shitting us.'

They both turned to him but Mac still couldn't speak.

'Call the police,' said the woman.

'Yes, Christ. A mouse? This is so messed up.'

'Will you stop saying that?' screamed Mac, suddenly finding his voice.

'I'm sorry, sir,' said the woman. 'It's just… well, a bit of a shock. I've never seen–'

'And you think I have?'

Her colleague dialled the police.

Back in the living room, the female medic asked, 'How old was she; what's her name?'

He told them. Marjorie McIntosh aged eighty-nine. 'Apparently, a nurse came to see her yesterday.'

'Really?' asked the woman medic. 'Were you here?'

He told her what Mrs Angelopoulos had told him.

'So we don't know what sort of nurse she was, or what hospital or surgery she was from?'

'No.'

'Was your grandmother expecting this visit? Were you aware of it?'

'No.' Mac rubbed his chin.

'You see, the thing is, I reckon your grandmother was suffocated.'

The word hit him like a fist. 'Suffocated?'

'I can't be totally sure but the autopsy will tell you.'

'Autopsy?'

'Of course. There has to be an autopsy.'

Mac reeled back; how come he hadn't noticed? Because he'd been too repulsed by that… that pink tail protruding from her mouth.

'Why would anyone do this?'

The woman shook her head. 'That I can't tell you.'

'Was she on any medication?' asked the male medic.

'Does it matter?'

'We have to ask.'

'She took Enalapril, is that what's it called?'

'High blood pressure.'

'Yes.'

'It helps relax the patient's blood vessels.'

'But what we need to know,' said the woman, 'is why a nurse was here.'

He sat on his grandmother's sofa while the two medics squashed in together on the settee to the side of him, all three staring at the switched-off television in front of them. If this got any more awkward, thought Mac, he'd actually turn the TV on. Every few minutes, one of their radios would bleep but they ignored them. He rubbed his eyes. This was beyond surreal.

Fifteen minutes later, Mac heard, for the second time that evening, the sound of a siren.

The woman leaned over. 'You ready for this? They'll do a good job; everything will be fine.'

He tried to smile as he heard the police car come to a halt outside, but he wasn't convinced. Something told him that, quite the contrary, everything was going to be far from fine.

Chapter 6: Derek

Tottenham Court Road, Central London, December 1982

It was another dull day at Supervision Televisions. Derek's colleague, Ruth Jones, was busy with her paperwork while Derek helped a young, well-to-do couple choose the best rental option for the new GoldStar set which came with the most sophisticated battery-powered remote control. The song *Mickey* by Toni Basil played on the speakers assaulting Derek's ears. He hated that sort of music. He'd have thought a young, trendy couple would be impressed by the GoldStar but, whatever he said, he knew they remained unconvinced. He spent a whole fifteen minutes trying to charm them. He needed to make the sale here; the end of the month was fast approaching and he was well short of his target – again. He knew Mr Smith, his boss, disliked him, and thought he sucked at his job. He didn't care on a personal level but he needed to keep on the boss's good side for the sake of his job. Miss Jones, on the other hand, could do no wrong in Smith's eyes, what with her eye shadow and her designer jackets and chiffon scarves, of which she seemed to have a different one for each day of the week, the sun positively shone out of that woman's arse. They weren't colleagues here; they were rivals.

The young couple stood and thanked him profusely for his time but said they wanted to 'consider their options' before committing. Derek smiled his rictus smile while inside he just wanted to tell them to fuck off. He knew he'd never see them again; they'd been a waste of his time.

The door swung shut behind the couple. He could see them putting up their umbrellas before heading off, probably down the road to Ready Rentals, the newer, shinier alternative to Supervision, a shop full of colour and glitz and staffed by men in sharp suits and women with shoulder pads.

'That went well, Derek,' said Miss Jones, a satisfied smirk on her phizog.

'They were never going to buy anyway. Not even you could have landed that one.'

'So why did you waste so much time on them?'

'Well, there's no one else here, is there, smart alec?' He lit a cigarette, blowing his smoke out in Jones' direction.

Jones waved the smoke away. 'You know Mr Smith doesn't approve.'

'He doesn't approve of your fat arse, but so what? He's out anyway, just the two of us.'

The jibe landed, he could tell. She tutted and busied herself with her paperwork. Derek hated his job here. The shop, long and narrow, reeked of desperation, its shitty-coloured brown decor made it appear like something from the seventies. And he was surrounded by televisions switched on all day, every day, different channels, with the volume turned off, unless turned up as part of a demonstration. He always went home at the end of the day with a headache, the flashing colours of all those bloody TVs penetrating his eyes, leaving him quite dizzy. And then the piped music. The same couple of cassettes on repeat all day, every day. Some crap by Wham! was playing right now.

He was still only twenty-five but he was working in a dead-end job more suited to someone twice his age. But he needed this job. Good knows, money was short at home and he needed the money to fund his guilty secret – an occasional flutter at the bookmakers.

Miss Jones carried on with her paperwork while humming along to some shambolic tune by the Madness. That was the other thing Derek hated about this place – they still used pen and paper and ledger books and little calculators and handwritten invoices, and Post-It notes, Tippex, posters written with felt-tip pens, everything so bloody old-fashioned. He'd long campaigned for a computer, one of those smart ZX Spectrum computers or, even better, a Commodore 64 with its daisy wheel printers, like they had in Ready Rentals. But Mr Smith wouldn't entertain it; said they were too expensive and, anyway, why pay all that when pen and paper served just as well?

'When's he back?' he asked a few minutes later.

'Who? Mr Smith? He'll be back before closing, he said.'

The final humiliation came at the end of the day, serving the last customers. Again, a couple, it usually was, but these two were quite old, perhaps in their sixties. They sat on the customer side of the desk from Derek, sipping the tea he'd made them both. They wanted to rent. An actual sale was always better but landing a rental deal was still OK. The woman didn't say a word, leaving it all to her husband. Again, Derek was pushing the GoldStar, hoping to impress them with its technology and its superior performance. They were certainly enthusiastic, and Derek, feeling confident, went for the closure. Miss Jones was earwigging, but he didn't care, let her witness how it's done. He sensed he'd impressed the man sufficiently to the point he simply had to have *this* model, whatever the price.

He was wrong. The sale fell apart the moment he mentioned the monthly rental cost.

'How much?' exclaimed the man. 'You're having a laugh. Look, are you seeing a handle on the side of me head?'

'I'm sorry, sir? I don't understand.'

'You think I'm a mug, is that it, mate?'

Miss Jones laughed out loud at this, unable to stifle her mirth. That's when the man noticed her. 'If I'm so funny, miss, what do you suggest, eh?'

'Ah, well, I was thinking, sir, maybe you'd be more comfortable, price-wise, with the…'

And she stepped in, she bloody stepped in and took over, making Derek look like a real dunce, a fixed grin plastered to her face. He caught the woman staring at him and he wanted to ask what the fuck she was staring at, the ugly cow, but he just about managed to hold onto his tongue.

Within a matter of minutes, Jones had sealed the deal. The contract was signed, a deposit paid and a delivery date agreed. The couple went out happy, the man thanking Jones profusely. The woman shot Derek a final, cutting look as she followed her husband out of the shop.

'Well done, Miss Jones,' said Derek. 'But I'm still gonna claim that one.'

'You what? Piss off, Derek, *I* sold it, not you.'

'Yeah, but they were *my* customers, not yours. After I warmed them up, you could have sold them *anything*, you could have sold sand to a sodding Arab.'

'Not that old joke again, Derek. But you're wrong. You'd totally lost them. If I hadn't stepped in, they would've walked out of here empty handed and you'd have lost us a sale – again.'

Mr Smith chose that moment, a couple of minutes before closing time, to return to the shop, shaking the rain from his umbrella. Sensing discord, although there was nothing new in that, he asked what was going on. Derek explained in an increasingly indignant tone, while Jones shook her head as if everything he said was absurd. With Dexy Midnight Runners playing in the background, Mr Smith listened to Derek and then, turning to Miss Jones, asked for her version of events.

Like a judge and jury, having heard both sides of the argument, Mr Smith made his decision. Turning to Derek, he said, 'Derek, have you lost it, mate, or what?'

'How do you mean?'

'Which staff member put their signature on that contract?'

That's when Derek knew he'd lost. If truth be told, he knew it from the off, he never stood a chance against pretty, pretty Miss Jones. 'Hers,' he said, looking down at his boss' shoes.

'Exactly. Not Mr Fuck-It-Up but Miss Jones.' He turned to her before heading off to his office at the back. 'Thanks, Ruth. Good work.'

'Pleasure, Mr Smith,' she said, looking directly at Derek, smirking.

Right at that moment, nothing, but nothing, would have given Derek greater pleasure than to smash his fist into her pretty, smug face and wipe that smirk off her face once and for all.

Chapter 7: Benedict

Camden, North London, February 2023

Tuesday evening. They took an unmarked pool car, a VW Golf, Benedict driving. 'Welcome to the mean streets of Camden,' he said, as he eased the car into the evening traffic.

'What sort of cases do you get here?' asked Jessica, casting her eyes at the passing shops.

'I imagine much the same as you're used to – a lot of burglaries, far too much domestic violence stuff, Saturday night brawls, and, unfortunately, a lot of gang-related turf wars.'

'Sounds familiar.'

'Holbrook House isn't too far.'

Ten minutes later, Benedict turned into the car park belonging to Holbrook House. The car's headlamps scanned three uniforms interviewing a group of youths near the entrance, a couple leaning on mopeds. No press though. It didn't surprise him; they wouldn't be interested in the passing of an old woman, even if it was potentially suspicious. The cars here were generally beat-up rust buckets with the occasional souped-up bit of bling, incongruously shiny in this down-at-heel part of the world.

They stepped out of the car and, passing the PCs conducting their interviews, entered the block.

'Eight floors, too far to walk so we're going to have to run the gauntlet of the lift. You ready for this?'

'Will I need to hold my nose?'

'Very probably.'

As it was, the lift was clean, smelling strongly of disinfectant, and, for once, graffiti-free. 'I've been told the lifts are only ever cleaned when they've got some kids doing community service,' said Benedict.

They found flat twelve on the eighth floor, a Police Community Officer standing guard at the front door. 'Good evening, sir. I was told to expect you. I've got your gloves and shoe covers for you.'

'Ah, good man, Thank you.'

He and Jessica slipped on their coverings. 'No damage to the door then,' said Benedict.

'No, sir.'

Suitably attired, Benedict and Jessica entered, only to bump into Dick Evans, the pathologist, heading out. 'Oh, DI Paige, didn't expect you. Would've thought this was too lowly for you.' Evans had a habit of talking to your shoulder so one felt the constant urge to check that an errant piece of fluff hadn't inadvertently landed there.

'We were just passing.'

'And who's this then?' he asked, his eyes flicking from Jessica's shoulder to her chest and back again.

'DS Gardiner, sir,' said Jessica, offering her hand. 'Started today.'

'Have you indeed?' he said, looking at Benedict. 'Well, a bit of an odd one to start you off.' He stepped back into the flat and Benedict noticed the large wooden crucifix hanging from the wall above the fireplace. Evans led them through to the bedroom where the old lady lay in her bed, having her photograph taken by another individual covered head to toe in protective clothing. The woman's arms rested on top of her duvet, her head thrown back, her mane of grey hair spread on the pillow. Above her, hanging from the wall, a rather large portrait of the late queen.

'She's been suffocated. Look at her bloodshot eyes, the discolouration around her nostrils and mouth.'

'What the hell is that?' asked Benedict.

'That's the odd bit – the killer saw fit to place a dead mouse inside the poor woman's mouth.'

'Why would…' He shook his head. 'That's just horrible.'

'Peculiar, isn't it?'

'Any other injuries?'

'Nothing to the naked eye. But the post-mortem will tell us, of course. So, where are you from, love?'

'Me?' said Jessica. Benedict could sense her bristle at his use of the word 'love'.

'Well, I wasn't talking to the old girl here.'

'Manchester.'

'Any sign of a struggle?' asked Benedict, wanting to tear Evans' attention away from Jessica.

'No, but I guess we'll find some DNA or at least some fibres under her fingernails if there was.'

'And the mouse?' asked Jessica. 'I mean, it's a horrible thought but did the killer force it in?'

'I think not. I think he inserted it afterwards. It's mind-boggling, isn't it?'

'Nothing else seems to have been disturbed?' asked

Benedict.

'You'll have to ask your CSM that. Next, you're going to ask me about time of death?'

'You know me too well, Dick.'

'Mm. Early guess, I'd say the best part of the day already, maybe a whole twenty-four hours.'

'OK.'

'Right,' said Evans, making a show of checking his watch. 'Now, if you'll excuse me, I have a more interesting place to be and it ain't here.' He patted Benedict on the shoulder. 'Good to see you again, son, and, er…' turning to Jessica, he added, 'and nice to meet you, DS… DS…'

'Gardiner, sir.'

'Ah yes, Gardiner. That was it. Cheerio now.'

'Strange, isn't it?' said Jessica, watching Evans leave. 'How is it all pathologists come from the same mould?'

'It's part of their job description. I do apologise.'

'Oh, it's not for you to apologise, sir.' She smiled. 'But thank you anyway.'

A knock on the bedroom door. 'I think we're about done here,' said DS Adrian Collins, the man appointed CSM (Crime Scene Manager). Benedict introduced Jessica.

'Oh, you're new, aren't you?'

'Started today.'

'Nice.'

'So,' said Benedict. 'Any sign of damage?'

DS Collins shook his head. 'Nope, not one bit. No damage to the flat door, no furniture turned over, nothing broken. Whoever it was, the woman opened the door to him.'

'Or her,' added Jessica.

'Or her. So, you may well be looking for someone known to her. But, having said that, her purse is empty. Nothing in it apart from some coppers, her library card and a blood donor card. Make of that what you will.'

'What happened to the man who found her? Her grandson?'

'Yes, her grandson.' Collins consulted his notebook. 'One Thomas McIntosh, thirty-nine years old, owns a barbershop on the high road, Mac the Clipper, or something like that. Lives locally. Visited his grandmother three or four times a week. Like you say, he was the one who found her. I know you'll want to interview him so I've told him to expect you at some point tomorrow morning. Is that OK? You can always re-arrange.'

'No, that's fine. Cheers, Ade.'

'No problem. Also, whilst you're here, you might want to say hello to the neighbour in number eleven, one… Mrs Angelopoulos. Apparently, she saw a nurse visiting the grandmother late yesterday evening, around ten o'clock.'

'OK, thanks.'

'We'll get the body moved shortly, and I'd suggest you keep a couple of uniforms posted inside the flat just for tonight – in case, I don't know, the killer comes back for whatever reason. Unlikely but…'

'You never know.'

'Exactly.' Collins patted his coat pockets. 'I think that's me done. Nice to meet you, Jessica. I'll wish you good night.'

'Looks like it's pointing to a burglary gone wrong, sir,' said Jessica.

'But she let them in, she opened the door to them.'

She shrugged her shoulders. 'Could still work. He knocks, she opens, he charms himself in, saying he's come to read the gas meter or something and shows her some ID, then… bang!'

'But he'd only kill her if she put up a struggle and I can't imagine a burly burglar, once he was in, feeling too threatened

34

by a frail old woman in her bed. So, why steal the contents of her purse?'

'Assuming it wasn't empty in the first place.'

'In which case, why?'

Benedict Paige had a nasty feeling that there was more to this case than met the eye.

Chapter 8: Mac

Mac was lying in bed conscious that about half a dozen of them were padding around on his bare chest, their little feet tickling his flesh, caught in his chest hairs, their horrible pink tails swishing. Get off me, he screamed, get off! But he couldn't move his arms, couldn't bat them away. Their noses twitched and their large eyes glistened in the semi-dark. Mac screamed. There seemed to be more every time he looked down, more and more of them, covering his torso, sniffing around, scuttering this way and that. He screamed for help, the tears gushing. A couple were inching up his chest, up his throat. No, no, keep away from my mouth. He clamped his mouth shut, but they were nudging his lips with their revolting noses, trying to force their way in.

Mac opened his eyes, his chest heaving. Where was he, where was he? He was at home, in his bed, it was OK, everything was alright, there were no mice on his chest, he was fine, just fine. Oh God, it was only a dream, an awful dream…

Later that morning, Mac visited his father in his care home and told him that his mother had died. He didn't say she'd been murdered; no point in upsetting him. But his father said nothing and, indeed, showed not a trace of emotion. He remembered when he told his father that the queen had died, his eyes welled up. Not this time though. Mac knew his father and grandmother hadn't seen each other for years.

Now, two hours later, Mac waited for his sister to show up, and the apprehension was eating away at him. He was in his small office at the back of the barbershop, Mac the Clipper, trying to tally up his takings but finding it difficult to concentrate, knowing Rebecca would come waltzing through any moment.

However he tried, he couldn't shake the image of his grandmother with that… that thing poking out of her mouth. His poor grandmother.

He wondered what he would have to do now. No doubt, his sister would go into overdrive and deal with all of it; she invariably did. The flat belonged to the council so she'd probably delegate the task of emptying it to him. Not that his grandmother had much, and certainly not by way of keepsakes. Did she have a will? He'd never thought to ask. And if she did, he imagined she'd leave what little she had to his father. But his father was in a care home now, and not doing too good himself. Still, any money forthcoming would help pay for his care.

Mac and Rebecca got on OK-ish. But, if truth be told, he found his sister overbearing and dismissive. As younger siblings, they rubbed along fine but were never particularly affectionate with each other. As adults, nothing much had changed. Rebecca lived in south London, technically not that far from Camden, but they rarely saw each other. And that was fine. Rebecca had a well-paid career as a marketing executive and was married to an equally high-earning husband. Mac, owning a small barbershop in Camden, earned little. And he knew exactly what she thought of his profession. He'd undersold himself, doing a 'silly' job. But, on the plus side, his sister was happy to pay Dad's care home fees, not an inconsiderable sum of money to stump up month after month.

But what really caused the rancour was that, while Rebecca was happy to let their father 'rot' in a care home, Mac hated the fact. Given a choice and time, he'd rather have him home and take care of him himself. He knew Rebecca thought it a ridiculous idea.

Their grandmother's death was about to bring them back together for the first time in almost a year. They had things to discuss, notably, the funeral.

'Who do we invite?' asked Rebecca once she'd waltzed in.

Together, drinking tea, they sat in his back office, big enough for a desk and a couple of chairs, and an armchair in the corner but little else. She'd aged a little, perhaps, the stress of a demanding job. At least she didn't have children. Just three cats whose names all began with an 'R'.

Mac saw her glancing up at his framed poster of ruggedly handsome Clark Gable and the lovely Vivien Leigh embracing for the film poster of *Gone With the Wind*. 'Don't they look gorgeous?' he said. 'Have you seen it? The film, I mean.'

'No, doesn't interest me. So, I repeat, who do we invite to the funeral?'

Mac shrugged. 'I don't know. She didn't have friends, you know that. Maybe Mrs Angelopoulos and her husband, not that I've met him.'

'Mrs who?'

'Angelopoulos, her next-door neighbour.'

'Did they get on?'

'Not particularly.'

She sighed. 'So no point inviting her, or her husband, then, is there?'

'Suppose not.'

'Did she never go out?'

'No.' Why, he wondered, did he feel responsible for that? Their grandmother's solitude seemed to reflect badly on him, at least in Rebecca's eyes.

They sipped their teas, the awkwardness hanging over them. 'So,' said Mac, 'looks like there'll be just the two of us then.'

'We could invite Uncle Geoff.'

'Uncle Geoff? We've not seen him in years.' He swept his arm across the table and, in the process, managed to knock over a pile of pound coins, sending them scattering all over his office. 'Shit.'

'Jesus, Mac, why are you always so bloody clumsy? You're just like Mum.'

He laughed. 'God, yes, she was always knocking stuff over or tripping over things.'

There was something Mac wanted to ask his sister, had done for… years. But the time never seemed right; it was somehow *too* big a question. But now, he decided, was the time. He stirred his half-finished tea for a long while choosing the words he'd already rehearsed many times in the past. His eyes focussed on his tea, he forced the words out, 'Do you ever think of her?'

'Who?' she asked without looking up. 'Oh, you mean Mum.' A momentary look of exasperation crossed her features. 'No, not really.'

It wasn't what he wanted to hear.

'You?' she asked. 'Do you think of her?'

Yes, he did, frequently; hardly a day passed when he didn't, at some point, think of her, wonder how she was doing, whether she was happy. But he couldn't say that, not now; he feared his sister would think less of him. 'No, not often, but you know.'

'Good. She's not worth thinking about. Anyway, she could be dead by now, for all we know.'

He hated the way she so casually threw that in. 'Surely, we would have heard.'

'From whom exactly?'

'I don't know; I…'

'What?'

'I don't know,' he said, feeling defeated somehow.

'Can I leave it to you to book a slot at the crematorium?' she said in a tone that implied that although delegating this task to her younger brother, she didn't quite trust him to do it properly.

'Yeah, sure. No worries.'

'Preferably as soon as possible. Get it over and done with. Can you manage that?'

'Yes, of course, I can manage that.'

'Right then, let's go see Dad and get it over and done with.'

'Actually, there's something I need to tell you.'

'What's that?'

He hadn't planned on telling her but she had a right to know, and, anyway, keeping it all to himself was eating away at him. He had to share the burden. 'Whoever killed Gran left a mouse inside her mouth.'

She didn't speak, merely stared at him, the shock there to see.

'A white mouse. Dead.'

'You've got to be kidding me? You mean, an actual mouse, a real one, in her mouth?'

He nodded and glanced down, unable to look into her eyes any more.

'What sort of fucked up, bat-shit person would do such a

thing?'

'I don't know, Rebecca. I don't bloody know.'

Chapter 9: Derek

December 1982

The old bastard of a man sat on the other side of the desk from him, with his pinched expression and nicotine-stained fingers. 'But this video recorder is still under guarantee.'

'No, Mr Johnstone,' said Derek. 'For the hundredth time, it is not. The guarantee ran out four days ago. Look,' he added, jabbing his finger at the contract. 'Four days ago.'

'Yeah, but it bust last week before the guarantee ran out. It was fine up to then but then, on Friday, it wouldn't work. It even chewed up a tape me and the missus were looking forward to. You know, that show with Les Dawson.'

'So, why didn't you bring it in straight away?'

'I was busy, wasn't I?'

'I thought you said you were retired.'

'I am but that don't mean I wasn't busy. Besides, that thing is bloody heavy to be lugging around.'

'It's not under guarantee any more, Mr Johnstone.'

'But, I'm telling you; it broke last Friday and–'

'We don't know that. You could be lying.'

'You what?'

'I said–'

'I heard what you said, you're accusing me of being a liar. What do you take me for?'

'Your word against ours.'

'I want to see the manager.'

'He's not in today. It's just the two of us,' said Derek, motioning to Miss Jones.

'Maybe I could help,' said Miss Jones, stepping over. 'I'm the assistant manager here. Derek, I can take over from here.'

'No, it's alright–'

'Thank you, miss,' said the man. 'He's calling me a liar; it ain't right, I'm no liar.'

'I'm sure you're not, sir. Let's see if we sort this out for you. Derek, if you don't mind…'

Derek glared at her but she held his gaze and eventually, he backed down and let her take over.

Five minutes later, Mr Johnstone left the shop with a new video recorder under his arm. He flashed Derek a grin as he left.

Miss Jones adjusted her pink chiffon scarf. 'Sometimes, Derek, good customer care is more important than making a quick buck.'

'We'll see what Mr Smith has to say about that.'

'I think he'll agree with me, don't you? That's why *I'm* the assistant manager here and you, Derek, are… not. Would you mind filing away Mr Johnstone's paperwork?' With that, she flounced off to the office at the back leaving Derek to absorb another humiliation at Miss Jones' hands.

He hated her, bloody hated her. How dare she show him up time and again? Who did she think she was? All flouncy, and permed hair and white teeth. And she was right – Smith would take her side, he always did. Rumours were that Smith would soon be promoted to area manager, meaning Miss Jones would probably take his place as manager here. The prospect filled him with dread.

The postwoman arrived with the day's post, most of it for the attention of Mr Smith. Derek took it through to the office to leave it on his desk. He saw Miss Jones in their kitchenette leaning against the counter, an empty mug in her hand, waiting for the kettle to boil. 'I've been thinking, Derek…'

He stepped into the kitchenette to hear what exactly Miss Jones had been thinking about. 'Yes, what?'

'I really feel you should work on how you interact with our customers. If you were to take a step back a little, and perhaps put yourself in their shoes, you might–'

'Stop, let me interrupt you there, Miss Jones.' He walked right up to her, uncomfortably close for her liking, he could tell. 'The fact is, I couldn't give a flying fuck what you think.' The kettle boiled but didn't switch off, it never did, they needed a new kettle.

'Derek, please don't use that sort of language–'

'Oh, Derek,' he said in a shrill voice. 'Don't do this, don't do that. Listen to yourself, you… you…' His hand grabbed her chiffon scarf, tightening it and yanking it up, pushing her head up against the overhead cupboards.

'Derek–'

'You think you're so clever with your stupid degree from Trent Polytechnic or wherever it was–'

'Please, Derek, you're hurting me.'

The kitchenette was filling up with steam now as the kettle continued to boil.

He tightened his grip on the scarf, squeezing her throat. Her face turned red, her breathing erratic. 'And I'll fucking hurt

44

you again if you carry on making me look like a dick.' He slammed her head against the cupboard and only then released her. She lurched forward, fighting for breath, her hand frantically trying to loosen the scarf, spluttering. He stormed out leaving her dazed in a room full of steam. His heart thumping with adrenaline, Derek marched through the shop and outside into the cold December morning.

He strode down Tottenham Court Road, smoking furiously, ignoring the hundreds of Christmas shoppers buzzing past him. He almost laughed. That'd put her in her place; she'd think twice now about the way she spoke to him. The look of fear on her face was precious! He'd done that; he'd caused her eyes to blaze with fright. There might be repercussions, he knew that, but it'd been worth it, just to see her expression, to know that whatever she thought, he'd reclaimed the power here. And it felt great, in fact, it felt bloody fantastic!

To think he once fancied her. Eighteen months back, when she first started, he made the mistake of asking her out. He never forgot the look on her face – or forgiven her. She laughed at him. 'You? You're asking *me* on a date?' 'Yeah,' he'd said. 'Why not?' She gave me a withering stare. 'I think not, Derek.' She laughed again.

Well, she would never laugh at him again, not after today, not now she knew who really was the boss.

*

Six o'clock; closing time. Usually, Smith locked up and Jones waited, making sure no one jumped out at him. Today, without Smith around, Jones did the locking up and Derek was obliged to hang around until she finished. She'd put on her jaunty red hat, the sort that looked like something women would wear at the races, and a sleek pair of red leather gloves. The hat looked nice on her but nothing on earth would induce him to pay her a compliment.

'Maybe we should start playing Christmas carols tomorrow,' he said.

She ignored him while she set the alarm. Job done, she dropped the shop keys into her handbag and marched off without a word disappearing into the crowds. She hadn't spoken to him or even looked at him since he returned to the shop from his earlier walk. 'Well, sod you,' he muttered to himself.

Tightening his woollen scarf, he headed off towards his bus stop. A 73 bus, his bus, roared past, heading for Stoke Newington. He'd have to wait for the next one. He could still see her hat a little further up the street. He saw her enter Tottenham Court Road underground station, and, for some reason, he followed her.

He followed her down the station stairs, through the ticket hall and, keeping about a dozen people behind, followed her down the escalator. She swung right, heading to the northbound Northern line. A tube train pulled in and he had to run to catch it, squeezing himself on through the closing doors against a wall of commuters. The carriage was packed and he remained squashed against the curved doors. Scanning the carriage, he saw her at the far end, standing, reading a newspaper with one gloved hand, the other, hanging onto the handrail. After Mornington Crescent, the fourth stop, the carriage emptied out a little and Miss Jones found a seat but Derek remained next to the doors.

Another five stops and the carriage was now only half full. Derek kept his back to her. Here, at Highgate, Miss Jones alighted, dropping the newspaper into a bin on the platform. Again, he followed her.

Miss Jones exited Highgate station and, heading right, walked briskly down Sheridan Road, passing various shops – a newsagent, a dry cleaner and a fruit and veg stall, almost bumping into a woman with a shopping trolley. They apologised to each other but Miss Jones didn't look back, not once. Derek did wonder what on earth he was doing. It had turned mightily cold, but, having come this far, he decided to stay the course. He tightened his scarf again and slipped on his leather gloves, a gift from his wife, Pat, last Christmas.

Another fifty yards or so, she took the second right onto Onslow Avenue, a quiet residential street lined with trees and large, mainly detached houses fronted by drives. This, thought Derek, is what you called a desirable area, a far cry from the scruffy terraced street he lived on with Pat and his mother. Here, beneath a streetlamp, Miss Jones slowed right up and then stopped altogether. No one else was about. Derek darted behind a tree just as she turned around. He heard her call out: 'Hello? Hello, is anyone there?'

He waited until he heard her footsteps again, walking away, but much slower now. Peering from behind his tree, he saw her head up a drive. Quickly, he darted up the street in time to see the front door close. So, he thought, this is where she lived – number sixty-four, Onslow Avenue. Stepping behind another tree, he waited for two minutes when he saw a light come on the first floor, followed by Miss Jones herself, drawing the curtains.

He crept up the drive and cast his eyes down a panel of door buzzers. Sure enough, there it was: *Flat 3: R. Jones.*

It took Derek almost an hour to get home to his flat in Stoke Newington from Highgate. He walked in, blowing on his hands, to the smell of something nice, beef stew perhaps.

'You're late,' said Pat, his wife, brandishing a tea towel.

'Did you get Daisy her mice?'

'Yes, Derek.'

He needed to feed her, his Royal Python, a beautiful creature. Being an adult, she only needed feeding once a week. Daisy liked her white mice. Pat worked as a dinner lady in a primary school and on her walk home passed a pet shop, so he always got her to buy Daisy's food, a collection of frozen dead mice, white ones, always the white ones.

'Is dinner ready?' he asked, realising just how hungry he was.

'Been ready half an hour.'

Yes, he was starving but, he mused as he stuffed his gloves into his coat pocket and hung up his coat and scarf, that had been a worthwhile exercise – for now he knew exactly where Ruth Jones lived.

Chapter 10: Mac

Camden, North London, February 2023

Sunny Grove, Dad's care home, wasn't too far away. They took Rebecca's car, a Hyundai Tucson.

The staff knew Mac by now. This was his second visit today. Normally, he tried to visit twice a week, the days he wasn't visiting his grandmother. He felt guilty even about that – was it enough? Should he visit more often? But he ran his own business and worked full time. He got tired, and visiting his father was always a draining affair. Some days his father's mind would be sharp and he'd recognise his only son and they could actually have a conversation, nothing very deep or interesting but a conversation, nonetheless. But sadly most days, he'd not recognise Mac and he'd ask who he was, or not even say anything. Mac would sit next to him, pat his hand occasionally, say the odd word that Dad wouldn't hear or not understand, and that'd be it.

Mac's mother deserted the family when Mac and Rebecca were still kids. Mac was nine years old, Rebecca ten. They'd not seen or heard from her since. Not once, not a single word. And even now, after all this time and as a grown man, it hurt; it bloody hurt. Why did she leave? Did she not have any sense of loyalty to them, to his father, to her young daughter and son? Obviously not. His mother had no loyalty to anyone – except perhaps herself.

Sunny Grove Care Home specialised in dementia patients. The home itself was two large Edwardian houses merged into one. It accommodated about fifteen residents. It was Wednesday late morning, still less than two days since his grandmother's death; the ground still wet after an earlier downpour. Mac pressed the buzzer next to the front door and the door swung open. They walked in and Mac breathed in the familiar smell of disinfectant and canteen-like food. One of the carers greeted them as she passed. Next, the home's manager, Mrs Hale, chose that moment to come out of her office.

'Ah, Mr MacIntosh. I was hoping to see you.'

Mac introduced his sister.

'Can I have a quick word before you go see your father?' asked Mrs Hale.

'Sure,' he said, not liking the sound of this one bit. They settled in Mrs Hale's office, a small but airy room, with several framed photos on her desk facing away from him. 'Is there anything wrong?'

'It's not easy to tell you this but your father's being abusive to the other clients again.'

'There's a surprise,' said Rebecca.

'We've been here before, haven't we? I have a responsibility to all our clients, Mr MacIntosh, and your father is causing considerable upset.'

'I'm so sorry, I–'

'Mrs Hunt's granddaughter is most upset. She visits her gran every day and she's witnessed your father's bullying behaviour.'

50

'Is that Maxine?'

Maxine Hunt was one of his few female regulars at Mac the Clipper. She had shoulder-length red hair and only ever wanted the ends cut off. Mac charged her a lot less than female hairdressers.

'Yes, Maxine,' said Mrs Hale. 'We'll be keeping a careful eye on him but I'm afraid to say unless we see a radical improvement in his behaviour, he'll leave me with no choice but to evict him.'

'Evict him?' shrieked Rebecca. 'You can't just kick him out.'

'We can in extreme cases and this, I'm afraid, is extreme.'

'So you just chuck him out on the streets?'

'We give you twenty-eight days' notice.'

'But he's not aware he's doing it–' said Mac.

'I'm perfectly aware of that, Mr MacIntosh, but it doesn't lessen any of the hurt he's causing. Anyway, I wanted to alert you before you go in and see him.'

'OK, I see. Well, thank you, Mrs Hale.'

They walked through to the lounge area. A number of residents, mostly female, sat around the perimeter, some vaguely watching the mounted television set that was permanently switched on, all day, every day. Father wasn't there. Mac walked through to the conservatory, Rebecca following, and found him sitting alone in an armchair staring out into the garden, watching a robin pecking at a bird feeder swinging from a low branch of the elm tree. He had a mug of something in his hand, and a plate on the little table next to him, empty save for a couple of tell-tale crumbs.

'Hello, Dad.'

'Hmm? Who's that?'

'Your son.' Mac pulled up a couple of hardback chairs and, together, they sat next to him. 'Look who I've brought today.'

Dad turned and clocked Rebecca smiling at him, but there seemed to be no recognition in his dull eyes.

'Hello, Dad,' said Rebecca. 'How are you?'

'Who's this bird?' asked Dad to Mac.

'Rebecca, Dad, as in your daughter. Remember?'

'So, you're Thomas, aren't you?'

'Yes, Dad.' His name was actually Thomas McIntosh, but people called him Mac.

'How old are you now?'

'Thirty-nine, Dad. Almost at the Big Four-Oh.'

His father often asked about people's ages. If anyone asked him how old he was, the answer varied from twenty-five to forty depending on where he was in the recesses of his memory at that particular moment. He was never older than forty. A carer called Charmaine, according to her name badge, with a face mask and a swirly tattoo around her wrist, popped in and offered Mac and Rebecca tea. Rebecca thanked her but said no.

'So then, Dad,' said Rebecca. 'The boss woman here says you're not behaving yourself. You've been a naughty boy.'

Another resident wandered in holding a cup and saucer. Mrs Hunt stooped; the poor woman Dad had been harassing. She wore a beige skirt and jacket with a large, leaf-shaped brooch. She looked dapper. She dressed the same every day. She looked like she had an important meeting to go to. But she hadn't. She simply walked around the care home all day, taking delight in seeing things or people for what she thought was the first time when, of course, she had seen them a thousand times already. 'Aha, Mr McIntosh, there you are,' she said to Mac's father as if she'd been genuinely looking for him. The cup tilted on the saucer. 'Soon be time for tea. I hope you're hungry.'

'Go away, you old bat,' said Dad.

'Hello, Mrs Hunt,' Mac said to her.

'Hello there. And you are…?'

They'd met several times before but he smiled and told her. 'I'm Thomas, Mr McIntosh's son. Nice to meet you.'

Satisfied with this, she about turned and ambled back the way she came, cup and saucer at a precarious angle.

'Hey, Mac,' said Rebecca, filling in a gap, 'are you still going out with that Kate woman?'

'Kath. No, we broke up months back.'

His father, leaning forward, patted him on the knee, saying, 'That's good.'

'What?'

'Women. Good riddance to them.'

Mac's mouth dropped: it'd been a while since he'd heard his father utter such an articulate sentence. 'What do you mean, *good riddance*?'

'You don't need a woman in your life, son. Waste of time. Love them and leave them, if you want, but whatever you do, son, don't ever fall for one. Because she'll be the death of you.'

OK, he needed to tread carefully here. Glancing at his sister again, he said, 'Like Mum, you mean.'

'Your mother was a bitch.'

Ow, his mouth dropped open. Did he just say that? Did he actually call his mother by that word? It was as if Dad had punched him in the stomach. How could he use such a foul, horrible word?

'That's a bit harsh, Dad,' said Rebecca.

'She was.' He folded his arms across his chest. 'A right bitch.'

'Why did Mum leave, Dad?' There we are, he thought, time to try again…

But his father looked confused again. He'd lost him. 'Do you

53

think they might bring some more of these nice biscuits?'

'Maybe we could ask Charmaine,' said Rebecca.

'They remind me of the biscuits we have at home.' Mac's father often made references to his childhood in the present tense. Now came the part about his father…

'I sit in the garden shed for hours sometimes. Best place to escape my dad. He's got a temper on him, that man. Best to lay low, avoid him, you know?'

Rebecca looked at her phone; she'd had enough. 'Well, Dad,' she said, standing up. 'We'd better be going. It's been great. Can't wait to do this again.'

He didn't respond, his mind now back to his childhood.

*

Mac and his sister sat in Rebecca's Hyundai. Mac sighed.

'Jesus, why do you bother?' said Rebecca. She pulled her vape out of her coat pocket and puffed on it.

'One of us has to.'

'Yeah,' she said, blowing out a plume of vapour which soon filled the car. 'But that still doesn't answer *why*. Answer me this, who exactly benefits from your visits? Cos it's certainly not Dad, that's for sure. So, why, Mac? Is it just to show the staff you're a caring, loving son? Is that it? Or is it to salvage something in your conscience? I mean, hell, Mac, that was awful. Just awful.'

She was right; he knew she was, and he had no answer for her – why, indeed, did he bother with a man who so casually called his mother a bitch?

*

Mac returned to his barbershop. It'd been an exhausting visit to the care home. It was good to get back to the sanctuary of

54

his shop. Both Eoin and Tony were busy with customers, while a queue of people waited, two of them wearing black face masks. Mac said hello to all the customers, most of whom he knew as returning customers. He had a quick catch-up with the boys. All was well although Eoin said they'd received a phone call on the shop's landline. 'Some woman asking for our email address.'

'We don't have one,' said Mac

'I know that. She wanted to write an email to you specifically, that's why she didn't want to use our Instagram or Facebook or anything, just email.'

'What have you been up to, eh, Mac?' said Tony. 'Your past catching up with you?'

'So, hope you don't mind, mate, I gave her your email address.'

'Did she say her name?'

'Nope. I asked but she refused. Just said she'd email you.'

'All right. Cheers, mate.'

Mac checked his email on his phone but there was nothing there that shouldn't be there, just a whole lot of junk and various newsletters he never read but never got around to unsubscribing. It didn't matter. Whoever this mysterious woman was, she'd get in touch if she needed to.

He turned to his customers with a smile. 'Right, who's next?'

Chapter 11: Benedict

Wednesday morning. Detective Inspector Benedict Paige sat at his desk, an almond croissant and a fresh cup of coffee at hand and logged onto his computer. Jessica was upstairs with HR again.

He checked the website for Mac the Clipper: basic, as far as websites go, but it did the job. He recognised the shop front from his travels; it'd been there for a while. He'd always shied away from it – it looked like a young man's place, not for middle-aged fuddy-duddies like him, and too expensive – looking at the price list. Who wants to pay this much for a basic haircut? Sonia would mock him, call him a 'tight wad', as she often did. He had no aversion to spending money; he simply didn't want to pay over the odds when he could get the job done just as well down the street with the old guy who'd cut his hair for years at seventy-five per cent the price. It made sense.

He called over to DC Jamie Kelly. 'How's it going with the hit and run, Kelly?'

'Not good, boss. We've knocked on every house along the

street and not one single witness, no one heard a thing, no screech of the brakes, nothing. And only one doorbell camera which, like you said, had limited reach. We've got posters going up today.'

'Someone might have seen a car going too fast. It was closing time at the pub, after all.'

'The other piece of not-so-good news is that we've drawn a blank on Zoe's clothing.'

'Nothing?'

'Nothing except lots of tarmac. She was wearing one of those shiny coats.'

'And any suspicious number plates?'

'Again, nothing. Nothing from the ANPR.'

Jessica returned from her meeting. 'Ready whenever you are, boss.'

'Great. Let's go get a haircut.'

*

Mac the Clipper wasn't such a young man's barbershop as Benedict had expected – two men his age waited their turn. But the staff were all twenty-somethings, two tattooed, bearded hipsters, cutting hair while some obscure dance track pulsed over the speakers. The thought of working with that music, or any music, pounding in your ears seven, eight hours a day would be enough to send Benedict over the edge. Everything there had been carefully thought about – posters of iconic names from the worlds of music and film: James Dean, Marilyn Monroe, The Beatles, Bruce Lee and more, plus a myriad number of knick-knacks decorating the place.

'Take a seat, guys,' said one of the young barbers. 'Someone will be with you in a minute.'

'Actually, we're here to see Thomas McIntosh,' said

Benedict, showing the barbers his police ID.

'Oh, you mean Mac. Yeah, go through,' he said, pointing to a door at the back of the shop decorated with a skull and crossbones. 'Just knock in case he's up to something he shouldn't be.'

His colleague laughed heartily at this. 'What? Like checking his horoscope in the *Daily Mail*?'

'Cooking the books, more like. Sorry,' he added with a nervous laugh. 'I shouldn't say that to a copper.'

Jessica smiled weakly. Thanking them, she knocked on the office door and entered upon hearing a gruff voice on the other side. They found Thomas McIntosh sitting behind his desk, his hand on a computer mouse. He beckoned them in. A good-looking man, an older version of his staff, tattoos visible beneath his shirt cuffs, a neatly trimmed beard, his hair gelled to within an inch of its life, broad across the chest, a man who worked out.

Benedict clocked the *Gone With the Wind* poster. 'Good film,' he said, sitting down. '1938.'

'Thirty-nine, but, aye, a classic.'

'It featured a black actress, didn't it? The first African American to win an Oscar.'

'Hattie McDaniel, that's right.'

'Is it on Netflix?' asked Jessica.

An awkward silence.

'Joke,' she said. 'Just joking.'

'Anyway,' said Benedict. 'First of all, Mr McIntosh, our condolences on the death of your grandmother.'

'Do call me Mac. Everyone does. But thank you. So, was she really suffocated?'

'We'll know more when we get the post-mortem,' said Jessica. 'But it does appear that someone unknown suffocated your grandmother.'

Mac shook his head. 'And what about that… that rodent? Why would anyone do that?'

'That we don't know at this stage. How did she get on with people? Did she have many friends?'

Mac laughed. 'Friends? Granny? You've got to be kidding, I've never known her to have even an acquaintance, let alone an actual, real-life friend.'

'Did she not get on with people?' asked Jessica.

'Nah, sadly not. She was your epitome of a cantankerous old bird. Never heard her mutter a good word about anyone. Whether it was people on the TV, politicians, her neighbours, family, the council, she didn't discriminate; she hated us all in equal measure.'

Benedict chortled.

'But listen, seriously, she never knew anyone enough to fall out with them so badly that they might want to *murder* her. That's too ridiculous for words. I don't understand it.'

'We were thinking it might be a burglary gone wrong—'

'But she didn't have anything worth nicking. Have you been inside her flat?'

'Yes, but a burglar wouldn't have known that.'

'Yeah, council house tenants are always loaded.'

'We take your point, Mr McIntosh,' said Jessica. 'But we can't rule anything out at this stage.'

'I suppose.'

'Did she owe anyone any money?'

'No way, no. I mean, she never bought anything. The TV was paid for and… well, she didn't have anything else. Unless she had a gambling addiction I didn't know about.' He laughed at the thought. 'But on account she never went out and didn't have a computer… it's not likely.'

'How often did you visit your grandmother, Mr McIntosh?'

'Once every two or three evenings. I never stayed long.'

'You didn't?'

His eyes moved to the poster. He sighed. 'It was never a particularly rewarding experience, to be honest.'

'Did she leave a will?'

'Yeah, half a million quid to me.' He looked from Jessica to Benedict. 'OK,' he said, putting his hands up. 'That was bad taste, I apologise. No, she had nothing, absolutely nothing. She survived on her pension and that was about it, as far as I know. No savings that I know of.'

'Were you her power of attorney?'

'No. She may have been physically incapacitated but mentally, she was fine. Just grumpy.'

'Do you have any siblings, Mr McIntosh?' asked Benedict.

'A sister, Rebecca. Do call me Mac. I can give you her number if you want but I'm telling you, she never visited. Last time, with me, would have been, I don't know, over a year ago.'

'Any other family? A husband, perhaps?' asked Jessica.

'Nah. Her husband ran off years ago, decades ago. No idea where he is. Dead probably. My mother ran off too and I don't know where she is either. Not heard from her since the day she left. I was nine.'

'I'm sorry to hear that,' said Jessica.

'Yeah well. But my dad is still around – just about.'

'Oh?'

'He's in a care home, got dementia. Now with Dad, I do have power of attorney.'

'Have you told your father that his mother's died?'

'Yeah, but it made no impact. He showed more emotion when I told him the queen had died.'

60

'OK.'

'I can't remember the last time he and his mother spoke. No idea. Years ago. Granny lived with my parents when they were in Stoke Newington, but then Granny got herself a council flat here in Camden. But that was back in the early eighties. I wasn't born yet. Chances are, Dad doesn't even remember her. Doesn't remember me most of the time.'

'Where is this care home?' asked Benedict.

'Sunny Grove. You know it? It's not far from here.'

'I know it.'

Jessica cleared her throat. 'Could we talk to your father?'

'Dad? You want to speak to Dad? Why? There'd be no point; I told you, he's got dementia.'

'Yes, I know, but… you never know. I've spoken to dementia patients several times before and, yes, their short-term memory can be… impaired but they can often have clear memories of their distant pasts.'

'I'm not sure about this. I mean–'

'I promise we'd keep it very brief and the moment he shows any distress, we'll stop.'

Mac bit on a fingernail. 'I'd better check with my sister.'

Jessica glanced at Benedict. 'Why? Do you hold joint power of attorney for your father?'

'No, either of us can make a decision. It doesn't need both of us but you don't know my sister.'

Benedict could see him thinking.

'OK,' said Mac finally. 'On one condition…'

'Name it,' said Jessica.

'That I'm there when you speak to him.'

'Absolutely.'

'We would have insisted anyway,' added Benedict.

Thomas nodded. 'OK. When were you thinking?'

'We'll arrange something in a moment,' said Benedict. 'Did your grandmother have any other children?'

'Yeah, my Uncle Geoff but I've not seen him since I was a kid.'

'Where does he live, this Uncle Geoff?'

'Dagenham. At least, he used to. I've got his number in my contacts, not that I've ever used it. Do you want it?'

They did.

'He also visited Gran on occasion but I never bumped into him there.'

'We spoke to your grandmother's neighbour last night—'

'Mrs Angelopoulos.'

'That's the one. She says she saw a nurse leaving your grandmother's flat yesterday evening, about ten. She was wearing a nurse's uniform. Did your grandmother often have nurses visiting her?'

'Occasionally. Usually, some health care worker from the surgery.'

'At ten in the evening?'

'I don't know. I doubt it.'

'We'll be checking that out, of course. Have you got the name of your grandmother's doctor?'

'Not on me but I can find it for you.'

'Please. Unfortunately, this Mrs Angelopoulos didn't see the nurse's face as she'd heard a door slam and, opening her door, saw the nurse walking away from your grandmother's flat heading towards the lift. So, technically speaking, she didn't actually witness the nurse leaving the flat, she simply made an assumption. Officers have spoken to all the neighbours and not one of them had a nurse to call yesterday evening. But, whatever, we need to find this woman, if only to rule her out of our enquiries.'

'How do you know it was a woman?'

'Mrs Angelopoulos says she was wearing a dress under her coat. But she was wearing tights, so we don't know the nurse's skin tone.'

'We're waiting on the council to release the CCTV,' said Jessica. 'Once we've got that, we should get a better idea of who she was, and if there was anyone else who might be of interest.'

'Well, I hope you find her.'

'We'll find her all right,' said Benedict. 'Whoever this nurse is, we'll find her.'

Chapter 12: Benedict

'Boss, we've got a bit of headway on the hit and run.' said DC Kelly, with one of his smiles.

Benedict hadn't even taken his coat off but he was all ears. 'Go on.'

'One of the residents near where it happened has reported a scratch on his car.'

'Aha.'

'Yeah. Apparently, it's fairly slight so he didn't notice it at first, but there's a definite scrape on the driver's side which wasn't there a couple of days ago. He said if it hadn't been for our posters, he might just have ignored it.' Kelly passed Benedict a Post-It note. 'That's his address and number.'

'Excellent. I'll get forensics to take a look.' He glanced up at the office clock. 'In fact, I've got a meeting with them in an hour. I'll mention it then. What sort of car was it?'

Kelly consulted his notes. 'A Dacia Sandero, royal blue colour, 2019. Regarding our mysterious nurse who we think visited Mrs McIntosh…' He paused.

'Yes? Go on, Kelly, tell me, this isn't some TV talent show, you don't have to insert dramatic pauses.'

'Sorry, boss. So I've emailed you a few seconds of footage. It's not brilliant but it's the best we have.'

'Good man. But my first priority right now is coffee.'

'Oh, I'm afraid, we got nothing suspicious back from Mrs McIntosh's medical records. She had some complaints, high blood pressure, which she had pills for, some rheumatoid arthritis, that sort of thing, but nothing unusual.'

'And did they say whether they'd sent a nurse out to visit her?'

'No. Nor did St Cuthbert's hospital.'

Jessica came in, a smile on her face. Someone was happy to be at work, mused Benedict.

Three minutes later, with a coffee on his desk, Benedict logged into his computer and found Kelly's email. Inviting Jessica over, he clicked on the first of two links and, enlarging the footage to full screen, saw the entrance to Mrs McIntosh's apartment block. The time on the scene said 22:00 hours. Evans had put the time of death around that time. A figure leaves, probably a woman, and bumps into the nurse coming in. The woman holds the door open for the nurse. The nurse was, rather incongruous, thought Benedict, wearing a brimmed hat. 'Why is she wearing that ridiculous hat?' asked Jessica. 'To hide her face? If so, it worked.' Beyond her chin, one couldn't see anything of her features. That was it.

'She's wearing gloves,' said Jessica.

'It hasn't been cold recently, has it? Windy perhaps. But not enough to blow her hat off.'

The second clip, thirteen minutes later, showed the nurse leaving. But this time, from behind, showed only her retreating figure.

'We need to find that woman who held open the door,' said

Jessica.

'Kelly, Prowse… a job for you…'

An hour later, Benedict and Jessica traipsed up two floors to meet their colleagues in forensics. Diana Pettigrew headed the department and welcomed them in, offering them a coffee. A woman nearing retirement, which she mentioned often, Benedict liked Diana, she had that no-nonsense, straight-to-the-matter attitude he admired. She also put up with no-nonsense for her number two, Dick Evans.

'No surprise here but Mrs McIntosh was, as we'd suspected, smothered. Hence, the bruising around the mouth and nostrils and the bloodshot eyes. There was also a small discharge of urine. The killer used one of the woman's own pillows, we found traces of its fabric in the victim's mouth.' Benedict opened his mouth, but Diana put her hand up. 'I know what you're going to ask me, Ben. Were there any signs of defence, and no, sadly not. Nothing under the fingernails.

'Did you find any medical traces?'

'Yes, but nothing alarming. She was on this stuff called Enalapril which is prescribed to people who suffer from high blood pressure. It's an enzyme inhibitor which reduces pressure by relaxing the blood vessels.'

'But she didn't have too much in her system?'

'No.'

'And the mouse?'

'Yes, very strange. Your ordinary white mouse. What I can't tell you is why the killer should place a dead mouse in the woman's mouth. Just a bit of theatre, I imagine. But… there's a big but here…'

'Yes?'

'The white mouse in the mouth. We've been here before.'

Benedict and Jessica exchanged looks. 'We have?'

'Before your time, Ben, but we sure have. Back in the early eighties, exactly the same signature.'

'Oh my god,' said Jessica.

'Yep, killed two in Stoke Newington, plus a third who survived. But he was caught. He was sent down for it.'

'Oh,' said Benedict. 'That rings a bell.'

'We know the motive for the first attack, in a word: jealousy, but never established a motive for the second or third.'

'Were they sexually assaulted?' asked Jessica.

'No.'

'And since released?'

Diana shook her head. 'That's the weird thing, he died in prison at the end of June last, eight months ago.'

'A good alibi then.'

Diana laughed. 'Thing is though, the victims were all young women. Mrs McIntosh, as we know, was old. She was eighty-nine. Also, she was suffocated, the previous victims were strangled. So, different type of victim, slightly different MO, different vicinity, and forty years apart. Nothing to link the cases together.'

'Apart from the mouse in the mouth.'

'Apart from the mouse in the mouth.'

'Copycat?' said Jessica.

Benedict nodded. 'Could be. Or could be just a coincidence. Who knows? OK, Diana, thanks for all that. Did DC Kelly mention the car with the scrape?'

'Someone's on their way over to speak to the owner.'

'Excellent. Thank you.'

Benedict and Jessica strolled back to the office. 'Thing is,' said Benedict, 'if you were a copycat killer, you'd do more than just copy the signature. It's the motive that gets me. It's not a burglary gone wrong because, after all, the killer wouldn't have arrived prepared with the dead mouse. And why kill an old recluse like Mrs McIntosh? I think we need to look more into her history. Who knows, perhaps she had some skeletons in her past?'

'I'll look into it.'

'Yes, do that. There's something odd about all of this. Whatever that is, it may well hold the key.'

Chapter 13: Derek

December 1982

Miss Jones came in late, looking flustered, bringing in the cold with her. Mr Smith asked her if she was OK. 'I'm sorry, Mr Smith,' she said, removing her red gloves. 'I'm fine now but I woke up feeling a little… shaky.'

Smith asked if she wanted to go home and take a sick day, but she declined and thanked him, stating that she was fine now. Derek wondered whether her feeling 'shaky' was anything to do with him. He hoped so. Miss Jones adjusted her chiffon scarf, momentarily exposing the visible bruise on her neck.

'Blimey, Miss Jones,' said Mr Smith, 'has someone tried to strangle you?'

She looked at Derek for a split second. He turned away, busying himself with paperwork.

'Ha, no! I got caught up with my scarf. It's nothing.' She squirted a couple of squirts of perfume on herself, infusing the shop with the smell of lavender.

'So, I was thinking, boss,' said Derek, keen to change the

subject, 'shall we play carols from now on?'

Mr Smith sighed. 'You're probably right. *O, Come All Ye Faithful* on repeat from now to Christmas Eve. Joy! But I'm telling you now, I refuse to don a Father Christmas hat until Christmas Eve.'

Derek forced a laugh and, grappling in the bottom drawer of his desk, found a cassette box labelled 'Xmas carols'.

The morning passed quickly with an unending stream of customers. A few times, it got so busy that Mr Smith had to come out from his office to lend a hand. Miss Jones didn't speak to Derek once. She looked miserable. He did wonder whether he had anything to do with her sullenness. But all he did was stand up for himself; it was *her* fault; she'd brought on herself. The look on her face when he tightened that scarf of hers around her neck still caused him pleasure.

It reminded him of the time, a few years back, when he beat the shit out of a kid who gave him too much lip. He'd been working on the shooting gallery at the funfair when he got into an argument with some mouthy kid. After finishing his shift, he wandered around the funfair and bumped into the boy. He followed him until he was able to grab him and pull him behind one of the large marquees. There, he proceeded to kick the shit out of him. The next day, while working at the gallery, two burly coppers came and arrested him there and then. He got away with that one, slapped with a two-year suspended sentence, while the kid recovered, by all accounts, albeit with a differently shaped nose.

Mid-morning, Derek asked Miss Jones if she wanted a coffee but she merely shook her head without looking up from her desk. He wondered whether now was a good time to remind Mr Smith that they still needed a new kettle.

Normally, Derek remained in the staff room during his lunch

hour, but today he was so wound up, he faced the cold and went for a walk. He strode down a side street behind Oxford Street and to his pleasant surprise, came across a pet shop. He simply had to go in and admire their collection of snakes. He left with a bag containing three frozen white mice and felt a whole lot better.

Early afternoon, during a lull, Miss Jones, still looking miserable, went to see Mr Smith in his office. Derek welcomed a couple of customers but found it hard to concentrate, kept glancing towards the back, wondering what she and Smith could be talking about for so long. He soon lost his customers and he knew it was because he'd been offhand in dealing with them – not that he cared.

Finally, after almost fifteen minutes, Miss Jones returned to her desk looking stony-faced and still refusing to meet Derek's eye. She settled down to her paperwork, twiddling a pen around her fingers.

'Everything OK, Miss Jones?' he asked, trying to keep his voice upbeat.

She didn't answer.

A spark of annoyance ignited within him. She'd maintained this ignoring act for long enough now. Glancing towards Smith's door, he strode over to her and putting his hands down on her desk in front of her, said, '*I said*, is everything OK?' This time his tone was purposefully malevolent. He wanted to see that look of fear in her eyes again, wanted that surge of power it gave him.

But she still didn't look up at him, still didn't answer. God, he'd happily strangle the bitch right there and damn the consequences. How dare she treat him like shit?

The shop door opened, and he returned to his desk, seething.

An hour later, the shop door opened again but this time it

wasn't a customer but a man Derek had met once before, a colleague from the Supervision branch in Paddington. Richard Prentice.

'Hello, hello, campers!' he said. 'How are we all today? It's brass monkeys out there, I'm telling you.' He shivered for effect.

'Hello, Richard,' said Miss Jones. 'Thanks for coming over at such short notice.'

What did she mean, thought Derek. Obviously, she knew Richard was coming over but hadn't thought to tell him. 'What are you doing here?' barked Derek.

'I've come on relief, mate,' said Richard, breezily.

'Why? We're all here. We don't need you.'

'Apparently do you, mate. *I am only acting under orders*,' he said in a fake German accent. 'Gotta report in with your boss first. Someone put the kettle on, be a love. See you in a min.'

Something was going on, and Derek didn't like it. Miss Jones knew about this but he couldn't bring himself to ask; didn't want to give her the satisfaction.

Three minutes later, Richard Prentice returned from the office. 'I'm here! I'm taking over your desk, Derek.'

'What for?'

'Don't ask me, mate, but the boss wants to see you.'

'He does?'

Richard laughed. 'Ha ha, bad luck. I wouldn't want to be in your shoes, mate.'

Derek trudged over while Richard took his place. 'Oo, nice warm seat, Derek. Thank you! So, Ruth, how goes it with you? Tell me all the gossip, will you?'

Derek knocked on Mr Smith's door and entered, taking the chair opposite his boss. Smith looked serious.

'I want to hear it from your side,' he said straight away.

'What?'

'Don't give me that. You know what I'm talking about. Miss Jones has made a serious allegation about you relating to yesterday afternoon. So, in your own words, what happened?'

Derek shrugged. 'Nothing happened, boss. I went to find Miss Jones because we were busy and I needed help. I found her skulking around in the kitchenette when she should have been helping me and working. So, I gave her a piece of my mind.'

'And?'

'That was it. Honest, Mr Smith. That was it. She sulked a bit but then she came through.'

Mr Smith considered him for a while and Derek forced himself to maintain eye contact. 'Did you, at any point, touch Miss Jones in any way?'

'Touch her? What do you mean, boss? No, I didn't touch her; I didn't lay a finger on her. Why would I do that?'

Mr Smith sighed. 'Miss Jones alleges that you tightened her scarf around her neck to the point it caused that bruising I commented on earlier.'

Derek laughed. 'That's ridiculous. I would never do something like that.'

'But you'll admit – she has a bruise around her neck?'

'Yeah, but so what? Nothing to do with me.'

'Hmm. OK.' He drummed his fingers on the desk. 'I've spoken to head office, and they've told me that they will be looking into this and, unless one of you retracts your story, there'll have to be a tribunal.'

'A tribunal? What does that mean?'

'To be honest, I don't know. I've never been involved in one before. Meanwhile, head office says you are to go home until someone from there contacts you.'

'Go home? Now?'

'Yes.'

So that was why Richard had come over. 'Will I still be paid?'

'Yes, you will still be paid.'

'For how long?' The prospect of being stuck at home with his mother all day every day did not appeal. She was still only fifty but looked about seventy and seemed to have the mobility of someone aged a hundred. She was a total thorn in his side; he couldn't stand the woman and having her at home all the bloody time was, as far as Derek was concerned, hell on earth.

'As long as it takes.'

The two men sat in silence for a few moments. Derek knew Smith didn't believe him. 'I really didn't touch her, you know, boss. She's lying.'

'Why would she lie?'

Derek shrugged, 'I don't know.'

Mr Smith leant forward. 'If it turns out you laid even a finger on her, Derek, you'll be out before your feet can touch the floor and, what's more, unless Miss Jones objects, the police will have no choice but to press charges.'

Derek swallowed. 'I can't lose my job here, boss. I *need* the money. My wife's pregnant,' he said, happy to lie. 'And my old mum lives with us. If you sack me–'

'You won't get a reference and no one will take you on. I know.'

'I need this job.'

'You'll need to give me your staff badge.'

Handing over his badge seemed so final.

'Head office will be in touch soon. They won't want this hanging over them.'

Derek went to the kitchenette to fetch his coat, scarf and briefcase. He was about to leave when he noticed Miss Jones' handbag under the small table where they ate their lunch. Looking around, making sure no one was coming, he quickly opened it up and sure enough found a key ring with three keys attached. He slipped the key ring into his pocket. About to leave, he also noticed Mr Smith's favourite Arsenal mug unwashed in the sink. He carefully lifted it up and dropped it in his briefcase. He wasn't sure what he was doing; he just knew that *somehow* he needed them.

He headed out into the shop, determined to leave as quickly as possible.

This time, however, Miss Jones did look at him. 'Going home, Derek?'

He didn't trust himself not to punch her lights out there and then.

Richard looked up. 'Hey, Derek, you off, mate? Before you go, can I ask you a question about this account?'

Derek ignored them both.

'Derek? Derek, wait up, mate…'

But Derek had gone.

He should have gone home but he didn't. Instead, putting his leather gloves on, he headed for the tube and caught the northern line from Tottenham Court Road north to Highgate. From there, he turned right onto Sheridan Road and then the second right onto Onslow Avenue to number sixty-four. By now, it was dark and turning cold. He knew what he wanted to do now.

With Miss Jones' keys in his hand, he unlocked the front door, then, deciding it was best not to switch the hall light on, walked quietly but quickly up the stairs to the first floor. He could hear people in their flats but no one came out. No one saw him. He found number three and let himself into the darkened flat.

A tabby cat came to greet him. He removed his coat and shoes but kept his gloves on and was relieved to feel the heating was on. Switching on Miss Jones' kettle, he made himself a cup of tea but, to his annoyance, couldn't find any sugar. With his gloves still on, he removed Mr Smith's Arsenal mug from his briefcase and left it unwashed in the sink.

It was a lovely flat, large, two bedrooms, nicely decorated with warm red or amber colours throughout, lots of family photographs on the walls and a large painting of snow-capped mountains in the living room. It was neat, everything in its place. He cast an eye over her collection of LPs and books. Miss Jones was a fan of The Eagles and Duran Duran, and romance novels, especially those by Jackie Collins, and a couple of Jeffrey Archers thrown in, plus a few cookbooks and, on the coffee table, a hefty volume of Monet's art. She liked her wine – a rack half full of red, and a couple bottles of white in the fridge. She also liked her herbs and spices – a whole rack of them in the small kitchen. He wondered whether Miss Jones had a man in her life, but if so, he didn't live here, she definitely lived alone with her cat who, according to its name tag, was called Twizzle. In the corner, Twizzle's cat tray.

He opened the bedroom door. A surprisingly big room with a four-poster double bed, so much nicer and cosier than his own. His eye was drawn to a shiny plain blue book on her dresser. It was a diary, 1982 written in big, golden letters. He flicked through to yesterday but the page was still blank. He flipped the pages and, in January, the name Neil jumped out at him. But this Neil wasn't Mr Smith, it was another Neil, a lover. He skim-read several passages, sitting on the edge of Miss Jones' bed. Heck, by the end of March, Miss Jones had finished with this Neil. But, oh no, Neil couldn't accept it, the word 'pestering' came up several times. And then, in July, a new name – Paul. Paul was now the love of her life. But Neil kept turning up unannounced and things were getting awkward at work. *Work?* The realisation hit him – Christ, this Neil *was* Mr Smith. Oh my God, he thought, how did he never realise? Smith and Jones together, and then not together, right under his nose, and he had absolutely no idea. Pat often said he was totally unobservant.

Ignoring the cat, he made himself comfortable on her settee, and, sitting down, sipped his non-sugared tea. He'd liked to have looked through the Monet book but it was properly dark now and he couldn't risk turning on a light

So he waited in the dark and slowly, very slowly, a new idea formed.

Chapter 14: Mac

Today, the sun was out, the shop loud and busy, The Killers playing on the stereo, the till constantly pinging and Mac felt good. The only blot on his otherwise sunny landscape was the thought of his father.

Whenever he thought of the man, he experienced a horrible rush of guilt. Everyone at the care home had taken against his father. The man was poorly, it wasn't his fault; he couldn't control his mind.

A customer came in, a young lad with a rainbow tee shirt. He was one of Tony's regulars. They fist-bumped each other. They knew each other well. No one shook hands in here any more, not since Covid hit. Eoin sauntered off to make the lad a cup of coffee.

The door opened again – another customer. Mac shrank back on seeing her, Mrs Hunt's granddaughter, Maxine. He'd only cut her hair recently; why was she back already? He feared this was going to be about his father.

'Hi Mac,' she said, nervously. 'C-can I have a w-word?' she asked. 'Please.'

'S-sure. Shall we go through to the back?'

She followed him through to his office. She was wearing ripped jeans and a black sleeveless top, exposing the gentle smattering of freckles on her forearms. She glanced up at his *Gone With the Wind* poster but didn't comment on it. She declined his offer of a coffee.

'How can I help, Maxine?'

'Yeah, right. Look, the thing is, I w-wanted t-to say sorry, you know, about earlier. I heard Mrs Hale gave you a hard time.'

'No, you don't have anything to apologise for.'

'It's just that…' She concentrated her attention on Mac's domed-shaped paperweight which had a photograph of Vienna inside it. She looked close to tears.

Mac leaned forward across his desk. 'My dad can be difficult, I know that. He's not had the easiest of times. And I'm sorry if–'

'It's… it's just that…'

'Go on.'

'She's all I got; you know. And… and… I don't know. I don't know how to say it.'

'It's fine. You don't need to. I get it, I do.'

'See, my dad died last year. He had pn-pneu… I can't say it, sorry.'

'Pneumonia?'

'Yeah, that's it. I don't even know what it means.' She pulled on her earring beneath her red hair.

'I'm sorry, Maxine.'

A flicker of a smile. 'It's all right. My mum died when I was small so Gran is my only family now, she and Charlie.'

'Charlie?'

'My cat. Gran's bonkers and all that, but still…'

79

'It hurts when you see someone being horrible to her.'

'Yeah, that's right, yeah.'

'Actually, we're quite similar, you and me. My mum left when I was small, and I was brought up by my father. My grandmother died just a couple of days ago.'

'Oh. I– I…'

He wished he hadn't said that now, it had only served to make her more agitated.

'You sure you won't have that coffee?'

'Nah, I oughta…' She checked the time on her phone. 'I gotta get to work.'

'Of course. Listen, Maxine, you really didn't have to come to say sorry. It's me that should be apologising.'

'It's not your fault though, is it?'

'No, but… it's like guilt by association.'

'I don't understand.'

'It's difficult having to care for parents and grandparents when they get old.'

'Yeah, true.' She stood up. 'Where is that?' she asked, motioning the paperweight.

'Vienna. Have you been?'

'Me?' She laughed. 'I ain't even been south of the river, never mind Germany or wherever it is. Thanks for doing my hair the other day.'

'It's fine. It looks good on you.'

She smiled at the compliment. 'Yeah, looks cool.'

'Will you be back?'

She looked at him for the first time, and the brightness of her green eyes took him aback. 'Yeah, I'll be back. If you'll have me, that is?'

He threw open his arms. 'The pleasure would be all mine, Maxine.'

Late afternoon. Harry Styles was playing on the stereo. Mac's next customer was a young boy of about eight or nine, dual heritage, small enough for Mac to fetch his crate and place it, upturned, on the chair. The boy wore a blue Chelsea football shirt with Christian Pulisic's name and the number ten on the back. His mother, or so Mac assumed, said hello. 'How do you want it?' he asked her as the boy climbed up onto the chair and considered his reflection in the mirror.

'Oh, short back and sides, please. A bit of a general tidy-up.' She flashed Mac a lovely, warm smile that made him feel warm inside.

'No problem.'

She was certainly attractive, long fair hair with blonde highlights, stylish jeans and a grey, sparkling top. 'His grandmother used to cut his hair but I decided he deserved a proper cut now so you might find it a bit ragged in places.'

'That's fine. Let's see what we can do.' He turned to the boy. 'What's your name then?' he asked as he tied an apron around the boy's neck.

'Marcus Elliott Cavendish.'

His mother laughed.

'Right! So, Marcus Elliott Cavendish, how do you do? Oh, wait, I'm sorry, I can't cut your hair.'

Marcus looked puzzled.

'It's against my religion, I'm sorry.'

'W-why?' asked Marcus, glancing over at his mother.

'Didn't you see the big sign on the door as you came in?'

The boy shook his head.

'It says, quite clearly, no Chelsea supporters allowed in this barbershop. Arsenal supporters only. Sorry, mate.'

Marcus grinned at his reflection. 'It's not true, is it, Mum?'

'I'm not sure, Marcus. I didn't see the sign. Maybe I should go check.'

'OK,' said Mac. 'Let's compromise. As long as you don't like Manchester United, that's the main thing.'

'Man U?' Marcus shook his head as if he'd tasted something foul. 'I hate Man U; they're rubbish.'

'Ah, great. That's something we can agree on. Maybe I can cut your hair, after all.' Mac picked up his shears. 'What do you think, Mum? A number two for the back.'

'Yes, that'd be perfect. Thank you.'

'No problem. Right, young man, ready for a proper haircut?' Marcus grinned and nodded.

'Let's do this then!'

*

Marcus and his mother had left. He realised she hadn't told him her name. He hoped they'd return; she really was rather nice. But no time to ponder such things – a queue of blokes wanted their haircuts. He was about to summon his next customer when he heard the ding-dong notification on his mobile.

He told the next guy in the queue he'd be with him in a moment. Disappearing into a corner, Mac looked at his phone and opened up his email, wondering whether this could be from the mysterious woman Eoin had mentioned. A new email had popped up in his inbox with the subject heading, *Hello*. His nerves on edge, Mac opened the email while Taylor Swift played loudly, too loudly, on the stereo.

Dear Thomas.

Thomas? Only people who didn't know him called him

Thomas.

Dear Thomas,
I know this may come as a bit of a shock but I am your mother.

Oh fuck. *Fuck.* He slammed the phone into his back pocket. The room spun; he needed to sit down. The music was too loud, his head was pounding. Tony, who was with a customer, noticed. 'Jesus, Mac, you all right? You look ill, mate.'

'Yeah, I'm not…' He was fighting for breath here, this was mad. 'I just need some air. It's too hot in here.'

'Sure.'

He apologised to his next customer, telling him he'd be back in a minute.

It was mild outside, the sky overcast. He walked towards the post office where he knew there were a couple of benches outside. Sure enough, one of them was vacant. He sat down, his legs like jelly. He didn't want to read this email but he knew he had no choice. It was there, on his phone, waiting for him, a message from his mother. It didn't seem true. He never thought this day would come. He looked up and caught the eye of a young mum passing by, holding the hand of a small boy of about four or five. It seemed like an omen. He held his breath as he started to read.

I hope you're OK, son. I think of you every day. I managed to find your
email address with the help of a friend. I've just returned to London. I
was living in Spain but since Brexit it's more difficult for us Brits.

Thomas, I know you may not want to see me, but I would love to see
you again. I know it'll be hard for you but please can we meet? I know
you probably still hate me for running out of your life like I did but please
believe me – if I could change things I'd do so in a heartbeat.

I still love you.
Mum.

He couldn't control his heart; it was thumping so hard. He wanted to be sick. He stared up at the sky, clenching his eyes shut. He couldn't believe he'd just read what he'd read. She'd been in Spain all this time. And now she was back and she wanted to see him. She finished her email with her mobile number and the address of a bed and breakfast where she was staying just up the road. This was incredible – his mother was barely a mile away.

There were times when he'd have given anything, *anything*, to receive this email. But now? After all this time? No, it was too late now. He wasn't interested any more. He was not going to jump at the sound of his mother clicking her fingers. No, not now. He read the email again, this time more slowly, but it made no difference. This woman had ruined his life, and he was not letting her back in to ruin it again. No way.

He deleted the email.

Chapter 15: Benedict

Benedict was about to leave the office for a drive up to Milton Keynes to talk to a retired copper, checking his pockets for his car keys and his mobile. It was already mid-afternoon.

DC Kelly spoke. 'Oh, before you leave, boss, I spoke to forensics earlier about that car with the scrape down its side.'

'Oh?'

'His car was scraped along the driver's side by a silver Volkswagen Polo, probably registered around 2015–2017.'

'Gee, why couldn't it have been some obscure make or model? Right, get on–'

'I already have, boss. Spoken to half the local garages in the vicinity, especially that German car specialist off Church Street. Nothing yet. Gonna speak to the other half today.'

'Good man.'

Kelly smiled to himself.

*

It took a good hour and a half to drive to Milton Keynes; the traffic coming out of London was predictably heavy. But once on the M1 motorway, Benedict enjoyed the drive, listening to a radio play and, following that, an album by Coldplay. He'd received some good news before leaving the station – the hospital rang through; apparently, Zoe Wright's condition had improved, and she was now out of the danger and rapidly gaining strength. He wanted DC Prowse to go straight over and interview her, but Prowse suggested they leave it a day, give her more chance to recuperate. Reluctantly, Benedict had to agree.

Benedict passed Bletchley Park, the country estate that, during the Second World War, had been home to Britain's crack team of code breakers. He always heard that through their efforts, they probably shortened the war by at least a couple of years and certainly aided the Allied victory. If he had time, he'd have loved to have gone in. But time was not a luxury he possessed right now. He had a man to see.

Former Detective Inspector Peter Grainger was more than happy to talk to him about Neil Smith, a case he led on back in 1982–83. Now a widower, Grainger lived alone in the suburbs of the city. Using his Waze app, Benedict found the address – Broughton Gate, an attractive set of new builds.

Grainger welcomed him in.

'Nice place you've got here, sir.'

'Ah, you don't need to 'sir' me anymore, Ben. I'm just a plain old civilian now. Have been for years. But yes, I'm lucky to have this place. It's all very high-tech, you know. Scandinavian design and technology, don't you know, energy efficient, high ceilings, everything voice activated. Those Scandinavians know what they're doing. Took me a while to get used to it, to be honest. Watch this…' He ordered the living room lights to come on, which they duly did, and then turn off again.

'Impressive!' It was indeed a spacious room with a high

ceiling and, despite a large amount of furniture, still managed to feel spacey. He liked it.

'Can I get you something?' asked Grainger.

'A cup of tea would be nice.'

'Coming right up. Let's have a biscuit too. Bathroom's right through there.'

'So,' said Grainger, once they'd settled. 'Neil Smith, the white mouse man.'

'Yes, sir.'

'Someone's copying his signature.'

'Yes.' Benedict brought the former DI up to date, carefully avoiding divulging more than would be strictly professional.

'So, really, apart from the mouse placed in the victim's mouth, nothing similar whatsoever.'

'No but…'

'I know. No stone unturned and all that. Totally understand.'

Benedict glanced around the room, seeing the large number of framed photographs of family members – grandchildren here, a woman he guessed was Grainger's wife there, more grandchildren.

'That's why me and Vicky moved up here after I retired – get to see more of the grandkids. They all live up here or nearabouts.'

'Nice.' He sipped his tea, far too weak for his liking, but the chocolate digestives were most welcome. Benedict loved a chocolate digestive.

'I'm thinking of downsizing though. Now that I'm all alone, it seems…' He waved his arms about. 'Too big just for me. So, the thing about Neil Smith was that there was a very obvious motivation for killing his first victim, but absolutely none for his second or the girl who escaped with her life.'

'The first victim was called Ruth Jones,' said Benedict. 'Aged twenty-nine at the time. Strangled in her own flat by her own scarf.'

'Yep, that's the one. Smith and Jones worked together in a shop selling TVs and video recorders on Tottenham Court Road. He was her boss. We discovered her diary, and from that, we learned that they had been in a relationship together, but she finished it. She'd met someone new, a Paul something. About two months before killing her, Smith made quite the scene outside her flat, banging on the door, shouting and swearing, that sort of thing. This Paul bloke sorted it out. She was frightened of him.'

'How do you know?'

'She wrote it all down in her diary.'

'So, one day, Smith nicked her flat keys from work, went round to hers, let himself in and waited for her. He made himself a mug of tea while waiting. I remember it was an Arsenal mug – that was his big mistake. Forensics were able to determine it was still fairly fresh and the traces of milk hadn't gone off or anything like that. And of course, it had his fingerprints on it.'

'DNA?'

'No, still too new. The bigger stations were using it on the high-profile cases, but it hadn't rolled out yet. Do you remember Colin Pitchfork, like Neil Smith, a double murderer?'

'Oh yes, he was the first to be convicted using DNA.'

'That's the one. In 1987. He killed his first victim in November 1983, nine months after Smith's final attack. They released Pitchfork recently and then, because he started approaching young women again, they promptly chucked him back inside. Good thing too, I'd say.'

'Any witnesses to the murder?'

'Nope, not a single one.'

'But, sir, no witnesses, no CCTV, I'm guessing, and no DNA…'

'No, it wasn't just circumstantial. We had enough, damn it. We had the diary, the fingerprints and, living alone, he had no alibi. We never found out where he bought his mice. We asked all the local pet stores but no luck. But then, his fatal mistake… we found an envelope at his second attack, the poor woman killed down that alleyway, Elizabeth Blinkhorn, known by her friends as Lizzie. It was a Christmas card with an address in Winchester written on the envelope. It was a card for his sister. *To Cheryl, Happy Xmas, love, Neil.* Kiss, kiss. Not only did the card and envelope have Smith's fingerprints all over them, we had a handwriting expert look at it, and yes, it was definitely Smith's handwriting. Smith denied it, of course, in fact, he was shouting his innocence to the very end by all accounts. Of course, if, at any time, he'd admitted his guilt, he'd have been released years ago. But he refused, silly bugger. We also found a mouse at the scene of the third attack. That young lady was very lucky indeed. Would you like a top-up?'

'Hmm? Oh, no thanks, sir. Thanks anyway.'

'Sure.'

'I'll have another biscuit though.'

'You go ahead, Ben. Help yourself.'

They sat in silence for a while. Eventually, the old detective said, 'I heard that Neil Smith got himself a pen pal while doing time. Apparently, he and this woman wrote numerous letters to each other.'

'Really? That's interesting. Do you remember her name? Or where was she writing from?'

'Oh, Ben, I'd retired by then. I don't know. Have you read through all the files? Is it in that?'

'I've made a start. There's a lot to go through. I've got one of my assistants on the case.'

'At first, I had a hunch it was Smith's subordinate that killed those girls. He had previous for beating up a kid at a funfair and earned himself a two-year suspended. We interviewed him but his alibi, although soft, would have been enough to convince a jury. That's what my chief at the time reckoned, and he was probably right, looking back on it. And, to be fair, we had nothing against him apart from the fact he was one of these men you immediately take against. You know that feeling you get as a copper?'

Benedict agreed. 'What was his alibi?'

'Home all night with his wife, his mother and his brother who was visiting. Never went out. They watched a film on TV. *Jaws*, I think.'

'Do you remember his name, sir? I can look it up, of course.'

'It was… Derek something. I can't recall the surname right now. It'll come to me. Another digestive?'

Benedict patted his stomach. 'I'd better not.'

Chapter 16: Derek

December 1982

Derek woke up and rubbed his eyes. He'd fallen asleep on Miss Jones' settee. It took him a moment to remember why he was here in her flat and for his eyes to get accustomed to the dark. He wondered what the stink was – when he realised that Twizzle had been busy in her cat tray. He was still wearing his gloves – that was good. Checking his watch with its luminous hands, it was almost half past five. Miss Jones would be back within the hour – unless, of course, she decided to go out for the evening. If so, he'd wait. He was a patient man; he'd wait for as long as it took. He stretched and yawned. The cat, Twizzle, padded up to say hello. He stroked the cat then went to the kitchen and rinsed out his mug and left it inside down to drain on the draining board. But, on second thoughts, he put the mug into his briefcase. Had he touched anything else? No. Apart from her keys, which he'd take with him, no. And he'd kept his gloves on. Everything was as it should be.

The image of the expression on her face when he asked her out came to mind. He was recently married at that point but that fact hadn't entered into the equation. If he wanted to have an affair, that was his lookout. It was an expression of utter contempt, but that was Miss Jones all over, so sure of herself. 'You're asking *me* on a date? I think not, Derek.'

And now, thanks to her he risked losing his job. Pat's job as a dinner lady paid a pittance. No way could they keep up with the mortgage payments if he lost his job. And having his mother living with them, an extra mouth to feed, certainly didn't help. His mother was a bitter old crone. It seemed like a terrible thing to say, but he couldn't stand the woman, and hated the fact she was always there. She never went out, just sat in that armchair passing judgement on everything he did – his choice of TV programmes, his hair, his slippers, the way he ate, bloody everything. He'd quite happily place a pillow over her head and suffocate the old witch.

Even as a kid, he hadn't liked her much, nor had Geoff, his older brother. He'd recently rang Geoff and asked him if he and his wife, Debbie, would take her in for a while. Geoff agreed, albeit reluctantly, but his mother refused to budge.

He and Geoff had never got on. It didn't help that his brother had always lusted after Pat. Pat told him. Geoff had even tried to persuade Pat to leave him and run off with Geoff.

The fact is, Derek had never had any luck with women. Pat only married him because he made her pregnant after a drunken night out at a working men's club. They got married and soon afterwards promptly lost the baby. That should have been the time to escape but frankly, he knew no one else would have him, and he sort of got used to having a sex life for the first time, even if they always did it in the dark because he hated the sight of her scrawny little body.

Miss Jones was a threat. No two ways about it. It was him or her. The tribunal would take her word against his, he'd lose his job and possibly face time inside, especially as he couldn't play the 'first offence' card. He'd used that up on that kid he'd beaten up at the funfair. He couldn't face prison. He'd never survive.

It was now half past six. She'd be back any moment. But, of course, without her keys, she wouldn't get in. He removed his shoes and. together with his briefcase, hid them beneath her settee. He left her door on the latch, which meant the door remained ever so slightly ajar. He only hoped someone would let her in outside.

He heard footsteps coming up the stairs, voices. A couple of women's voices but neither of them hers. He held his breath and listened as they passed Miss Jones' flat, chattering amicably.

Twenty minutes later, he heard another couple of voices coming up the stairs – and this time one of them was Miss Jones. This was it. His heart hammered as he heard them approach and stop outside the flat door. Miss Jones was thanking the woman for letting her in, and worrying about where she'd mislaid her keys.

'If you want to call the landlord from mine, you're more than welcome,' said Miss Jones' companion.

'Oh, look, the door seems to be open. I must've… Well, that's something, I suppose.'

'You've not been burgled? Do you want me to come in with you?'

No, thought Derek, hiding behind the door, please don't come in, please don't…

'No, I'll be fine but thank you all the same.'

'You sure now?'

'There's no damage to the door so no one's forced their way in. I must've left in a hurry this morning.'

The woman said good night, see you again, before walking on. Derek squeezed himself against the wall behind the door.

Miss Jones entered her flat, carrying a plastic bag of shopping. Sighing, she flicked on the light. She removed her hat and knelt down to greet Twizzle. 'Hello, sweetie, how's your day been?' The cat purred, arching its back. 'Good girl.'

Derek heard a door close further down the corridor, presumably Miss Jones' friend entering her flat.

Miss Jones straightened. Derek could see her stiffen. She knew all of a sudden that something was amiss. 'Hello?' she called quietly. 'Is anyone h-here?' She removed her coat and stepped cautiously into her living room.

It was at that point, perhaps hearing footsteps behind her, she turned around and clapped eyes on Derek.

She didn't even have a chance to scream…

Chapter 17: Benedict

It took Benedict and Jessica over an hour to drive the twenty miles from Camden to Dagenham. It didn't come as a surprise though; Waze had pre-warned him. 'This traffic is mad,' he said to Jessica. 'You know, they say it was quicker getting around London during Victorian times with a horse and cart.'

'Imagine all that horse poo, though.'

'Less harmful than our fumes.' He stopped at a red light. 'So, how are you finding it down here?'

She took a while to answer. 'Yeah, I'm enjoying it. I have lived in London before though. I was at university here, Middlesex. But yeah, the job's very much as I expected it to be.'

'And is that a good thing?'

'Oh, totally.'

He was mightily relieved to hear that. 'Well, I have to say, Jessica, you're doing very well. You've fitted in with the team from Day One. Everyone likes you and, far more importantly, they *respect* you. I've been impressed.'

'Why, thanks, boss. That... that means a lot to me. Thank you.'

'I speak only of the truth,' he added in a pompous tone.

'Seriously though, we'll talk more at your first one-to-one. I don't want to make this journey into an impromptu meeting. Have you found somewhere to live yet?'

A motorbike speeded by, its exhaust making a racket. 'No, not yet. I'm couch surfing with some old uni friends until I find somewhere proper to rent. Where do you live, boss?'

'Me? I live in St John's Wood.'

'Oh, isn't that posh?'

'So they say although our patch is somewhat less posh than the rest of it.'

'Are you married?'

'Yes, and I have three kids, one fifteen and a full-blown teenager, another ten and already a full-blown teenager, plus a six-year-old. It's hell!'

'I'm sure you love it really.'

'Of course I do.'

Five minutes later, Waze displayed the black and white chequered flag showing that they'd reached their destination. 'And here we are,' said Benedict, parking on the street. 'Let's see what Geoffrey McIntosh has to say for himself.'

Jessica had phoned the day before using the number given to them by Mac so Geoffrey McIntosh was expecting them. He lived on the fifth floor of a tower block, Jarrow Tower, another sixties construction. He welcomed them into his flat, a council property. One whole wall of his living room was bricked and fronted by a massive television and above it a low-hung wide mirror. Everything was black and silver, it screamed bachelor pad, but it was clean and tidy. They accepted Mr McIntosh's offer of tea and, together, settled on the green, squashy settee.

'Digestive?' asked McIntosh.

'Chocolate?' asked Benedict, hopefully.

'Sure.'

'Good man. I have a weakness for chocolate digestives. Thank you.'

Once they'd all settled and Benedict had a chance to moan about the traffic, they began. Jessica started by offering McIntosh their condolences on the death of his mother. He didn't seem that perturbed.

'Did you visit your mother?' she asked.

'Oh yeah. I mean it was an effort getting there, as you've just found out, and my old Vauxhall Viva complained like hell. I've had that car for years. My mother hated going around in it; said she was ashamed to be seen in a "shit-coloured car" but yes, I visited the old girl. Not that often, mind you, but, you know, I did my bit. Took her to her appointments, that sort of stuff. More than I could say about my lazy brother.'

'We'll come to your brother in a minute. Did you ever bump into your nephew while there?'

'Mac? Nah, I didn't. I knew he popped in though. He bought her stuff, like food and that. Essentials, you know. I let him do it; he's got a job. I don't. Cost me enough in petrol, even more now, what with this bloody cost of living.'

'You won't have to go any more,' said Jessica.

'You're not wrong there, love.'

'How was your mother?' asked Benedict. 'In good spirits?'

'Mum in good spirits? The only time she was ever in good spirits was when someone died. Lionel Blair, Prince Philip, Leslie Phillips, that drummer from the Rolling Stones; I'm telling you, a celebrity death positively made her day.'

'The queen?'

'Ah no. That was different, like. She liked the queen. Had a portrait of her in her bedroom.'

'Of course.' Benedict remembered now. 'But otherwise?'

'What? Oh yeah, nah, to be honest with you, she was a bad-tempered old bat. Never smiled, never said thank you. I don't even think she liked me visiting.'

'Why did you bother?'

'Well, I didn't want her to change her will. Joke! Really, I was joking.' He slapped his own wrist. 'I must not joke in front of the old bill.'

'We haven't seen her will yet,' said Jessica.

'You won't find anything in it. She never had two half pennies to rub together.'

'So, where were you Monday night, about ten, Mr McIntosh?' asked Benedict.

'I knew you was going to ask me that – I was at the social having a drink. Just down the road, a two-minute walk. Loads of witnesses, including two old mates. You ask them, they'll tell you I was there, and the folk behind the bar.'

'From what time to what time?' asked Jessica.

'Oh, let's see. I reckon I got there about eight and left around half ten, actually, more like a quarter to eleven.'

Benedict was about to ask whether he'd popped out at any point, but he couldn't have driven to Camden and back without him being missed. Instead, he asked, 'When was the last time you saw your mother?'

'Erm…' He scratched his chin. 'Probably Tuesday last. Yeah, definitely.'

'How was she?'

He shrugged. 'Same as always. Her usual charming self.'

'Will you be going to the funeral, Mr McIntosh?' asked Jessica.

'I don't even know when it is, love.'

'Not until we release the body, I'm afraid.'

'I imagine Rebecca will be organising it. That's my niece.

Yeah, reckon I should go. It'll be good to see Becky and Mac. God knows how long since I last saw them.'

'What about their mother? When was the last time you saw her?'

'Pat? Now, you're talking. Nigh-on thirty or more years. Not heard a peep since she walked out on my brother, and that must've been… ninety-one, ninety-two?'

'Talking of whom,' said Benedict, finishing his tea, 'when was the last time you saw your brother?'

He sighed. 'We never got on, if truth be told. My brother and me, we… we never saw eye to eye, you know what I mean?'

'But the last time–'

'I can't honestly remember, but years back. And I'm talking about the time Pat fucked off… oh, I'm sorry, love, didn't mean to swear.'

Jessica almost smiled.

'So, we're talking thirty years or so,' said Benedict.

'That's about the measure of it, yes, I'd say so.'

'So, the big question, Mr McIntosh… why would anyone want to kill your mother?'

He shook his head. 'Beats me. I mean, yeah, she was an old witch but, you know…' He threw his hands apart.

'You've no idea?'

'Baffled.'

'You know your brother's in a care home now with dementia?' said Jessica.

'Yeah, I knew *that*. Mum and me *did* talk sometimes.'

'Of course. I apologise.'

'Don't worry about it, love.'

Benedict and Jessica looked at each other. Did they have anything else for Mr McIntosh? No, that was about it. They thanked him for his time and Benedict handed him his card.

Jessica nipped to his bathroom to use his toilet while Benedict helped himself to a last chocolate digestive.

Chapter 18: Mac

Mac still couldn't believe that after all this time, his mother had contacted him. He'd deleted the email, having no desire to see her again. Why should he allow her this chance of redemption when she'd forced him into a childhood of misery? He didn't want to see this older version of his mother begging him for his forgiveness. It was too late now, woman. He didn't need her now.

It was that time of the week when Mac visited his father. It was early evening, the sun fading, the shadows long. What he really wanted to know was what his father meant last visit when he called his mother a bitch. He hated him for saying it, and it'd been bugging him ever since. He could understand it, in truth, his wife walking out on him, leaving him with two young children to look after and bring up by himself. It must've been hard but still, 'bitch' was such a harsh, unforgiving word, and hearing him say it brought out a protective streak in Mac; he wanted to protect the very woman he'd not seen since he was nine years old. He often wondered whether she'd run off with another man and started anew. Did she have more children, did Mac and Rebecca have half brothers or sisters somewhere? Surely, she would have let them know; she wouldn't have kept such a thing from them. But who knows, she was hard-hearted enough to leave without by your leave, she had to be capable of anything.

Stepping into the home, he immediately bumped into the carer, Charmaine, the carer with a swirly tattoo around her wrist. But instead of greeting him with her usual cheery smile, she appeared a little off with him, as if he was an unwelcome guest. That, in itself, was the first indication that something wasn't quite right. He could hear the sound of someone, a woman, sobbing. He crept forward. Turning the corner into the dining area, he saw Maxine's red hair. She was crouching next to her grandmother's chair, rubbing the old woman's hand. She was crying loudly, and Mac knew why. He took a deep breath and prepared himself for facing his father.

Mac found his father as usual in the conservatory staring out into the garden. 'Hi, Dad, how's it going?'

His father looked up at him and Mac could see for himself that this was not a good day – his eyes looked clouded and he definitely didn't recognise him. Mac patted the back of his hand and drew a chair up and sat next to him. 'Hello, Dad.'

He looked up. 'I'm telling you, I'm gonna fucking kill that woman.'

Mac glanced around. 'Dad, don't use that language. Who are you talking about?' He knew the answer.

'That Hunt woman.'

'What about her?'

His father didn't answer and seemed to turn inwards. So, Mac resigned himself to sitting with his father as if he was a total stranger to him. They could've been fellow travellers on an underground train, sitting next to each other for a few minutes, ignoring each other, when the train pulls up at a station and he'll get up, vacate his seat and exit the train, and the man next to him won't give him a second thought.

Time passed slowly. Mac checked the time on his phone numerous times. Charmaine offered him a cup of tea. He smiled and said no thanks. After a while, Mac decided to leave. It'd not been a good visit; his father had not said a single word since and had kept his attention entirely focused on the garden outside. Mac was rather depressed by it all. He patted his hand again and stood up. 'Oh well, Dad. I'll see you in a few days, OK? Look after yourself.' He still didn't answer. 'And for God's sake, Dad, please behave yourself. Stop upsetting the others. Please, Dad.'

Please acknowledge me, please look at me, even if it's just for a second. He did not, and Mac left with a pebble in his heart.

As he was leaving, Mac heard his name being called. 'A minute of your time, Mr McIntosh.' He knew that stern voice.

'Yes, Mrs Hale.'

He followed the manager into her office. She told him to sit. 'He's upset Maxine's grandmother again, hasn't he?'

Pushing her keyboard to one side, she leaned forward. 'More than that, I'm afraid, Mr McIntosh.'

'What's he done now?'

She paused, as if for dramatic effect. 'He tried to strike her.'

'*Strike her*? Are you sure?'

She tilted her head to one side but didn't answer, as if the answering was beneath her, in other words, yes, she was sure.

Mac rubbed his eyes.

'I did warn you, Mr McIntosh–'

'Was she hurt?'

'Luckily not, but of course she's terribly shaken up, and so's her granddaughter.'

'Oh God. I'll have to apologise.'

Mrs Hale looked at him pityingly. 'I fear it's a bit late for that now, Mr McIntosh.'

'The man has dementia. I talk to him; I tell him to behave…' He used air quotes to emphasise the last word. 'But he's forgotten what I've said within minutes. You have to take his condition into account, surely?'

'I'm perfectly aware of how dementia works, Mr McIntosh. And we have taken his condition into account, but, as I've told you before, I have a moral and legal responsibility for *all* our clients here. Your father's actions and his outright bullying, whether conscious or not, cannot be tolerated a moment longer.'

'A moment longer? You're evicting him, aren't you?'

She nodded. 'I'm afraid so. Legally, I have to serve you–'

'Twenty-eight days' notice, I know.'

He sat back in his chair, deflated, exhausted. He hadn't wanted his father to live his final days here, but Rebecca had always insisted. He wanted to have him living in his flat. But now the time had come, it hit him exactly what he'd be taking on. He'd have to become a full-time carer for him, and let Eoin and Tony take over the everyday management of the shop. He could still do the financial stuff from home. But for how long? There was no way back from dementia, everyone knew that. Just a one-way ticket to oblivion. He needed Rebecca. What would Rebecca say if she was here? Well, she wouldn't take this lying down as he was. She'd fight, tell Mrs Hale she couldn't simply throw him out, however much notice she gave, that she'd take it to appeal, take it to courts if necessary. But he wasn't made like his sister, he was weaker, he knew that. And his sister wasn't here, was she? He was. Only him.

'OK.' he said.

'I'm sorry it's come to this, Mr McIntosh. But I hope you understand that your father's behaviour has left me with no option.'

'Yeah, well, he won't care, will he? He'll just have a different four walls to stare at all day. Won't make much difference to him.'

'We do provide excellent entertainment for–'

'Yes, I know, I'm sorry, I didn't mean to imply anything.' He stood. 'I'd better go.'

As he was leaving, he bumped into Maxine, also about to leave. 'You'll be pleased to know,' he said, 'they're evicting him. You'll be OK soon. We've got twenty-eight days to move out.'

'Twenty-eight days?' said Maxine. 'He'd have killed her by then. He tried to hit her earlier, you know that? My gran, at her age, hit by... by... *him*.'

Mac's face flamed up in shame. 'I know, Mrs Hale said. I'm sorry, Maxine.'

'Yeah, I know. You always say you're sorry but it doesn't change anything.'

The words hit him. She was right; he was forever apologising to her but it did no good whatsoever. She needed more, both her and her grandmother, they deserved it. Twenty-eight days seemed an age. Too long, far too long. God knows what Dad could do in that time.

He knew then he had no choice. He had to take his father out of Sunny Grove straight away, today, this minute, now.

Chapter 19: Derek

December 1982

Five minutes later, ten minutes, and he couldn't stop shaking. Had he really done it? Had he really killed her? It didn't seem possible; he never thought he had it in him, but yes, Miss Jones was lying on her back on the floor in the doorway between her hall and living room, her chiffon scarf wound tightly around her neck, her eyes bulging from their sockets, a damp patch where she'd wet herself. Then, without thinking about what he was doing, he placed one of his newly acquired white mice in her mouth. It was, he decided, a nice if rather macabre touch. Her bag of shopping lay on its side, spilling its contents: a packet of lamb steaks, some vegetables, a frozen strawberry cheesecake and a bottle of red wine. Was she cooking for someone tonight? It seemed too much for one person.

He retrieved his shoes and briefcase from under Miss Jones' settee and put his shoes back on. Next, he locked the flat door and switched the lights back off. He needed a drink but, finding his way in the dark, couldn't find anything besides a half bottle of white wine in the fridge, but he needed something stronger. Returning to the living room, he heard the faint rumble of music coming from a neighbour's flat, *Come On Eileen*. Twizzle came to see what was happening, meowing loudly. Poor thing; she was hungry. Stepping over Miss Jones' corpse, Derek went through to the kitchen again and after some rooting around, found a box of dried cat food. He poured a generous amount into a bowl and made sure the cat's water bowl was full.

It was time to leave.

But as he was about to leave the flat, the intercom buzzed. He swore. Her dinner guest, perhaps? Derek closed the living room door, shoving Miss Jones into the living room in the process.

Two, perhaps three minutes later, someone knocked on the flat door. 'Ruth?' A man's voice. 'Ruth, are you in there?' Another knock, much louder this time. The man lifted the letterbox flap and called through. 'I've brought wine. Ruth? Ruth, are you there?' He had an edge to his voice now.

Then, he heard the neighbour's voice. She told him how Miss Jones had forgotten or misplaced her house keys and she'd let her in outside but she found her front door unlocked and went in. No, she hadn't seen or heard her since, and that was about half an hour ago. Maybe she went out again, maybe to find a locksmith or the landlord? 'So, who are you?' the woman asked.

'Paul. I'm Ruth's boyfriend. We were going to have dinner together, lamb steaks.'

The woman said something but Derek didn't hear it.

'Something's wrong here,' said Paul.

'She's probably just popped out. I'm sure it's nothing to worry about. Do you want to wait in mine until she comes back?'

'Do you have a phone? I might need to call the police.'

Derek stiffened on hearing the p-word.

'Of course,' said the neighbour. 'Come through. I can do you a coffee, if you like.'

OK, thought Derek, so this was going to be the difficult bit. He had to leave now, as quietly as possible, knowing this Paul's ears would be on stalks listening out for Miss Jones. A siren rang out and, for a moment, he feared he might keel over with dizziness until he realised it couldn't conceivably be about him.

Pressing his ear against the flat door, he reckoned the landing was empty. There was no light beneath the door so the temporary landing light had turned itself off. He needed to leave straight away, this minute. Hopefully, the neighbour's kettle might hide any noise.

Gently, he turned the lock and inched open the door. The corridor was still dark. He held his breath, conscious of every movement, as he closed the door behind him. It made a click as it closed, deafeningly loud. He clenched his eyes shut. Quickly, he walked across the landing to the stairs and ran down the staircase. He crossed the darkened communal entrance, with the main doors ahead of him. No one was about but he still had to fight the urge to run, to get out of here, but he forced himself to walk, albeit as fast as he could.

He was outside now, the sharp, cold air hitting him. Oh, the relief. He walked, head down, across the gravel driveway and onto Onslow Avenue. Every step he took, brought him closer to freedom. He saw a dog walker coming up the pavement, so he crossed the road to the other side. Five minutes later, he was at Highgate tube station and entered the warmth of the station. Once inside, he had to stop himself from punching the air with delight.

He laughed out aloud. He ought to stop; people would think

him a madman. This feeling was utterly fantastic; as if he was soaring above the clouds. He was buzzing; he could dance, such was the rush. Is this why people took drugs, to get this high? He'd never taken drugs, had always been a little afraid of it, and, anyhow, he moved in the wrong circles, on account he didn't move in any circles outside work. But he couldn't imagine any drug giving him such a high as this!

He'd got away with it.

*

An hour later, he arrived home. He'd never been so relieved to step through his door and close it behind him. He even smiled at his mother sitting in her usual armchair in front of the television. She didn't like it. 'What are you grinning at, you goon?'

'And a good evening to you as well, Mother.'

He was incredibly hungry and absolutely exhausted. The excitement of it all, the fear, the pure adrenalin – it had left him feeling weak and, heck, even a little tearful. He went through to the bathroom and stared at his reflection. A murderer was staring back at him, a cold-blooded murderer. A tear escaped. What had he done? Turning on the hot tap at the basin, he washed his hands and his face. What was done was done, no turning back now. It made him a bad man, an evil bastard. He looked at himself again and whispered to himself, 'And I don't care.'

Satisfied and feeling better, he sat on his favourite armchair next to Daisy's glass tank. Daisy was a royal python, also known as a ball python due to them rolling into a ball when frightened or stressed. He'd always thought her beautiful, with her black, yellow and gold markings. He could watch her for hours and feel the strains of life ebb away. Although she was four feet long, it wasn't a big tank, pythons liked enclosed spaces, they felt stressed by too much space. He checked the thermometer – twenty-eight degrees. Perfect. It'd soon be time for her next dinner of white mice.

Pat came through from the kitchen. 'Oh, hello, stranger,' she said. 'You're late – again.'

'So what? Had a drink with a colleague from another branch who came by today.'

'Oh, yes? And does *she* have a name, this colleague?'

'Yes, *he* does. His name is Richard. Is that OK with you? I reckon he's a poof, actually.'

'You're too weak with him,' said his mother. 'You need to put your foot down more often.'

'Yes, Marjorie.'

'What, you mean like you used to with me and Geoff?' asked Derek. 'Give me a break.'

His barb cut; he could tell. His father had run off when he was still a boy, found himself a younger, less bitter model. He never heard from him again and that was fine by him because his father beat him regularly, usually with a leather belt. He'd always hated the old bastard.

The mention of Geoff hit home with Pat too. Whenever the name Geoff came up, they both remembered that his brother had asked her to run off with him.

'Is my dinner ready?' He sat at the small, Formica dinner table.

Pat dropped a plate of fish cakes, chips and peas in front of him.

'So, listen, I've got a day off tomorrow,' he said, his mouth full.

'Have you?'

'Yeah, maybe the day after too. Possibly all next week as

110

well.'

'Oh Gawd,' said his mother. 'That's all we need – you cluttering up the place.'

'Well, why don't you go and see your friends,' said Pat. 'Oh wait, you don't have any.'

'Yes, I have. Richard. Richard's my friend.'

'I thought you said he's a poof.'

'Yeah but that doesn't mean we can't be friends.'

'You like poofs now, then, do you?'

'Oh, bugger off.' He tucked into his, frankly, fairly revolting fish cake that tasted of sawdust, dry as a bone. 'I'll go out,' he said, thinking about taking a trip down to the bookmakers.

'I thought…' said Pat. 'I'm sure you said you'd used up all your leave.'

'Well, you heard wrong, didn't you? Just a week or so.'

He hoped to God it wasn't any longer.

Chapter 20: Benedict

Thursday morning. Carol Russell worked as an assistant manager of a high street accountancy firm. They sat on either side of a wide desk in her office on the seventh floor of a new build office block in London's St Pancras. Benedict had read the statement she gave DI Grainger back in early 1983 but he wanted to interview her himself, see whether, after all these long years, she might remember things differently. He found that occasionally, with the passage of time and with the benefit of perspective, a witness or victim could see things from a slightly different, more objective angle.

Carol Russell's assistant brought Benedict a coffee in a mug emblazoned with the words, *I "heart" Jamaica.*

'So, how long have you been working here?' he asked.

'Why, is it important?'

'No, no, just... making conversation.'

'DI Paige, if you don't mind, I'm a busy person... and, frankly, you're about to ask me about something I've spent the last forty years trying to forget. This is not easy for me.'

He put his hand up. 'I do apologise. OK then. So... if I've

got this right, you'd been to a party that night in January 1983 but left early.'

'Yes. I lived in Stoke Newington at the time. It was the eighth of January, a Saturday. But I wasn't feeling too good, so I left early. To be honest, I wished I hadn't gone in the first place; I was too bunged up with a cold. But it was my friend's party and I didn't want to let her down; I didn't want to appear a wuss. My boyfriend at the time offered to walk me home. I liked him. Sebastian, his name. But…' She paused here, the memory returning to her. 'It was one of those *if only* moments, you know? I've thought about it every day since, it never leaves me. *If only* I hadn't gone to that party in the first place, *if only* I'd stayed at the party, *if only* I'd accepted Seb's offer. But I didn't. I was seventeen, life was exciting, and I didn't want a small inconvenience like having a cold stopping me from enjoying life. And that's something I'll *always* regret, inspector.'

He nodded.

'It was a short walk from the party to where I was living at the time.'

'And where was that?'

'I lived with my parents on Albion Road. Fifteen minutes, if that, but only by taking that shortcut down that alleyway. And it wasn't late; it was only about ten o'clock. What could go wrong, as they say these days. What could go wrong? Quite a lot, as it happens.'

'You were attacked down the same alleyway as the previous victim.'

She sighed heavily. 'I know. Stupid–'

'No, no, not stupid–'

'No, but it was. But I was young, caught in my own orbit. I never listened to the news in those days, took no interest. So, I didn't know. I remember my mother mentioned it and

113

probably told me to take care, but I took no notice. You know what it's like at that age? You just dismiss it as your parents worrying as usual. You never think it could happen to you.'

'Yes, I know exactly what you mean. Look, I know this will be difficult, but can you describe what happened?'

'You haven't told me why you're here? Why are you asking again after all these years? Has something happened again?'

'There's not much I can tell you at this stage, Miss Russell–'

'Ms.'

'Ms Russell. But we've got a new case that… well, it involves… let's say certain similarities with your own terrible experience.'

Carol Russell stared at him, blinking. 'Shit.'

'Yeah. Exactly.'

'But the man who did it, Neil Smith…' She put her hand on her chest. 'God, I've not said his name aloud for years. He died in prison.'

'I know. In late June, eight months ago. We're thinking it's just coincidental but… well, we have to follow these things up.'

Carol gazed out of her window for a few moments. Without looking at Benedict, she began: 'I was just walking home feeling heavy with this cold and fed up. God knows what I looked like. My nose was bright as a beacon, and I was wearing earmuffs. Of course, walking was a mistake but how was I to know? I could've waited for a bus because it stopped right outside my house, but, you know, in those days we didn't have any apps or indicator boards telling you when the bus was due, so I figured it'd be quicker to walk, and I didn't want to be waiting for ages in the cold. It was freezing that night; the ground was glazed with a thin covering of sleet. I was vaguely aware of someone behind me but at first I took no notice. And of course, I did cut through that alleyway. Only then did I start to get worried about this bloke behind me, so I got my house key and gripped it.'

'You didn't run?'

'I know, I should have. But I remember thinking, I'm just being paranoid here, it's just a guy walking the same way as me, nothing to get worried about. I didn't want to appear stupid.' She shook her head. 'I didn't hear his footsteps catching up with me, didn't hear a thing. And then…' She paused and wiped an eye with the back of her hand.

'And then this gloved hand went over my mouth and pulled me down backwards. I couldn't scream. He said something but… no idea what, no idea. I felt something around my neck, and that's when I really started to panic. I wet myself, I honestly pissed myself. And, you know, that's what made me fight back. I scratched him with the key. And then this other bloke appeared and he ran away.'

'This scratch? Was it an actual scratch or a cut?'

'I don't know. I've never known.'

'Whereabouts did you scratch him?'

'On the face.' She turned to face him. 'Now, this is where I feel ashamed because at the time I didn't tell the police about this.'

'Can I ask why?'

'Wow, this is difficult. Because… because silly as it seems, but I *forgot*. I'd blocked it out. They kept pressing me for details, the coppers. They weren't exactly gentle, they *frightened* me. I imagined they'd be more considerate now, better trained. I was still only a kid, inspector.'

'I'm sorry.'

'And the more they pressurised me, the less I could think. It came to me a few days later, I remember I was in the shower, standing there shaking, when I remembered I'd scratched him. He called me a bitch. I had to tell the police but then I thought, "I can't tell them now; they won't believe me – it's too late; they'll think I'm just adding it as an afterthought." And, like I said, I was frightened of them. So, I never said.' She shook her head at the memory of it. 'I never said.'

'I understand.'

'I *should* have told the police about it. I should've told my parents. I should have told the court, but I was scared, so scared. So, I'm telling you – now. You're the first person I've ever told, inspector, and, you know, the relief is…'

'It's OK, Ms Russell, it's OK. It's fine.'

They sat quietly for a while, the silence broken only by a distant telephone ringing in an adjoining office.

'You see, I don't know how deep a scratch it was; it could have been nothing. But then I thought, it couldn't have been nothing if it hurt enough for him to call me a bitch. And when I saw him in that court, I forced myself to look at him, to see whether I'd marked him. But I couldn't see anything. Nothing at all. It'd healed. That's assuming there was something to heal in the first place. Of course, at the time, they didn't have DNA.'

'It was around but still wasn't widely used. Another couple of years, mind you…'

'Yeah. The funny thing is, he looked so sad standing there in the dock, that as much as I hated him, a tiny, *tiny* part of me felt sorry for him. And that fucked me up as well. How dare I harbour those feelings after what he'd done to me and those other women? He was a monster, and there was I…'

'It's OK now, it's OK.'

'Boy, this is hard.'

'I know. I've almost finished. Are you OK to continue?'

116

'Oh God yes, let's get it over and done with.'

'So, at the time, how did you describe this man to the police?'

She puffed out her cheeks. 'White. Stocky. Young-ish. Dark eyebrows.'

'Well, that description matched Smith.'

'Yeah, him and about a million others. At first, I thought maybe it'd been racially motivated but then I found out about the other women, and they were white.'

'You found the mouse.'

'Yes. I found the mouse. He'd dropped it in his hurry to escape. And that's what's given me a lifetime of nightmares. Knowing what he had planned; that that white mouse should have ended up in my dead mouth. That if he hadn't heard that man shouting from the end of the alleyway, he'd have killed me there and then. That man, Winston Abrahams, saved my life. I wished I could meet him now, say thank you again. I sort of said thank you at the time but it was rather half-hearted, and I've always felt bad about that. But at the time, I just wanted to hide under my duvet and never get up.'

'We tried to trace Abrahams. He emigrated soon after to St Lucia and apparently died about six years ago.'

She nodded, absorbing this piece of news. 'I wonder if he ever thought about that night.'

'I'm sure he did. He was a witness at the trial, after all.'

'I guess.'

Benedict reached for his phone on the desk and switched off the recorder. 'Ms Russell, I can't thank you enough. I'm sorry to—'

She put her hand up. 'It's OK, you don't have to say it. In some ways, you've helped.' She reached for a handkerchief and blew her nose. 'After all this time, I'm fine; I've got over it. It feels as if it happened to someone else. But its shadow has loomed long. I finished with Sebastian after it happened because I hated him even though he'd done nothing wrong. I *hated* him because he was a man, no other reason. Yet, he was a thoroughly decent kind of guy. And he was really *into* me, you know? I remember we kissed as I was leaving the party. I never kissed him again. I heard he was devastated when I finished with him and beside himself with guilt. He's married now, got a whole brood of kids. He won't have forgotten, I know that. I'm there forever, like a dark stain on his conscience. And he doesn't deserve that. He was a good man.'

'And you?'

'And me? It was years before I half trusted another man. I've never married, never had kids, never really had a relationship worth the name. I tell myself that was always my destiny, but I know I'm kidding myself. It wasn't so much the attack itself that fucked me up, because, you know, I was only tumbled to the ground; it's not as if I was raped or knifed or anything like that. But it's the knowledge that, if it'd gone to plan, if Winston Abrahams hadn't happened to be passing, I wouldn't be here today. I'd have been left for dead in a freezing cold alleyway with a dead mouse in my mouth.'

Chapter 21: Mac

Mac remembered when his father used to take him to the betting shop occasionally. Back then, people could still smoke indoors and those places always stunk of smoke, the ceilings were yellow and the carpet pockmarked with countless cigarette burns. Dad would pick him up after school and they went straight to the bookies, despite Mac's protests to go home first since he was hungry. Mac remembered the first time. Dad wanted to bet on a particular horse in a particular race. The odds were good and Dad was feeling confident. The race started and Dad was on his feet, hopping from one foot to the other, watching the race on one of those large, overhead TV screens. Mac knew that despite his father's bravado, now that the race had started, Dad was worried. He didn't see how much money his father had given the woman behind the cashier's desk but he reckoned it was a lot, more than he should have been gambling. That's when Mac knew that the outcome of this race would have a direct bearing on his immediate future too. The horse was called Arpeggio, his jockey wore purple with a large diagonal orange stripe. Mac's heart sank to see him in almost last place. Dad started shouting at the TV. Mac was on his feet too, his heart in his mouth, wanting to be sick. The horse had to win, just had to. Other men who'd bet on other horses in the race started shouting and the noise got louder and louder and the tension palpable. Mac willed Arpeggio on. With only a few fences to jump, he seemed to be catching up. But one horse in particular, Genie in a Bottle, was a long way ahead. Arpeggio was now in second place, doing well and far ahead of the horse in third place but with one fence to go he was too far behind. Dad was pulling his hair out. And then – a miracle: Genie in a Bottle fell at the last fence. All Arpeggio had to do was clear that last fence… Dad and Mac held their breaths, their eyes on stalks, glued to that TV screen. And he did it! Arpeggio was over, and way ahead of all the other horses. He trotted home in first place and Dad and Mac jumped in the air and screamed with joy. Dad collected his money from the cashier who laughed at what she called his beginner's luck, and they left the bookmakers on cloud nine. Dad took Mac to their local McDonald's and told him he could order anything he wanted. They ate like kings that night, and for the first time since his mother had left, Mac went to bed happy.

Of course, what Mac didn't appreciate at the time was that it was nothing but a false victory, a Pyrrhic victory, and that it would have been so much better in the long run had Dad lost that bet. Because, like the cashier said, it was beginner's luck, winning with his first go. It gave Dad a taste of what it was like to win easy money. Mac didn't realise at the time but Dad went back to that same bookmaker again and again hoping to recapture the euphoria of that first win, and occasionally he did, but it was rare. Mostly, he lost and lost badly. Soon, he'd lost everything he'd won with Arpeggio and more, much more.

And life at home became harder. They never had any heating on at home. If Mac complained, Dad would simply tell him to put another jumper on. Getting up for school in the mornings was horrible because the house was so awfully cold. And yet every week Dad still went off to the bookmakers with his social security money and lost it all. He'd come back in a foul temper and take it out on his son. Once, when Mac dared to ask if they could go back to McDonald's, he thought his dad was going to slap him, he was so angry. He never asked again and they never went again.

*

Today was Mac's turn to pop to the bakery a couple of doors down from the barbershop to buy pastries for himself, Eoin and Tony. He left the bakers with a paper bag containing three different flavoured pastries and bumped straight into a woman. He stepped back, apologising, and realised it was the Chelsea fan Marcus' mother. 'Oh, hi, hello.'

'Oh, Mac, hello. How are you?'

'Oh, fine, just got these pastries for me and the boys. An essential part of our diet.'

She laughed. 'Of course. Got to keep your strength up.' The breeze played with her hair.

'Absolutely. How's Marcus?'

'Oh, fine, thanks. He loved coming to get his haircut with you. He thought you were very funny.'

'Doh! I try my best.'

'Great haircut too. He loves it, keeps preening in the mirror.'

'That's good to hear.'

'He can't wait to come again.'

'Well, we'll be here whenever you're ready. You live around here?'

'Yes, just a few roads up,' she said, pointing behind her. 'Recently moved in after my…' She hesitated, leaving the sentence unfinished. 'Have you always had your barbers?'

'Yes, well, a few years now. It's a job, you know. Helps keep the wolves at bay.'

'Yes, I know what you mean.'

They looked at each other for a few moments, the silence stretching between them.

Mac broke first. 'Look, I'd better get these back,' he said, holding up his paper bag. 'Otherwise, the boys will think I've done a runner with their pastries.'

'Oh no, that wouldn't do.'

'Telling me. Anyway, it was nice to meet you again.'

'And you.' She smiled a huge smile before turning to leave.

'Oh,' he shouted after her. She turned, still smiling. 'What's your name? Sorry, I don't know your name.'

'Caroline.'

'Caroline. Well, nice to meet you, Caroline.'

Mac returned to the shop with a skip in his step and handed out the pastries to his grateful colleagues.

On his way back, he'd seen a poster with Taylor Swift, advertising her latest single. It was the same song on the stereo when he opened that email from his mother. He could visualise the video for the song. He knew though that whenever he heard that song it wouldn't be the video that came to mind but the memory of him reading those words written by his mother. *If I could change things I'd do so in a heartbeat. I still love you.* Jesus.

He snatched up his phone and opened up his email app. He scrolled down the deleted messages, finding the one from his mother. I'm doing this, he thought, and I'm doing it now. He knew if he hesitated, if he thought about it for a single second, he'd back out. He found her email, the name of the bed and breakfast she was staying at near the bottom, and below it, her mobile number. He pressed it and let it ring, his heart hammering inside his chest to the point of causing him physical pain. And then someone answered.

'Hello? Patricia Roberts here. Who's that, please?'

'Hello, Mum. It's your son here.'

Chapter 22: Derek

December 1982

That night Derek dreamt of Miss Jones, he could see his hands tightening that chiffon scarf of hers around her neck, the way she tried to fight him off, weakening by the second as he choked the fucking life out of her. He visualised her eyes, positively popping out of her head, the terror within those eyes. She tried to hit his hands off, to scratch him, whatever she had in her limited arsenal. He dreamt of her fingernails scratching his face, drawing blood. He woke up in an instant, the sweat running off him. He threw off the blankets and lay, panting, trying to quell the panic in his heart. He touched his face; it felt smooth, no scratches there, and then he remembered – she hadn't had a chance to remove those red leather gloves. Even if she had scratched him, she wouldn't have left a mark, there'd be no blood, no flesh under her fingernails. He was safe. Oh, the relief, thank Christ for that! His breathing calmed, his heartbeat slowed down. His illuminated alarm clock showed half past three.

Pat lay next to him, fast asleep, total silence. She had never been a snorer, his wife. One of the few things he actually liked about his wife.

So, he tried to remember – no one, as far as he knew, saw him come or go, it'd been dark, and he was wearing ordinary, dark clothes. He hadn't spoken to anyone, not even a grunt. No one heard him, or her. He'd kept his gloves on at all times. He had disturbed nothing except make a cup of tea and fed the cat. He'd walked around her flat in his socks, so not even a footprint. No one missed him except his wife and his mother – but that was OK, they'd do whatever he told them to. They depended on him too much. Yes, people would've seen him on the tube but he'd kept his eyes down at all times, and they would've seen thousands upon thousands of people on their commutes home. No one would remember him. He'd heard that some of the central London underground stations now had surveillance cameras, or CCTV as they called them, but surely not at Highgate station, it was too small for that.

Nothing was wrong. Everything was fine. He'd soon get his job back and, without Miss Jones on the scene, there'd be no tribunal, no permanent sacking. He was safe, absolutely safe.

But he still felt sick.

*

The following day, Derek had another dream – the one he often had. The swooshing sound of that leather belt as it sliced through the air, the terrible pain as the leather pounded his bare buttocks. His father yelling at him for being 'stupid', 'useless fucker' and 'worthless shit.' His mother always slipped away, too frightened to protect him from this monster. But it wasn't the cruel words that hurt so much, nor even the physical pain, it was the indignity of being forced to pull down his trousers and underpants, leaving him exposed and

125

humiliated. He never got over the shame of it.

Derek woke up at seven. He had never needed an alarm, just his natural body clock. He was about to get out of bed when he remembered… he didn't need to go to work. He groaned. That was the problem with work – he disliked the job and having to go to work, but as awful as it was, it was still preferable to being at home all day with his wife and mother. He had to think of something to do – anything to get him out of the house. But what? Yes, he'd go to the bookmakers later in the afternoon, perhaps buy a newspaper and have a coffee in a local café, but that was about it.

He lay in bed, trying to relax but his stomach churned with anxiety. He had no idea what lay ahead, and that worried him. It was the waiting that was churning him up. Waiting for someone to discover Miss Jones' body, if her boyfriend hadn't discovered it already, waiting for Mr Smith to find out, waiting for it to be made public.

He wondered whether it was the sort of thing that made the news. Did all murders make the news, local or national? Maybe some didn't; he had no idea. Would the police want to interview him? As someone who worked with her and saw her on the day she died, they would surely want to. The prospect chilled him. He remembered the last time – when the police interviewed him about that kid he beat up; he almost went to pieces under the pressure. Lying had never been his strong point. He'd been crap at it even as a kid, and, as a result, earned routine beatings from his teachers or, even worse, his father. His father never needed an excuse to thrash him, it was a regular occurrence. A slap across the bottom felt like he'd got away with it; it was the belt that he dreaded.

Half an hour later, Pat stirred. It took her a few seconds also to remember why her husband was still in bed and not getting ready for work. She too groaned, not relishing the idea of him hanging around all day, being bad-tempered and getting under her feet. She had her own work to go to but, as a dinner lady, not for a few hours yet.

'Suppose you'll be wanting me to get you your breakfast,' she said, her sleepy breath assaulting him.

'Bloody right,' he said. 'Quick as you like.'

*

Derek was eating his fried breakfast when his mother appeared in her dressing gown, looking like death. The sight of her revolted him. She was still only fifty, but God, she looked like a hundred and one.

He quickly finished his breakfast, having no desire to eat with her sitting opposite him.

Afterwards, he went out to the newsagent nearby and returned with *The Mirror* newspaper and a packet of salt and vinegar crisps. He settled down in his armchair. 'So, what has Thatcher done now?' he asked of no one. He opened his crisps when the telephone rang. Derek's heart speeded up. Was it the police? Could this be the start of it?

Pat strode in and answered it; she always did.

'It's for you,' she said, holding out the receiver.

He took it from her, bracing himself and said hello.

'Derek, sorry to bother you at home.'

'Oh, Mr Smith, it's you,' he said, almost weak with relief. 'No problem at all. Do you want me to come into work?' he asked hopefully.

'No, well, at least not today. I've still got Richard. Thing is though, Miss Jones hasn't turned up. I know it's unlikely but she didn't say anything to you, did she?'

'Miss Jones? No, not at all. Did she take the day off as leave?'

'No, I know that for a fact. But she's very late and, you know Miss Jones…'

'Punctuality is her middle name.'

'Exactly.'

'Maybe she took ill?'

'Perhaps but she'd call in, wouldn't she? Plus the fact that she's never had a day off sick in all the time she's been here.'

'There's always a first time, Mr Smith.

'You could be right.' He paused, his concern transmitting itself down the line. 'Well, look, Derek, if you should happen to hear from her—'

'It's not likely though.'

'No. I guess not, but, you know, just in case, you'll let me know, yes?'

'Of course, Mr Smith. You can count on me.'

He put the receiver back in its cradle and realised he was sweating.

'Everything OK?' asked Pat.

'Hmm? What? Yeah, of course. Never better.'

Chapter 23: Benedict

Friday morning Having spoken to DCI Lincoln to update him on his current cases, Benedict sat down at his desk and logged onto his computer.

DC Kelly came through, a smile on his face. 'Oh, hello, boss, we've got some good news. I got a call from a garage on Kitchener Road, not the German specialist. Some bloke brought in a car with an unsightly scrape down its left side – a silver Volkswagen Polo, 2016 reg.'

'Excellent. Well done, Kelly, good work.'

'Thanks, boss.'

'Ring Diana Pettigrew and ask her to send someone over to that garage. If that Polo bears any trace of a blue… what was it again, the car that was hit?'

'A Dacia Sandero.'

'That's the one. If they match, we'll have enough to make an arrest.'

'On it like a car bonnet, boss.'

*

Benedict and Jessica drove over to Sunny Grove Care Home, Benedict driving. The day, which had started sunny, had turned wet, the wipers working overtime. Traffic moved slowly. But it was fine; they were early. They'd arranged to meet Thomas McIntosh at the care home at half past one, a good hour after the residents had their lunch.

Benedict decided to ask Jessica the question he'd been meaning to ask for a couple of days now but was worried about the answer. Keeping his eyes on the road, he asked, as casually as possible, 'When you told Thomas McIntosh that you'd spoken to dementia patients several times before – was that actually true?' He paused at a pedestrian crossing and acknowledged a woman's waved thanks.

'Well, when I said *several...*'

'Yes?'

'Hmm, well, I may have exaggerated a bit.'

'*Exaggerated?*' He drove on slowly, taking a sharp right turn. 'You haven't interviewed one, have you?'

'They say there's going to be a thunderstorm tonight.'

'*Jessica?*'

'No.'

As he feared. 'Right. Great. Let's hope we can pull this off then.'

'Oh, it'll be fine, boss, a piece of cake.'

'Sure. I'll let you take the lead; a woman's touch and all that.'

'Fine by me.'

The last time Benedict had been inside a care home it seemed like some sort of Victorian asylum; he'd been to dog homes that were more comfortable but this place, Sunny Grove, was totally different. With large windows, the place was infused with light, it smelt fresh, and everything gleamed with cleanliness.

They were told that Mrs Hale, the care home's manager, was off for the day. Instead, a carer called Charmaine with a tattoo around her wrist and wearing a face mask, took their coats, commenting on the rain, and led them through to the conservatory where they saw Thomas McIntosh sitting silently in a hardback chair next to a man in an armchair looking out at the garden. Thomas stood on seeing them and quickly approached. 'Mr McIntosh,' said Benedict, offering his hand.

'Mac, please.'

'Mac.'

'Hi. Welcome. Look, before you start, I need to tell you something.' He glanced back at his father. 'I haven't told Dad you're police. I just thought it might... I don't know, worry him.'

'Perfectly understandable,' said Jessica with a reassuring smile.

'I told him you were a couple of distant cousins of mine who are researching a bit of family history. I hope that's OK?'

'No problem,' said Benedict. 'But won't he know who his nephews and nieces are?'

'No, frankly. That's why I think you're wasting your time but as you insist...'

What immediately hit Benedict was the man's age. Being a dementia patient, he had a certain expectation – but this man could have been no more than sixty-five. His skin was still relatively clear, his hair neatly combed. He wore a dark green cardigan, corduroy trousers and a pair of slippers. But he took no notice of the visitors, maintaining his vigil on the world outside the large conservatory windows.

'And this is your father?' asked Jessica.

'Yes.' Mac leaned down towards his father. 'Dad, these are the cousins I was telling you about. You remember?'

Only now did Thomas' father look at them, and Benedict had to stop himself from falling back, such was the intensity of the man's stare.

'You what?' he barked.

Jessica took the seat Mac had vacated. Benedict, standing next to Mac, hung back.

'Good afternoon, sir. My name is Jessica.' She offered her hand, but he ignored it. 'This is my friend, I mean, brother, Ben. He likes to be called by his full name, Benedict, but everyone ignores that. How are you today?'

'Bugger off.'

'Dad, please, stop that. Be nice to the lady.'

'Bugger off.'

'I'm sorry,' said Mac to Jessica.

'It's fine. Really. So, sir, I understand your son has told you that your mother has passed away.'

'Has she? Oh yeah. So what? She was old. No great loss.'

'What was she like, your mother? Did you get on?'

He seemed to mull this over. 'When's dinner?'

'You've just had lunch, Dad. Remember? Fish fingers. Jessica was asking whether you got on with Granny.'

'Who's Granny?'

'Your mum, Dad.'

'She got herself a council place, didn't she? Buggered off. The happiest day of my life, that.'

'OK,' said Jessica. 'Your mum, did she have any visitors in her new council place?'

'Visitors? I don't bloody know.'

'OK, fair enough. I understand. So, you wouldn't know if she ever fell out with anyone? What I mean, did your mum have people she didn't like?'

'I said I don't know. You deaf, or what?'

Benedict could see that this was going nowhere fast, the man was already getting agitated, a sheen of sweat forming on his brow. He could sense Mac's agitation too. Mac was right. They were wasting their time.

But then, for the first time, the old man looked directly at Jessica. 'But she did what I told her to.'

'Sir? What do you mean by that?'

'What I just said: she did what I told her to. I told her; you tell them I was *here*. You bloody make sure you tell them I was here. And she did, as good as gold, although she knew there'd be hell to pay if she didn't.'

'When was this, sir?'

He shrugged. 'Don't know. Can't remember. A few weeks back?'

'And, er, who's *them*?'

'What?' He was properly sweating now.

'You said you told her to tell *them* you weren't there. Who's *them*?'

'I don't know. Those bastard cops.'

Mac glanced at Benedict. 'OK, I think that's enough now. Ignore him; he's confused. He watched some detective series on the telly last night; he's getting mixed up. It happens – fact and fiction get blurred, you know?'

'What series was that, Mac?' asked Benedict.

'I wouldn't know; I wasn't here. Something on Netflix. American.'

'What bastard cops, sir?' asked Jessica.

'No,' said Mac, stepping forward. 'I said that's enough. You said you'd stopped if–'

Jessica stood. 'It's fine,' she said with a smile. 'You're right; it's time we left you in peace.' Looking back at Mac's father, she said, 'It was nice to meet you, sir. Thank you.'

The man didn't say another word, returning his attention to the garden outside.

Benedict and Jessica thanked Mac, apologising for going too far.

Collecting their coats, they thanked Charmaine on the way out.

Back in the car, Benedict inserted the car key into the ignition. Leaning back, he said, 'Good work, Jessica.'

She smiled. 'Thanks, boss.'

'*You tell them I was here.*'

'Yeah, what was that about?'

'I don't know.' He turned the ignition and flicked the wipers on. 'I don't know but I reckon it's time we paid more attention to what exactly happened forty years ago, don't you?'

Chapter 24: Mac

Mac put his father in the passenger seat of his car. He hadn't told the detectives he was moving his father out; it was none of their business. His poor father looked confused as hell. When was the last time his father had been in a car, he wondered. Possibly years. Dad struggled with the seatbelt, and gave up, swearing. Mac had to help.

'Where are you taking me?' he asked as Mac drove.

'I'm taking you to my flat, Dad, your old home.'

'But I liked it there.'

'And you'll like it with me as well.'

Dad didn't answer.

Having parked up, Mac led his father up the stairs to his first-floor flat. 'Here we are, Dad,' he said, unlocking the flat door. 'Come in, come in.'

His father paused on the threshold, as if reluctant to step inside. 'Whose place is this?' he barked.

'Mine, Dad. It used to be yours and now it's yours again. Here, come through.'

He settled his father in an armchair, handed him the free

Metro newspaper he'd picked up earlier and went off to make Dad a cup of tea. By the time he came back, his father had fallen asleep, the newspaper unopened on his lap.

'Welcome to my new life,' said Mac.

*

Mac couldn't remember much from his childhood. He recalled snatches here and there but there were these long lapses where he had only a vague sense of what was happening in his life, like the vaguest of Impressionist paintings. He remembered his mother as a loving and warm person but of course that memory of her was totally sullied. At nine years old, he'd reached that age when he no longer wanted to be cuddled by her because he was too big. But boy, once she'd gone, he'd have given anything for one of her hugs.

He remembered she always wore a lot of make-up. Bright red lipstick and stuff around her eyes. He didn't like it. Yes, it made her look pretty but he didn't want pretty, he wanted Mum. He remembered she was also very clumsy. Still, to this day, whenever he dropped anything or tripped over something, he'd think, *just like Mum*.

Every girlfriend he had ended in tears because he knew what he was like: terrified they'd run off one day, that they'd get bored of him sooner or later and go off to pastures new. He could not, must not, allow that to happen again, he could not afford to be emotionally ripped apart like that ever again.

He remembered so clearly the day Mum left. Every day when he came home from school, Mum would greet him with a big hug and a kiss. And then came the day that would always remain imprinted in his mind, the day he knew that her love was worthless; the day his mother left and never came back. He'd returned home from school and opened the front door with his key. He knew straight away that something was off, that the house was too quiet. And that's when he saw the little white card propped up against the cold kettle with his and Rebecca's names on it. He flipped it over and the words pierced him, leaving him gasping for air:

My dearest Becky & Thomas, I'm so sorry. One day I hope you will forgive me, Mum.

That was it. But it was enough – he knew she'd gone. He didn't know what to do. Rebecca was out at gymnastics and a friend's mother wouldn't drop her off for a while yet. He just had to wait for him to return from work. He knew he didn't want to show him Mum's note, he knew Mum had meant it for him and his sister only. So he hid it in one of his books, his old Winnie the Pooh book.

Dad came in about five o'clock, his usual time, by which time Mac was starving. 'Where's Mum?' was the first thing he asked. 'What's for dinner?'

Mac shook my head. 'I don't know where Mum is, she wasn't here when I got back.'

That stopped Dad in his tracks. He looked at his son weirdly as if what he was saying didn't make sense. He ran from room to room shouting her name. He pounded upstairs and Mac could hear each door opening and slamming shut. Then, he returned downstairs and repeated the whole circuit again, even going outside to check in the garden shed, as if she was hiding in there. He finally stopped, looking grey and exhausted.

He slammed his fist onto the dining room table. 'The bitch,' he yelled. 'The bloody bitch.'

Mac knew Mum had done wrong by running off but he still didn't like it when he used that word. 'Where is she, Dad?'

His father shook his head, the sweat pouring off him, catching his breath. 'I don't know, son. I don't bloody know.' He wiped his brow. 'All I know is if I ever catch her...' He didn't even finish the sentence, just left it hanging there, and for years Mac wondered about those unsaid words.

They looked at each other and Mac willed himself to hold his father's gaze. He so wanted to tell him he was weak with hunger. Then, without a word, Dad scooped up his coat he'd thrown on the back of a dining room chair and charged out, slamming the front door behind him. Mac stood there, wondering what to do, how to feed himself, who to ask for help. And I realised he had no one to help... no one at all.

And that's when he collapsed on the armchair and sobbed.

Chapter 25: Maxine

Saturday morning. Maxine was sitting in the living room of Sunny Grove care home, applying varnish to her grandmother's fingernails, lilac and a small star on every other one. The ITV lunchtime news played quietly in the background on the super-large television in the corner, something about climate change. 'Almost finished, Gran,' said Maxine. Granny was wearing a sparkling pink cardigan and had recently had her hair permed. She looked lovely, thought Maxine, so elegant. She'd had lunch and looked rather sleepy. She felt so much happier now, now that Mac had moved his horrible father out. She couldn't understand what Granny had done to annoy the man so much. But it didn't matter now; they'd never see him again.

'There, all done!' She finished the last nail and leaned back to admire her handiwork. 'You'll have to leave them to dry for a few minutes.'

Her grandmother smiled. 'Thanks, Maxie. They look so pretty, don't they?'

'They do. So pretty.'

'I love the stars.'

'Thanks, Granny.'

'I'll just sit still, shall I, until they dry?'

'That's right.'

'I might just have a shut-eye.'

'That's fine. I've got to go now anyway. But listen, I'll be back the day after tomorrow.'

'Oh? Not tomorrow.'

'Sorry, Gran, I'm working tomorrow.'

'Where do you work again?'

Maxine had told her a hundred times or more but patiently, she reminded her grandmother.

'You're a nurse? How lovely. Good girl.'

Maxine smiled. 'Thanks, Gran.'

She gathered her coat and leaned down to kiss her grandmother goodbye. She wondered what to do with the rest of the day. She needed some feminine products so she'd pop by the chemist on the way home.

As she left Sunny Grove, her mobile rang: unknown number. She didn't like unknown numbers so she ignored it, slipping the phone back into the pocket of her jeans. She stepped outside, another grey day but not at all cold. She wondered whether it was to do with this climate change they were always talking about on the telly. She felt her phone vibrate in her pocket. Unknown number again. Whoever it was, was obviously keen to speak to her. Maybe she'd won the lottery. This time she answered. But before she could say hello, she heard a number of electronic-sounding beeps that she'd never heard before. Then a voice came over. 'Hello, hello? Is that Maxine?'

Oh, that sounded like Jean from work, Jean Mulholland. She liked Jean. 'Is that Jean?'

'Jean? No, my name is Rebecca.'

'Who?'

'I'm Mac's sister. I hope you don't mind but he gave me your number.'

'Mac from the barbers?'

'Yes, Mac the Clipper. Have you got a moment?'

'Erm, yes, I suppose.'

'Thing is, Mac's told me about how horrible our father's been to your mother–'

'Grandmother.'

'Grandmother, yes.'

'But he's left the home now.'

'I know. He's living with Mac. Anyway, Dad's been feeling awful about the way he treated your grandmother; he's quite upset with himself.'

'Are you sure you're not Jean?'

'No, Rebecca, I said, Mac's sister.'

'OK. Sorry.'

'No worries. So, as I was saying, my father wants to apologise to you. He'd like to apologise to your granny but he knows he won't be allowed back into the home. So, I wondered, would you mind coming over to Mac's flat?'

'Mac's flat… oh, I d-don't know, I mean…'

'Mac wants to say sorry too. Look, I know it's a lot to ask and everything but he really is feeling sorry and, you know, he's not a well man. The home kept giving him these pills and I think that's the reason he was so horrible to your gran because ever since he stopped taking them, he's like a different man, so much nicer.'

'Oh, that's good.'

'Yes. So, what do you say? It'd mean so much to him. He's even bought you a box of chocolates but don't tell him I've told you that!'

'I suppose.'

'Where are you?'

'Now? I've just left Granny. When do you want me to go?'

'Are you free now by any chance? Mac will be there so you won't be alone.'

'Erm, I guess so. But I don't know where he lives.'

'It's sixty-two Richmond Avenue, not far from the home. Flat three on the first floor. Can you remember that? You could walk it in fifteen or catch the thirty-one bus from outside Sunny Grove. Could you get there now-ish? Would that be all right?'

'I know where Richmond Avenue is.' She wasn't keen but didn't know how to say no.

'Oh, even better. That's great. Remember, it's number sixty-two, first floor, flat three.'

Those strange beeps sounded again.

'Oh, heck, give me a minute… Christ on a bike.'

Maxine laughed at her expression; she'd never heard it before. The beeps stopped.

'You still there?'

'Yes, I'm still here.'

'Would that be OK then?'

'OK.'

'Thanks so much, Maxine. Dad will be so happy to see you. Mac said he'll leave the house key under the doormat outside and the flat door unlocked. It's because they have to have the telly on so loud because Dad's rather deaf now and sometimes Mac doesn't hear the door. So if no one hears you knocking, just come in. They won't mind; they'll be so happy to see you.'

'OK.'

'Thanks for this, Maxine. It'll mean so much to Dad; he's so embarrassed about everything. I'll tell Mac to expect you soon. Is that all right?'

'Yeah, OK. What did you say was your name again?'

'Rebecca. Rebecca O'Sullivan.'

'OK then. I'll walk over now.'

'Good girl. Bye-bye, Maxine, and thanks again.'

Well, thought Maxine, at least she had something to do now. She'd been so sure it was Jean from work but it hadn't been a great line.

Chapter 26: Derek

December 1982

Mid-morning and Derek didn't know what to do with himself. He actually missed being at work. The phone rang. He answered and was astonished to hear his brother's voice. He couldn't remember the last time he'd seen Geoff. He wanted something; Geoff always wanted something. Geoff asked how their mother was getting on – as if he cared. 'Listen,' said Geoff. 'I need a favour.'

'Really?' said Derek, feigning surprise. 'Don't tell me, you want money.'

The silence at the other end of the line only confirmed it. 'Look, I hate asking you, Del. It's just to tide me over until my next social comes through. Not much, and I'll pay you back within a week; I promise.'

He wouldn't lend the bastard a penny but he still asked how much.

'A hundred.'

Derek laughed. 'You think I'm made of money? Nah, sorry, mate. Not happening.' He put the phone down.

By lunchtime, Derek had read the newspaper from cover to cover and even tried, without success, to start reading one of his wife's Jilly Cooper novels. Pat had been out most of the morning but, out of some sort of principle, although he wasn't sure which one, he didn't want to ask where she'd been. She *did* have friends and he knew, or at least suspected, that they met for frequent coffees. But she'd returned in time to do him and his mother a cheese on toast each for lunch.

His mother switched on the television, telling him she liked to watch the lunchtime news, as well as the teatime news and the late news. For such an informed person, thought Derek, she still had bugger all to say about anything. The national news led on a massive earthquake in Yemen that had killed almost three thousand people. Next, the news that the population of the People's Republic of China had recently passed one billion. 'Apparently,' said Derek, 'if they all jumped at the same time, we'd have a massive earthquake. Tell that to the people of Yemen, wherever that is.'

Pat made three mugs of tea, handing them around, before sitting down to join them in front of the television.

The local news started with the stabbing of some black kid in Clapham, but its second story was about a twenty-nine-year-old woman called Ruth Jones who'd been found strangled in her own flat in Highgate. Derek coughed up his tea. 'You alright, Derek?' asked Pat.

'Shut up,' he barked. He gazed at Daisy and tried to quell his panicked breathing.

The screen flashed up a photograph of the victim, a studio shot of her wearing a fetching red jacket with large lapels, her hair freshly permed, her bright lipstick matching her outfit. Derek thought he might die of a bloody heart attack, it beat so hard.

'She looks gorgeous,' said Pat.

Her boyfriend, the reporter said, who had come over to have dinner with her and who later alerted the police, was 'helping police with their enquiries'.

'Ha!' snorted Mother. '"Helping police with their enquiries." That's doublespeak for he did it.'

'Not necessarily,' said Pat, her hands cupped around her mug.

'What do you know? It's always a man, and it's nearly always someone the victim knows. You mark my words, the boyfriend did it.'

The police, the news reporter said, were looking for witnesses.

'How sad,' said Pat, shaking her head. 'Derek...'

Derek sat staring at the television, something about the threat of strike action on London's buses, but wasn't listening, couldn't focus. Seeing Miss Jones' photo on the television, hearing her name, had brought it home. He'd been responsible for that. He was a murderer now; he'd crossed that line, and it wasn't a line one could return across. But he had to do it – he would have lost his job, and that had been her fault. If she hadn't snitched on him, gone running to 'sir', he wouldn't have risked losing his job. His whole life would have crumbled like a house of cards – without a job, he would've lost the house. He'd be out on the streets sleeping in doorways. He'd never get another job, not without a reference and what with his previous record hanging over him. Killing her had brought no joy; it'd been easily the hardest thing he'd ever done, but he had to do it; she'd left him with no choice, the silly bitch.

'Derek? Are you OK? Derek?'

'What? Sorry?' He shook the dark thoughts from his head. 'Sorry, I was miles away.'

'Are you feeling OK?'

'He looks guilty,' said Mother. 'Mark my words, Pat, he's been up to something.'

'Yes, Marjorie.'

'Out late two nights running, I'm telling you–'

'Shut up, Mum, will you?' He jumped up from his armchair, his face red, his fists clenched by his sides. 'Just… just for once in your miserable life, put a sock in it, will you, and shut the fuck up.'

'Derek,' said Pat, leaning forward. 'What's got into you, love? Calm now, now, calm now.'

Mother looked up at him, her mouth open, the shock clear in her eyes.

He stormed into his bedroom, slamming the door shut behind him. He fell onto his bed, close to tears, squeezing the bridge of his nose.

A few seconds later, the door inched open, and Pat stepped into the room. Quietly, she lay next to him. 'Derek, tell me, is anything wrong, love?'

Her gentle voice soothed him somewhat but he couldn't cry, not in front of her. 'Yeah, sorry. I'm – I'm fine, just feeling… I don't know.'

'Maybe you're coming down with something.'

'Yeah, I think you're right. There's a bug going around at work, that's why Richard had to come on relief. I think I may have caught it.'

'Well, perhaps you should stay here and close your eyes for a while. I'll draw the curtains for you if you like. Sleep's always the best medicine.'

'Yeah, you're right. Thanks.'

She patted his arm. 'That's OK, my love. You know…' She hesitated. 'You shouldn't speak to your mother like that.'

'I know but I can't bear her any more, just sitting there all fucking day, day in, day out. I just want her to go, to fuck off out of our lives. Why can't she go live with Geoff? I hate her being here.'

'I don't know what to suggest.'

His mother was on the waiting list for her own council flat but having a comfortable home already, as far as the council was concerned, she was not a priority. When Derek last asked, a housing officer joked she'd probably be a hundred and one by the time she got a place.

Pat drew the curtains and crept out.

It was only after she closed the door that Derek allowed the tears to come.

Chapter 27: Benedict

First thing on returning to work Saturday afternoon, Benedict rang former Detective Inspector Peter Grainger in Milton Keynes to ask him whether he remembered if Neil Smith had a scratch on his face at the point of his arrest. Grainger was adamant that he hadn't. 'We would've asked him about it if he did,' came the curt reply.

DC Kelly had tracked down the woman who'd opened the door at Holbrook flats to the mysterious nurse. Unfortunately, the woman, a resident of the flats, had no recollection of her, apart from what Benedict already knew – namely, that she was a nurse wearing a wide-brimmed hat, which struck her as rather odd. But as to what she actually looked like – the woman had no idea. So much for that.

Now, with the time approaching three p.m., Benedict and Jessica were due to visit St Cuthbert's hospital to try and track down this mysterious nurse, but he had things to do beforehand. First, having been supplied with a telephone number, he rang Neil Smith's sister on the landline at the address in Winchester found on the Christmas card Smith had

149

dropped during the second attack. But, according to the daughter who answered, her mother had died two years ago. She had never truly recovered from the shame of her brother's notoriety. Following his conviction, she never uttered her brother's name ever again; the subject became totally taboo. As far as her mother was concerned, her brother had never existed.

*

Benedict and Jessica were directed to a Mrs Idowu in St Cuthbert's Hospital's HR department. A bosomy woman with half-moon glasses, Mrs Idowu welcomed them with a toothy smile. Jessica showed her the screenshot taken from the CCTV at the entrance of Holbrook House, showing the woman in a nurse's uniform entering the block. 'She's wearing a white uniform with navy stripes and white piping. That means she's an auxiliary nurse.'

'Do you recognise her?'

'Of course not, you can't see her face properly, that hat's in the way.'

'Yes, but she has rather distinctive red hair.'

'It's probably a wig.'

'Oh,' said Benedict. 'I never thought of that. Does it look like a wig?'

'You're asking me? It's hard to tell.'

'So, you don't recognise her?'

Mrs Idowu shook her head, no, she didn't recognise the person in the photograph. She showed it around to her colleagues and not one of them recognised her.

Without having to look up the numbers, the HR woman informed the detectives that St Cuthbert's hospital employed some 312 nurses, a mixture of permanent and agency, 72 per cent of whom were female and 52 per cent white. If memory serves, she said, the hospital employed some 200 auxiliary nurses. 'How many are redheads, I couldn't tell you. Quite a few are agency staff or locums which could prove difficult for you because, obviously, they come and go. Are you sure she's from *this* hospital?'

'No. But, being the nearest, we thought we'd start here.'

'Well, good luck,' she said in a tone that implied they would need it.

Benedict asked if they could ask around in the wards. Mrs Idowu couldn't see a problem with that. They thanked her and headed downstairs to the first ward they came across on the first floor. Using the calculator on his phone, Benedict reckoned that roughly 150 white female auxiliary nurses worked at the hospital.

'We'll make a start but if we don't get anywhere, we'll ask Kelly and Prowse to take over.'

'Surely, it won't be difficult to identify her. She is, as the HR woman said, rather distinctive.'

'I went out with a redhead when I was younger. She shunned the sunlight like a vampire.'

'What happened to her?'

'She migrated to Australia.'

'Oh right. No sun there.'

'Mm.'

They showed the photo to numerous staff in three wards without luck. 'Maybe it *is* a wig,' said Benedict.

'In that case, we're probably wasting our time.'

'Let's try this last ward. Then we'll call it a day.' The ward, the Fraser Booth ward, specialised in kidney and transplant care.

They approached the first nurse they saw, a young black man

in the uniform of a staff nurse. He peered at the photo, twisting his head. 'You know what, I think I do recognise her. Wait a minute.' He approached a colleague. Benedict heard him say, 'Hey, Nigella, does this look like Maxine to you?'

The woman, Nigella, also twisted her head and squinting, said, 'Could be. Hang on.' She found her glasses and took a second look. 'It's hard to say but yeah, it could be.'

'That's what I thought.' A third and fourth opinion was sought – all agreed, it *could* be a colleague called Maxine, but none were sure.

The nurse returned, handing the photo back to Benedict. 'We reckon it might be Maxine Hunt just from the hair. She's an auxiliary.'

'Is she here today?'

'No. I can have a look at the rota, see when she's next in, if you like.'

'Please.'

He returned shortly. 'She's back on Sunday, starting at nine. Seven-hour shift. She doesn't work that often though because she looks after her mum.'

'Not her mum,' came a voice from afar. 'Her grandmother.'

'Oh yes, her grandmother. She's in a care home.'

'Oh?' said Jessica. 'Do you happen to know which one?'

'Hey, Nigella, what home is Max's gran in?'

'Sunny Grove, isn't it?'

'There you are. She talks about her gran a lot.'

'Sunny Grove? Thanks,' said Benedict. 'Is Maxine a permanent member of staff here?'

'Agency. She's been here about a year or so.'

'OK, thanks for that.'

Benedict and Jessica returned to the HR department to ask Mrs Idowu for Maxine Hunt's address and telephone number.

Back outside, they rushed to the car to get out of the rain. 'Well, that's interesting,' said Jessica, securing her seatbelt.

'Indeed, it is. Sunny Grove, who'd have thought it?' He typed Maxine's address into his Waze app. 'Eight minutes away. I think it'd be a good idea to go visit this Maxine.'

Chapter 28: Mac

Mac met his sister at the entrance of Holloway underground station. She was dressed in a blue and white striped top and rather shapeless black trousers. It was a shame, he thought, that she hadn't made more of an effort. He, meanwhile, was wearing his smartest jacket, dark blue with thin red lines, and a collared shirt and paisley-patterned waistcoat, and his shiniest black leather shoes. Rebecca noticed: 'You look smart. Got a meeting with your bank manager after?'

'How are you feeling?' he asked.

'Alright.' She took several puffs of her vape.

'Is that it?'

'What would you have me say, Mac? That this is the most momentous occasion of my life; that it's gonna have this massive profound effect on me? Is that how you feel?'

'No. I'm nervous though, I mean, it is a sorta big deal, isn't it? it's not every day you get–'

'Oh, do shut up, Mac. It is what it is.' She looked at the time on her phone. 'Come on then, smart boy, don't want to keep Her Majesty waiting, do we?'

Bertie's Café on the Holloway Road was half-full when Mac and Rebecca got there at a quarter to eleven, fifteen minutes early. He'd wanted to be early; he needed time to prepare himself, get used to his surroundings. He followed his sister inside and breathed in the delicious aromas of coffee and cinnamon. He'd been to Bertie's before. George, the camp, high-pitched barista with a ponytail, greeted him like a long-lost friend. The place wasn't too dissimilar to Mac the Clipper in terms of its feel: brick walls, wooden floor, low-hanging lampshades, movie posters and framed prints of moody Parisian street scenes. Mac was worried in case the music was too loud, but it was pleasant: a laid-back jazzy number.

They took a seat and waited. He knew this was going to be tough – and they were far too early. His mouth had turned dry, his palms damp with sweat. He couldn't stop his leg from jigging up and down. Every time the door opened, his heart did a somersault. He knew instinctively that he would recognise her, of that he was sure. She was his mother, after all, his own flesh and blood, *and she still is.* Yes, he hadn't seen her for thirty years but he'd know her anywhere.

He reached for the menu and, in doing so, knocked over the salt cellar.

Rebecca shook her head in exasperation. 'Clumsy boy.'

'Just like Mum,' he said, brushing away the granules of salt that had escaped the cellar.

He wondered whether she still wore as much makeup as she used to. What would they talk about? He was pleased Rebecca was here. But where does one start after so long? He would have to tell her about Dad, how the dementia had crept up on him at such a young age, took his mind horribly early.

The door swung open: a woman wearing a headscarf, her face obscured. Mac thought this was her. He jumped up from his seat, his legs weak. He opened his mouth but the woman removed her headscarf and he saw his mistake. He sat down again and drummed his fingers on the tabletop.

'For fuck's sake, Mac, just relax, will you? Hells bells.'

'How can you be so calm?'

'Just because.'

George approached them. 'What can I get you guys?' he asked.

'We're waiting on someone,' said Rebecca. 'We'll order then.'

'Ok, ok,' he said, retreating quickly. 'No worries.'

George turned to leave and bumped into someone, a woman. He apologised and spun off like a top. The woman looked at Mac and his sister. 'Hello, Thomas; hello, Becky.'

Mac jumped up again. 'Oh, hi. Hello.'

Rebecca stood also. 'Mum. Hello.'

She smiled at them. 'G-glad you could make it,' said Mac. 'Here, take a seat.'

'Thank you.'

They all sat. She removed her coat, its collar caught momentarily in her dangly earrings. She wore an off-white blouse under a grey jacket.

'Lovely place this,' she said. 'Is it one of your regulars?'

'Not me,' said Rebecca. 'I live south of the river. Blackheath.'

'Oh nice.'

'I've been here before,' said Mac.

She shuffled in her seat, twisting a ring around her finger. Yes, thought Mac, she'd applied a bit of lipstick and a hint of eye shadow but nothing much.

'Thanks for agreeing to see me, Thomas, Becky. I know this isn't easy – for any of us.' Mac remembered why his sister had always insisted on being called Rebecca – because her mother had always called her Becky and she didn't like the memory.

156

'You're here now,' said Rebecca.

'Would you like a coffee?' asked Mac. 'They do all the different types. And a cake maybe? George's carrot cake is famous in these parts.'

She looked up at the huge blackboard behind the counter. She was exactly as Mac remembered her, as if she hadn't aged in the last three decades, apart from her hair, which was short, and almost grey. It gave her a rather severe look. Her eyebrows were finely arched, crow's feet around her eyes, nice teeth.

George sauntered over, a large grin fixed on his face, and took their orders.

Mum talked about the area and how it had changed since she left. But she'd seen a couple of shops that were here in her day and still, by the looks of it, going strong. 'I even popped my head around the door of your barbershop, Thomas. It's very nice but did you not go to university?'

'University? No. Never even considered it.'

'Oh, now that is a shame. I thought all children of the nineties went to uni. Maybe you inherited your father's lack of brains. And are you married, Thomas? Children?'

'No, Neither.'

'Do you have a girlfriend?'

He shook his head.

'Oh, dear. You're forty now, you're not getting any younger.'

'Thirty-nine actually.' He gripped his leg.

'Oh, you're not *gay*, are you?'

'No, Mum, I'm not gay.'

'Well, that's one thing to be thankful for. Not that I got anything against gay people, mind you, but you know… And you, Becky? What is it you do?'

'I work in marketing for my sins. I am what's called a "marketing executive",' she said, using air quotes. 'And I'm married. No kids.'

'Oh? Well, that sounds nice although a shame about the kids. You ought to get a move on, Becky. Nature's ticking. Do you have a photo of my son-in-law?'

Rebecca pulled up a few photos of her husband from her phone to show her mother. Meanwhile, George arrived with their order. Only Mac thanked him. 'Oh, he is rather dishy.'

'Yes, I suppose he is. He's called Gabriel. He's Irish, like Gabriel Byrne.'

'Like the angel Gabriel.'

'Ha! I'd hardly describe Gabriel as angelic! He's called O'Sullivan. I've taken his name, like the good old-fashioned girl I am, so I'm officially Rebecca O'Sullivan now. Just so that you know, Mum. Although, actually, I maintain McIntosh professionally.'

'Did you keep McIntosh as a name, Mum?' asked Mac.

She didn't answer. Instead, still focused on Rebecca, their conversation continued apace while Mac quietly drank his coffee and ate his pastry, his foot keeping time with the jazz music still playing.

'Gabriel and I went skiing in Bulgaria a couple of months ago. We should have gone two years ago but what with Covid and everything, it kept being postponed. I've got some photos if you want to see?'

'Oh, yes, I'd love to.'

That led to more photos – Maldives, Marseilles, Madrid. Gabriel and Rebeccas liked their holidays.

Mac finished his coffee. He took a sneaky look at the time on his phone – almost midday. Had they really been there almost an hour already? He'd hardly spoken yet he was still smarting from her comments about his lack of education and his relationship status. After all this time, he'd wanted to make her feel proud of him and he'd failed – spectacularly.

'Have you come back?' asked Rebecca, causing a flutter of nerves batting in Mac's stomach. 'Or is it just a visit?'

'I want to come back, yes. Perhaps not…'

'Yes?' said Mac, speaking for the first time in ages, aware of just how important her answer was to him, how, despite everything, he wanted her to say that she was staying here and not returning to Spain.

'Well, perhaps not to this area. It holds too many… memories for me. But to England, to London, yes, certainly. I hope so.'

It's a start, he thought, the intention was there.

She sipped her coffee, surely now cold, and eyed Rebecca over the rim of the cup. 'So, how is your father?'

'Thomas is better placed to answer that one.'

'Yeah, well,' said Mac. 'It's, erm, a long story.'

She shrugged her shoulders. 'I have the time if you have…'

'I think I'll nip to the loo,' said Rebecca.

Mac took a deep breath, fortifying himself. 'OK, if you're sure…'

And so he told her everything while having the nasty feeling she wasn't too interested.

'Oh dear, Thomas, you sound as if you had it rather rough,' she said, once he'd finished. 'Anyway, all water under the bridge now. I wonder where your sister's got to. Look, there she is, talking on her phone.'

'But I guess, looking back, Dad was ill, Mum. I…' He stopped, realising this is the first time he'd called her that to her face in thirty bloody years: *Mum*. Just saying it sounded weird.

'This coffee is stone cold. What do you mean he was ill?'

Rebecca returned to the table. 'Sorry about that. Work call.

159

Honestly, the place would collapse if I'm not there to steer the ship. Who was ill?'

'*Is* ill… Dad. As it happens, I've already moved him out. I've got my neighbour keeping an eye on him.'

'Fuck!' screeched Rebecca. 'They've evicted him already? We can appeal. And they've got to give us twenty-eight days' notice.'

'What's the point though?'

She buried her face in her hands. 'Right, OK, you do as you see fit, Mac, but I'm telling you, this is on your head, alright?'

He nodded.

'What's your place like, Thomas?' asked Mum. 'Do you have room for both of you?'

'It's the same flat you and Dad lived in, Mum.'

'Oh my. Richmond Avenue?'

'So, what happened, Mum?' asked Rebecca. 'Why did you leave us?'

She sighed heavily. 'You know why I left you. I told you.'

'What?'

'Did you never read my letters?'

'Letters?'

And they all knew in that same moment what had happened here. 'You never got them, did you?'

Mac shook his head. They sat in silence for a while. George was busy serving a table of three girls seated behind Mac. They giggled as George flirted with them with his campness on full display. But right now, Mac had a very large hole in his heart as the realisation hit – his father had hidden all his mother's letters. The more he thought of this, the more something bubbled up inside of him. How dare he? Did he think he was protecting him? It didn't matter how young he was; Dad had no right to hide them; Mac was entitled to read his mother's letters.

'How often did you write?' he asked.

'Two or three times a month. At least to begin with.'

He allowed himself time to absorb this. 'So, why did you leave, Mum?'

Mum stared out of the window watching a man push his bicycle up the street. She took a deep breath and exhaled. Finally, she turned back to face them both. 'Your father was a violent man.'

Her words hit Mac like a fist. 'Dad?'

She ran her hand through her short hair. 'Yes.'

Mac couldn't process this. 'He hit you?'

She nodded again. He believed her. He didn't doubt her for a second; he knew she was telling the truth. His accident-prone mother, always falling over, always bumping into things, always tripping over. His mother who always wore so much make-up. Of course, it all made sense now. She wasn't accident-prone at all, and she had no choice but to cake herself in make-up. His bastard father. He wanted to stand up, to pace around. He wanted to shout, to scream this place down.

Mum played with a paper tube of sugar. 'I knew I had to leave. But... I once made the mistake of threatening to take you both with me. He said he'd kill me. Your father said he'd track me down and kill me. And, you know, I believed him. I knew I'd never be able to protect you, not properly, and we'd forever be on the run, looking over our shoulders. I knew I was leaving you behind with a violent man but I knew he never hit you. I just had to pray that he never would.'

'No, he never hit us, did he, Rebecca?'

'No, he never hit us.'

'I had to choose. I had to decide what was the safest option, to leave you with this man or take you both with me into an

161

uncertain future. I called social services once but nothing came of it. I had very little money, he made sure of that, and no idea of where to go. But I did it, Thomas, Becky. I had to go. Kissing you both that last morning before school was *the* hardest thing I've ever had to do. Please...' She reached for Rebecca's hand. 'Forgive me...'

'You ended up in Spain?' asked Rebecca, happy to withdraw her hand. 'Did you remarry, have another family?'

'No. I was seeing a man for a while but... it never worked out. I regret it but, God's own truth, nothing on earth compares to the regret I felt on leaving you, Rebecca. Thomas. Nothing...'

The conversation turned to more mundane matters and finished with what they each planned on doing that afternoon: Mum flat hunting on her iPad at her bed and breakfast, Rebecca working from home and Mac spending the rest of the day at the barbershop, hoping his neighbour looking after Dad wouldn't mind.

It hit Mac then that taking his father out of the home was possibly the biggest mistake of his life.

Chapter 29: Mac

After his mother had told him about his father's violence towards her, Mac's anger simmered below the surface, threatening to erupt at any moment. He managed to keep a lid on it while he and Rebecca said their goodbyes to Mum. They'd scribbled down their respective addresses and telephone numbers on napkins and promised to keep in touch.

After his mother left, he pulled Rebecca back to their table, already cleared of their debris and waiting for the next set of customers. 'So, what do you make of that?'

'What, the hitting bit?'

'Yes, the hitting bit, *Becky*.'

'Don't call me that, you know–'

'Your name isn't the issue right now.'

They both sat again. 'It doesn't really surprise me, to be honest.'

'You're fucking joking?' An older woman pushing a toddler in a buggy stared at him, shocked, perhaps, by his language. He leaned in towards Rebecca. 'What do you mean, it doesn't surprise you?'

'Lots of men whack their wives every now and then. I know I've thumped Gabriel in the past, doesn't make me a husband-beater.'

'It does if it's continual. For Christ's sake, Rebecca. So, what, you think she's *exaggerating*?'

'I didn't say that—'

'Because it was obviously bad enough for her to walk out on us in fear of her life and *our* lives.'

'Yes, exactly, she left us to take our chances with a monster. What sort of mother does that make her?'

'A frightened one, perhaps? Jesus, Rebecca, I don't believe I'm hearing this. What sort of cold, cynical gene did you pick up along the way?'

'Look, Mac, I understand why you're upset—'

'Upset? Bloody right I'm upset. I want to kill the fucker—'

'But it was thirty years ago, Mac. It's all in the past now, you can't change it. Let it go.'

'What d'you mean, let it go? I only found out ten minutes ago.'

She checked the time on her mobile. 'I've got to go. I've got a meeting this afternoon, and a hundred and one emails have come through since I've been here—'

'Oh, poor you. And what should I do? I've got the fucker—'

'Hey, hey, hey,' said George, suddenly appearing next to them. 'What is all this with the swearing? You're upsetting my customers. You need to leave.'

'We're about to,' said Rebecca.

'No, now. You leave now and take your…' He glared at Mac. 'Take your potty-mouthed companion with you.'

So much for being treated like a long-lost friend, thought Mac.

'Come on, Mr Potty Mouth,' said Rebecca, 'Let's get out of here.'

Outside, Mac buttoned his jacket against the cold. 'So, I ask again – what should I do? I've got him living under my ceiling now.'

'Yeah, and whose choice was that, Mac? I could've told you, you were making a big mistake.'

'Yeah, and I told you, he was about to get kicked out anyway.'

'And I *told you*, we could've appealed. But no, you went goose-stepping in, threw your toys out of the pram and marched the fucker, as you call him, home. Sorry, mate, you made your bed, now–'

'Yeah, yeah, alright, I don't need any more metaphors or whatever you call them.'

'Look, I'm really running late now. I'll talk to you again about it – if I ever get time.'

Mac watched her march off, checking her phone and vaping as she headed back to Holloway tube. His mother's words came back to him: *your father was a violent man*. The bastard, the bloody bastard.

*

Mac was in his office, knowing he had to get back to his father at some point, that he couldn't leave him with his neighbour for too long, when a gentle knock sounded on his door. 'Come in.'

The last person he expected was the lovely Caroline. She stepped in, holding Marcus' hand. The boy, wearing his school uniform, grinned at him.

'Hello, Mac,' said Caroline. 'So sorry to disturb you–'

'Something wrong? Is it the haircut, don't you like it any more, Marcus?' But Marcus was distracted by Mac's domed-shaped paperweight with the photograph of Vienna inside it.

'No, no, nothing like that. It's just that, well, it's Marcus' birthday today and he's got something he wants to show you.'

'Oh? I'm honoured. What is it?'

Marcus pulled out a strip of folded cards from his blazer. 'Mum got me a ticket to see Chelsea play.'

'Oh, wow, that's brilliant. Let's see.' Sure enough, Marcus held up three tickets for a Chelsea game. 'How exciting.'

'Yeah.' The boy could barely contain himself. 'It's brilliant.'

'Will you wear your Pulisic shirt?'

'Yeah. Mum said she'd buy me a programme too.'

'That's great, Marcus. Oh no, wait a minute, they're not playing Arsenal, are they?'

'No, it's Notts Forest. It's at Stamford Bridge. Saturday.'

'Saturday week,' said Caroline, correcting him.

'Well, that's one great birthday present.'

'Yeah, Mum's taking me.'

Mac guessed the third ticket was for Marcus' dad. 'So, is it your birthday today?'

'Yeah. I'm nine.'

'Nine? Oh, what a lovely age. I wish I was nine. Happy birthday, mate.'

'Thanks.'

Caroline smiled. 'I hope you don't mind us coming in, I can see you're busy.'

'No, no, not at all. It's… it's lovely to see you again.' Turning to Marcus, he added, 'And like I said, I'm honoured.'

'Marcus really wanted to come tell you all about it.'

'So, you're going home now for a bit of birthday cake?'

'Yeah! I've got some friends coming over too.'

'Well, that's lovely.'

'You can come too if you want!' said Marcus.

'Me?'

'Oh, Marcus, Mac will be too busy with work.'

'Yeah, you won't want an old duffer like me cluttering up your party. But listen, mate, have a great birthday and maybe come back and tell me all about the game, yeah?'

Marcus smiled up at his mother. 'Yeah, sure.'

'I can't believe I'm about to say this but… I hope Chelsea win.'

Marcus guffawed. 'Of course they'll win. Chelsea are the best!'

'Yeah, well, second best, but yeah!'

*

Caroline and Marcus' visit had made Mac feel a whole lot better. What a lovely kid, and what a stunning woman. Her husband, or boyfriend or whatever, was one lucky bloke. What must it be like to go to a football match with your son? Something he'd never experienced with his own father. His dad had never shown any interest in football, and would never have thought of taking him to a game. Marcus didn't know how lucky he was to have such parents.

Thinking of his father darkened his mood again. He knew he should go out into the shop and cut some hair. Instead, he remained in his office and took out his phone. Opening Safari, he started typing into Google. He spent only twenty minutes weighing up the different options. Previously, three and a half years ago, he spent hours on this – comparing costs, reputation, health and safety, staff experience, customer reviews, distance, and, most importantly, what the Care Quality Commission had to say about it. He'd made a spreadsheet comparing lots of different options with a list of pros and cons against each, and shared it, via a shared drive, with his sister.

This time, all that mattered was cost. He couldn't give a shit about the rest of it, not this time. He found what he thought was the cheapest, one with OK-ish reviews, and a less than flattering report on the CQC's website. Perfect. He rang the number listed on their website.

'Good afternoon, is that Beeches Court Care Home?'

Chapter 30: Derek

December 1982

The next morning, Derek feigned sickness in order to have an excuse for why he wasn't going to work. He only hoped Mr Smith would allow him back soon because he couldn't maintain this for long without Pat becoming suspicious.

He stayed in bed and asked Pat to go out and buy him a newspaper, preferably *The Mirror*. And, on account, he was staying in bed all day, the local newspaper which only came out once a week but today was the day. Ideally, he'd liked to have read through every newspaper available, but that would've looked odd, but he certainly reckoned the local rag would have picked up on Miss Jones' demise.

Pat returned with his two newspapers and brought him a lemon drink that contained paracetamol.

He waited until she left the room before quickly flipping through the pages of *The Mirror*. He wasn't sure whether to be disappointed or not. Perhaps, on reflection and putting his ego to one side, it was better that they hadn't. If it became a leading, national story, the police would throw more resources at it in their attempt to solve it. Better that it remained low-key and of low priority. The local newspaper however did report on it, and included the same studio shot as the television report featured yesterday, but it was still brief. He hadn't learned anything new.

He heard the telephone ring. He sat up in bed and strained his ears as Pat answered it. She heard him say 'Mr Smith'. Derek swivelled out of bed, grabbing his dressing gown. He took a deep breath; he knew this was going to be difficult.

He took the receiver from his concerned-looking wife. 'Mr Smith, good morning. How can I help?' His mother, damn her, sat there watching him.

Mr Smith didn't answer straight away. Derek could hear a sniff at the other end. 'Have you heard, Derek?'

Derek cursed himself for having sounded so upbeat. 'Yeah, I saw it on the news yesterday,' he said, speaking slowly and quietly, conscious of his mother listening to every word.

'It's… it's hideous,' said Mr Smith. 'I c-can't believe it. It's just so, so…'

'It's hard to believe, yes. The poor woman.'

'I mean, she had everything to live for. Who'd do such a thing, what sort of monster would do that? In her own home, as well.'

Derek made a few appropriate noises. Then asked, 'Do you want me to come in today, Mr Smith? You know, in the circumstances.'

'What? Today? No, no. We're shut. I'm at work with the police here. They want to go through all her paperwork and stuff and ask me loads of questions. Head office didn't think it was a good look, having the police swarming around the place, so we're not opening today. I've put a sign up.'

'And tomorrow? I can come in tomorrow if you want me to.'

'Tomorrow? Yeah, I think I will need you. I've already got Richard covering, I can't ask for two covers. I'll speak to head office just to make sure. But I reckon they'll be fine with it. At least you won't have to face a tribunal now, Derek.'

'Oh, yes, I hadn't thought of that. I guess not.'

'I'd better go, I think I'm needed again. Oh, just to let you know, the police want to speak to you as soon as.'

'All the more reason for me to come in tomorrow.'

'No, today. I had to give them your address. They'll be there shortly.'

Derek suppressed a 'fuck'. He replaced the receiver. His mother shuffled out. Derek immediately made another call. 'Geoff, do you still need that money?'

'I do as it happens.'

Derek took a deep breath. 'OK, I'll *give* it to you. A hundred quid.'

'Give?'

'Yes. See it as a brotherly gift. But in return, I need to ask you a favour...'

His mother returned, Pat following her. 'Is everything OK?' asked Pat.

He sat and indicated Pat should sit also. 'Listen, Pat, Mum, there's something I didn't tell you yesterday.'

'What is it now?' said his mother.

He glanced out the window and saw the dark clouds scudding by. 'I know that woman they found. Or *knew* her, should I say.'

'You knew her? The woman murdered in her flat?'

He nodded. 'Ruth Jones. I worked with her.'

'Oh, Derek,' said Pat. 'No wonder you're feeling poorly.'

'Fact is, we had a bit of a... an argument, let's say. Nothing major,' he added quickly. 'It was about... whether a sale was mine or hers, you know? It happens. We both claimed it and Mr Smith had to decide and he decided for her – as always. And, last night, I didn't go out for a drink with Richard, like I said. I was upset, what with everything, so I just went out by myself, had a couple of pints, maybe three, I can't remember. I don't know if anyone saw me but if no one did…'

'What are you saying, Derek?'

'Look, I know it's a lot to ask, but…'

'He wants us to say he was here,' said his mother triumphantly. 'If the police come asking.'

'Erm, well, yes. That's about it. The police are on their way now.'

Pat looked puzzled. 'You want us to give you an alibi. Is that what you're saying?'

'Yeah. I know, I know I'm asking a lot but otherwise it doesn't look good, does it?'

'Someone will remember you. At the pub, I mean. Which pub was it? The barman or woman or whatever will remember you, especially if you had three pints. Surely, you remember the people who served you, can't you? Or at least picture them? Derek?'

'Well, no, that's it, I can't. I was in a state, wasn't I? What with the argument we had and everything. I just kept my head down and didn't look at anyone. Geoff's going to vouch for me too.'

'Geoff?'

'He's going to say he was here from five o'clock to ten.'

Pat and his mother exchanged worried glances. His mother made a sort of *phah* noise. 'He wants us to lie to the police for him.'

He turned on her: 'Yeah, just for once in your life, show me some support, will you? It's not as if I've done anything wrong but if no one can say they saw me, well, it doesn't exactly look good, does it?'

Pat cleared her throat. 'OK, I suppose we can do that, can't we, Mum?'

He never liked it when Pat called his mother 'Mum', her name was Marjorie, but now wasn't the time to berate her. 'The thing is, I was so upset, I sort of left work early.'

'Early? How early?'

'Three. Thereabouts. So, I would have got back about three forty.'

'So… you want us to tell the police you were here from three forty? And that Geoff got here about five and you never went out.'

'Yes. I'm sorry.'

'It's OK. It's fine. Do you remember what we had for dinner last night?'

'What? Why?'

'They might ask.'

'Oh. Yes, you're right. Erm… we had fish cakes and chips, didn't we? And peas.'

'We watched *Jaws* on TV last night, didn't we, Mum? It was on ITV. You've seen *Jaws*, Derek.'

He liked her way of thinking; he'd got her on board. 'Yes, you're right. We all watched *Jaws* together.'

He could have kissed her, such was his relief. He'd have to phone Geoff back about watching *Jaws*. But what about his mother? Surely, despite everything, she'd play along. Christ, he was her son, after all.

Derek pulled his chair closer to the tank and gazed lovingly at Daisy.

He'd always had a snake. As a kid, he pestered his parents until they got him one. It'd been their only act of kindness

173

towards him. It was a Kenyan Sand Boa, a tiny little thing, only twenty centimetres or so. He called it Basil, after Basil Fawlty in Fawlty Towers. In the end, as a teenager, he sold Basil and replaced him with something new, a beautiful red milk snake with red bands and black and yellow rings. He called this one by the more prosaic name of Peter. But poor Peter died young, leaving Derek distraught. And after Peter, came Daisy. Snakes always soothed him, made him appreciate what was important in life. He'd stare at them and for a while at least, everything would feel right in Derek's world.

Chapter 31: Maxine

Half eleven. Maxine Hunt approached number sixty-two, Richmond Avenue. She paused at the gate and looked up at the house. She so wished she didn't have to do this now; why had she agreed? The front door opened and a woman struggling with a cumbersome double buggy appeared, looking harassed. The buggy had two toddlers in it, twins perhaps. Maxine smiled her best smile. 'You OK there? Do you want a hand?'

'I'm fine. I'm used to it. Are you coming in or what?'

The woman held the front door open. 'Thanks,' said Maxine, skipping into the house. 'Bye,' she said to the woman as she swivelled the buggy through the gate. She didn't respond. Maxine remembered Rebecca saying the key was under the doormat. She wondered whether to just leave it there now that she was in. Yes, she'd leave it there.

She walked up the stairs.

First floor. Flat three. She took a deep breath, wanting to get this over and done with, and knocked. No answer. She could hear a television blaring away inside, just as Mac's sister had warned. She couldn't see a bell so she knocked again, harder this time and waited. Still no answer. What did Mac's sister say? That Mac would leave the door unlocked so if no one answered, she could walk straight in. She tried opening the door but it was locked. She tried again. No, definitely locked. Christ on a bike, as Mac's sister had said. She knocked for a third time, much louder this time. Still no answer. Oh well, she'd tried. In some ways, she was relieved, but she didn't want to have to do this again.

Then, she had an idea. She found Mac's sister's telephone number on her mobile and rang it. The number rang and rang for ages, no answer and no voicemail either. She stopped the call and checked the number. Yes, it was definitely the right number, no one else had called her today. In truth, no one had phoned since a call from the care home ten days ago. She tried the number again. Again, it rang and rang but this time, finally, someone answered – a man's voice.

'Oh, hello,' said Maxine. 'Is, erm, Rebecca there please?'

The man laughed. 'Sorry, love, you've come through to a payphone.'

'A what?'

'I just happened to be passing.'

'I'm sorry?'

'For fuck's sake, love, you've got the wrong number. No one here called Rebecca.' The line went dead.

Maxine knocked on the flat door one last time – just for good measure. And then, feeling rather deflated, she returned downstairs and left the house.

'Well, that was a waste of time,' she said to herself as she walked briskly back down Richmond Avenue. 'Christ on a bike.'

Chapter 32: Mac

The high-pitched woman who answered the phone at Beech Court Care Home put Mac through to the manageress, as she called her. The manageress, a Mrs Abiola, in contrast to her colleague, spoke with a surprisingly deep voice, heavily accented, possibly Nigerian. She seemed pleasant enough, falling over herself to sing the home's virtues. Mac, making no mention of the OK reviews and reports, responded enthusiastically. Mrs Abiola suggested that Mac brought his father in for a visit; would tomorrow do? Yes, indeed, said Mac, tomorrow would be great. Anytime. They agreed on eleven am. Mac thanked Mrs Abiola and, closing down the call, a bit of weight lifted off his shoulders.

Mac felt exhausted; it'd been an emotionally draining day. He simply wanted to go home and crawl into bed, fall asleep and forget everything.

He found both Eoin and Tony busy with customers and with a line of customers sitting, awaiting their turn, Dua Lipa playing on the stereo.

'You alright, Mac?' said Eoin. 'Hope you don't mind me

saying but you look like shit.'

'Cheers for that, mate.'

Eoin forced a laugh. 'Seriously, mate, are you OK?'

'Yeah. Difficult day, you know, what with Dad and all.'

Mac went back to his office and sat at his desk. 'Frankly, my dear, I don't give a damn,' he said aloud, looking up at his *Gone With the Wind* poster. But in truth, he did give a damn and he suffered a stab of guilt. With him out of the picture so much, his boys had that much more work to do. It wasn't fair on them, but what could he do – except perhaps employ a third employee, even on a part-time basis to help cover the busy periods? But could he afford it? Maybe, maybe. He'd have to do the sums again. Even now, he thought, he could go through and help out, cut some hair, help bring the queue down. But, again, he couldn't face it. He logged onto his computer and whiled away the time looking at his social media accounts and deleting the junk from his email.

Eoin and Tony were good blokes but, at the end of the day, they were not his friends; they were his employees and though he was sure they liked him – they too saw him not as a friend but as their boss. He knew they socialised together, that their girlfriends were mates, that they all went to the pub together, but never thought to ask him along. The realisation hit him hard. So, who, exactly, did he have in his life that he could count on as a friend, not an employee, not a sister, but a genuine 'let's go out and have a pint' sort of friend. He had no one. Absolutely no one.

There was no point being here; he was of no use, a spare part.

Having said goodbye to Eoin and Tony and thanked them for working so hard, Mac traipsed home. At least he'd managed to organise an appointment at this potential new care home tomorrow. He promised himself he'd remain civil with his father. Whatever his past crimes, he was vulnerable now and he had to take that into account. He knew he'd failed. He'd had Dad at home just one day and he was already throwing in the towel but that was before he knew what sort of man his father really was, a despicable low life.

He popped into the small Turkish supermarket halfway home and bought milk, tea bags and a packet of frozen chicken breasts.

He returned home. On closing the door, he could see his father in his armchair watching the early evening TV news, the volume deafening loud. 'God, Dad,' he shouted. 'You'll have the neighbours knocking on the walls at this rate. What are you doing having it so loud?' His father didn't answer. A reporter was interviewing a Labour politician about illegal migrants crossing the Channel in flimsy inflatable boats.

Mac reached for the remote and brought the volume right down. 'Wow, that's better. I've got us some chicken for dinner. Just need to defrost it in the microwave. Fancy it? I'll put the oven on.'

He went through to the kitchen, switched the oven on and emptied out his shopping bag. He placed the chicken in the microwave and started cleaning the carrots. 'Dad?' he shouted through to the living room. 'You OK with carrots and broccoli? I'll do some frozen chips too. It'll be ready in half an hour or so.'

Having put the chicken pieces in the oven to heat up and chopped the carrots, leaving them for now in a pan of cold water, he went through to the living room. 'You're very quiet, Dad. What's up? Cat got your t...'

He saw it, the translucent pink tail of a mouse poking out from his father's mouth, the scarf wrapped tightly around his

179

neck, his eyes bulging from his head, the wet patch on his crotch. 'Shit, oh, shit, shit, hit.' He ran over to his father. 'Dad? Dad.' He shook him. His father's limp body fell forward.

'Dad, Christ's sake, Dad, wake up, wake up, please, Dad. Dad, Dad… please, no, not you, not now, Dad. Shit! Daddy, Daddy…'

Chapter 33: Derek

December 1982

Derek paced his bedroom. Yes, he'd got Pat to agree to lie for him, and he reckoned, when push came to shove, his mother would come around, but he'd made a mistake, an awful mistake. He said the argument that he and Miss Jones had had was about the sale, and whose it was. It was because he couldn't face telling them that Miss Jones had put in a complaint about him, about him pinning her to the cupboards in the kitchenette. He couldn't tell them that Mr Smith reckoned he'd be put up in front of a tribunal, her word against his. It sounded too bad. It *was* bad. But the police would know this; Mr Smith would have told them. He had to be honest with them, and then Pat and Mum would know; and they'd look at him all funny, and stutter over their answers, and that would cause alarm bells to ring.

He decided the best thing was to go tell them now, quickly, before the police arrived, tell them the truth about his contretemps with Miss Jones, get it out in the open. He paused at the bedroom door, but he couldn't do it, couldn't face it. He went to the window and, opening it, leaned out, breathing in the fresh air, or rather, the London air. Still felt fresh to him. He had to do it, he had to tell them. Better that it came from him than from the police. Right, he'd do it now.

He found Pat and his mother sitting in silence in the living room, the atmosphere heavy with awkwardness. He glanced at Daisy. He couldn't leave her here, not with the coppers coming in; he'd have to move her; he couldn't risk them asking what he fed her on. She wouldn't like it but tough. He lugged her into the bedroom and placed her on the floor on the far side of the bed, so if anyone looked in from the door, they wouldn't see the tank.

'You OK?' asked Pat. 'Why are you–'

'Apparently, you're meant to move them every now and then.'

Pat shook her head. 'I still can't believe it – that she was a work colleague, that you saw her day after day, and now she's dead, and some awful person strangled her. You must be so upset, Derek.'

It hit him that he hadn't been looking or sounding particularly upset, and that might come across as rather strange. 'Yeah, it hasn't hit home yet. I think it must be the shock, you know?'

'Yes, of course. You poor love.'

'It'll probably hit me later.'

'Yes.'

He took a deep breath, glancing at his mother's pinched expression. 'Actually, there is something I need to tell you, something else.'

Pat looked up at him, the concern written on her face. 'What is it, love?'

He opened his mouth to speak just at the point he heard a

knock on the door.

The two plain-clothed police officers sat awkwardly together in Derek's living room, making the room feel rather cramped, their notebooks at hand. The leading officer, Detective Inspector Peter Grainger, was huge – six foot something, with a huge belly, a ruddy face, and short, cropped hair. His companion, Detective Sergeant Barbara Milner, a woman perhaps in her forties, was, in comparison, painfully thin with a sharp nose and plucked eyebrows. They apologised for calling in unannounced but hoped, given the situation, that Derek would understand.

DI Grainger asked if they could speak to Derek alone. Derek tried not to let the relief show. The two women made themselves scarce. Derek only hoped they didn't try listening at the door, his mother in particular.

'Right,' said Grainger. 'Do you mind if we call you Derek'?'

'No, no, I mean, yes, that's fine.'

'So, Derek, let's make a start. Tell us, how long have you been working at Supervision Televisions?'

'Erm, about three years.' He made a show of mentally calculating it. 'Yes, coming up to three.'

'Coming up to three years,' repeated DI Grainger, writing it down slowly. 'And in that time, have you always worked with Ruth Jones?'

'Yes. Actually, no. I'd been there a few months before she started.'

'Were you senior to her?' asked DS Milner.

'No. We were the same scale.'

'Did you know each other outside of work?'

'No.'

'You didn't socialise?' asked Grainger. 'Work drinks, Christmas parties, that sort of thing?'

'Oh, yeah, maybe a couple of times, but I never saw her without my colleagues there.'

'Have you ever been to her flat?'

He shook his head and, trying to keep his voice level, said, 'I couldn't even tell you where she lived.'

'Did you get on with Miss Jones?' asked Milner.

'Yeah, on the whole, you know.'

'On the whole?'

'Yeah, I mean we had some, erm, professional disagreements sometimes, but nothing special.'

'Nothing special?' said Grainger. 'Yet on the very day she died, she accused you of assaulting her.' He referred to his notes. 'That, on the day before, you grabbed her scarf and almost strangled her.'

'Yeah, but I didn't, it's not true,' he said, tripping over his words.

'And that's exactly how she met her end – strangled by her own scarf, a chiffon scarf.'

'But I didn't touch her. She made it up.'

'Why would she do that?' asked Milner, playing with her shirt cuff. 'Mm?'

'I don't know; you'd have to… I suppose, you see, we did have a bargie the day before that. I'd made a sale but because she stepped in at the last moment to help, she claimed it for herself.'

'And who adjudicated on the matter? Your manager?'

'Yes, Mr Smith.' He sighed. 'He gave it to her,' he added quietly. 'But he would. They used to be *together*, you know, as in seeing each other.'

'Oh?' said Milner.

They didn't know that. So Derek pressed home the point, telling them that Jones had finished with Mr Smith and he hadn't got over it and was extremely jealous of Jones' new boyfriend. They jotted down everything he said.

'So, if Mr Smith gave this sale to Miss Jones, she wouldn't be holding any grudges against you. On the contrary, any grudges to be had would be held by you. So, the question is, why would she lie about you assaulting her the following day?'

'Because I told her I was going to take it to head office. But she made up that stuff about me touching her before I got chance.'

Milner asked, 'Why is claiming a sale important? Are you on commission?'

'A small one, yeah, but it's because we have targets, you know, monthly targets.'

'Which you were failing to meet, Derek,' said Grainger aggressively. 'In fact,' he added, again referring to his notes. 'You have failed to meet your target…' He flipped a page. 'Four months running.'

'We all have dips. The more we sell, the more the targets increase, and the more difficult they are to reach.'

'Had Miss Jones ever accused you of anything like this before?'

Derek shook his head.

'Have you ever been suspended before?'

'No, of course not. She lied, I'm telling you, because she was worried head office would believe me. I shouldn't have been sent home.'

'How do you get on with Mr Smith?' asked Milner.

'Fine. He's alright as bosses go. A bit up himself but…'

'Up himself?'

'You know – self-important, I don't know.' He was doing well, he was sure of it, but he had to maintain it, keep going.

'Were you worried about losing your job?' asked Grainger.

'No.'

'This alleged assault could have gone to your work tribunal, and ultimately, had they found against you, they may have referred it to us.'

'I know but...'

'Yes?'

'I... I was confident they'd see she was lying.' He shook his head. 'I don't like talking about her like this, calling her a liar and all that, it seems...'

'Disrespectful?'

He looked up at the man. 'Yeah, exactly. Disrespectful.'

'But it wasn't the first time,' said Milner. 'We know about your suspended sentence, Derek.'

'I was just a kid, a hot-headed kid.'

'Twenty-one.'

'Still a kid. I'm married now, and I look after my dear mother. You know, I've... I've had to change – for the better.'

Grainger coughed. Milner leant back. 'Right, so where did you go after Mr Smith sent you home, Derek?'

'I came home. I didn't have anywhere else to go and I was feeling pretty pissed off, to be honest, so I just came home.' He could feel the trickle of sweat inching its way down his back.

'Straight home then? No detours, didn't meet anyone or bump into anyone you know?'

'Nope.'

'And your wife and mother were in?' asked Milner.

'Yeah.' He forced himself to maintain eye contact with the woman. 'And my brother came over.'

'So they can corroborate this?'

'Of course. You can ask them.'

'Oh, we fully intend to, Derek,' said Grainger, snapping his notebook shut. 'We fully intend to. What did you do last night?'

'We all watched *Jaws* on ITV, the four of us. Ask them.'

Grainger turned to DS Milner. 'I think we're done here for now. Yeah?'

DS Milner nodded and with a flash of a smile, said, 'Yes, I think we have.'

DI Grainger pulled himself up from the armchair with some difficulty. Pulling the creases from his jacket, he looked down at Derek from his towering height and beamed. 'Thank you, Derek, for your time. You've been most helpful.'

Chapter 34: Benedict

Benedict drove quickly to the address on Richmond Avenue, following his Waze app. Drawing up, he could see the flashing blue lights of two police cars and an ambulance parked near the house. He braced himself. He was a policeman; he'd seen many corpses over the years, it was part of the job, but that never made it any easier. Seeing a dead body always left him with a deep sense of melancholy.

'OK, ready for this?'

Jessica nodded. 'Let's do it.'

Flashing their ID cards at the uniformed scene guard, they walked up the flight of stairs to the first floor. The flat door was open but cordoned off with police tape. Another uniform lifted the tape, allowing them inside. 'Any sign of damage to the door, constable?'

'No, sir. None whatsoever.'

'Right. Thanks.'

The first person Benedict saw, being interviewed by the Crime Scene Manager, DS Adrian Collins, was Thomas McIntosh. Beyond them, officers in white overalls were busy

– taking photographs, dusting for fingerprints, another filming the crime scene, the very image of quiet industry. And in the midst of it all, an armchair, its back to Benedict, a limp arm hanging down on the left-hand side.

Collins thanked Mac for his time.

'Mr McIntosh, Mac,' said Benedict. 'I'm sorry we have to meet again under such circumstances.'

Mac swept his hand through his hair, upsetting its carefully laid parting.

'DI Paige. DS Gardiner.'

'Please accept our condolences, sir.'

'Yeah, it's difficult but thank you. I thought discovering my dead grandmother was bad enough. And now… now this.'

'Yes, it must be difficult. This is your flat, I assume.'

'Yes.'

'OK, let me speak to some of my colleagues. Can we catch you later for a quick chat?'

'Sure, but I've already spoken to…'

'DS Collins, I know but nonetheless…'

'OK, sure. I'm going to… I don't know. Do you want a cup of tea or something? No? In that case, if it's OK, I think I'll go lie down on my bed. Just knock when you're ready.'

'Actually, no. I'm sorry but while this remains a crime scene, we're going to have to ask you to hang around here. I'm sorry.'

'Yeah, of course. Sure.' He stuffed his hands into his jean pockets. 'I'll hang around here.'

Benedict and Jessica picked their way past the officers in white and found Dick Evans, the pathologist, examining the body.

'Ah, DI Paige, we meet again. And DS Gardiner, a delight to meet you again.'

Jessica forced a tight smile.

'Dick,' said Benedict. 'How's it going?'

'Never better,' said Evans, his eyes focused on Benedict's shoulder.

Benedict looked down at Mr McIntosh in his armchair, his head fallen to one side, his mouth open, the pink tail of a white mouse clearly visible poking out of his mouth, his eyes wide open, the scarf still unbearably tight around his neck.

'I'll tell you this for starters,' said Evans. 'This is a carbon copy murder of his mother's death. Same bruising, same bloodshot eyes, a urine leakage, not to mention the… rodent.'

'Obviously the same.'

'Oh God, yes, absolutely, otherwise my name is Hannibal Lecter. Same MO, same signature, victim same member of the family. No sign of a break-in, according to your CSM. So, just like his mother, Mr McIntosh opened the door to his killer.'

'Or his killer had a key to the flat,' said Jessica. 'And the grandmother's flat.'

'Indeed.'

'Forensics will tell you,' said Evans. 'But I reckon both were killed where we found them – bed or armchair.'

'Implying that they felt comfortable with whoever it was.'

'Looks like that. Regarding time of death, it's recent, a matter of hours, maybe this morning. So, how are you fitting in, DS Gardiner? Ben treating you well, I hope.'

'Very well, thank you.'

'Ah, he's a decent sort despite what people say.'

'Hey?' exclaimed Benedict. 'What do people say, exactly?'

'No regrets about leaving Liverpool?'

'Manchester, sir. No, not at all. Although it seems to rain just as much down here as up there.'

'Ha! That might be to your advantage here. If the killer came in with damp shoes, forensics would know. Meanwhile, I'll do the PM on this poor blighter in due course. I hope you find the killer soon, Ben. We don't want another like this, now do we?'

Benedict thanked the old pathologist. Turning to Jessica, he said, 'Let's go speak to Mac.'

The three of them stood in the kitchen. 'The last time we saw you, Mr McIntosh, your father was living in the care home,' said Jessica.

'Yes, but I moved him out yesterday.'

'Yesterday?'

'I decided it was for the best.'

'So, what happened here?' asked Benedict.

'I left Dad asleep in the armchair around ten-fifteen to meet my sister and, er, my mother.'

'You met your mother?'

'Yes, she got back in touch out of the blue. Wanted to meet us, Rebecca and me.'

'Right. That must've been–'

'Weird, yeah.'

'How long were you with your mother and Rebecca? And where did you meet?'

'Bertie's Café in Holloway. We met at eleven. We were there for a good two hours or so.'

'Then what?' asked Jessica.

'I popped into work for a while and chatted with a couple of customers, then came home via the shops–'

'What shops, Mr McIntosh?'

'Hang on.' His eyes narrowed. 'Are you actually interviewing me as a suspect here? Because if–'

'No, no,' said Benedict, his hand up. 'We just like to get as full a picture as possible. I'm sure you must understand.'

'OK,' he said, looking unconvinced.

'Do carry on, Mr McIntosh,' said Jessica. 'You were about to tell us which shops you went to on your way home from your barbershop.'

'Right, yeah. So, let me see, I bought milk and tea bags and a couple of other things at the local convenience store just at the corner of this street.'

'Card or cash?'

'Jesus, you really are interviewing me. Card. I hardly ever use cash these days. I didn't take the receipt, but I guess you'll be able to check.'

'If we feel the need to, yes,' said Benedict.

'And then what?' asked Jessica.

'I came home. This must've been about two. Put the key in the door, called for Dad, and saw his arm drooping to the side of his armchair so at first, I assumed he was still asleep. He does sleep a lot nowadays. And that's when I found him. I puked. I saw the mouse in his mouth, and it caught me.' He looked down as if embarrassed by this admission of being unable to control his bodily functions. 'And that's when I called 999. Just like the other day, when I found Granny. It's like Groundhog Day. I mean, will they come for me next? Christ.'

'Did you notice anything when you came home, Mr McIntosh?' asked Jessica.

'What do you mean?'

'Was anything out of place here?'

'No, not that I noticed.'

'Did you see anyone on the staircase or leaving the house when you returned?'

'No, not that I remember.'

'A nurse perhaps?'

'A nurse? No, no nurse. Oh, you mean like the one who

visited Gran? No, I didn't see any nurses.'

'Have you told your mother or sister yet?'

'No, I was waiting for your guys to leave.'

'They might be a while yet.'

'I'll ring Rebecca now. Mum, I think it'd be better if I went to see her. Not the sort of thing one should say down the phone, even if they have been separated for thirty years.'

'Good idea. OK, I think that'll do for now. OK, DS Gardiner?'

'Boss.'

'But, having said that, you have discovered two murder victims in the space of days, Mr McIntosh. I think, in light of that, we should carry on this conversation under a more official environment. Can you come to the station tomorrow morning?'

'Christ, are you arresting me?'

'No, no, not at all. You'll be helping us with our inquiries.'

'Right. Do I have a choice?'

'Frankly, no.'

'What time?'

'Shall we say ten?'

'If I must.'

Chapter 35: Mac

Mac asked one of the uniformed officers if he could leave the flat; he didn't want to see his father's body being carried out. The woman said as long as DI Paige was happy, he could do as he pleased. First, and again with the officer's permission, he gingerly approached his father. It seemed wrong somehow to say goodbye to him while so many people milled about, but what could he do?

He looked down at his father hoping to see an expression of peace on his face. People often said that, didn't they? *He's at peace now.* But no, he couldn't see it; nothing serene about his expression, just that same angry look he always had, that same bitter look he always wore. It hit him then that he'd never seen his father happy. Not once. Actually, he was happy while he had his snake but once she'd died, Dad couldn't afford to replace her. Also, that one time his father won at the bookmakers with Arpeggio. That snake and Arpeggio had made Dad happy in a way that no human had, not that Mac could remember; and he certainly hadn't. A glowing school report, a goal scored at football, a cake made in cookery class

194

at school, his exam results, a new girlfriend, not that that happened too often, opening his business, none of it registered with his father, all of it met with a shrug of indifference. Thinking about it, looking at his father's corpse, he doubted that he'd ever made his father proud. Not once. But he felt no resentment, no anger, only a deep sadness that his father was not a man who took any joy from life; from his children, from… anything. What a waste, an utter waste of a life.

'Goodbye, Dad.' And with that, Mac left his flat. He didn't look back.

Stepping outside, he turned his collar up and rang his mother. She answered straight away.

'Mum, I need to see you. It's important. Can I come over now?'

'I don't see why not, yes. I'm at the B and B. I gave you the address, didn't I?'

'Yes. OK, I'll be with you shortly. Thanks, Mum. See you in a bit.'

He waited for a pair of elderly women to walk by. One with one of those pugs on a lead, snorting and struggling to breathe, poor blighter. Then, he rang his sister.

'Rebecca, can you talk?'

'Sure but be quick, I'm expecting a work call and–'

'It's about Dad.'

'Oh shit, what's he done now? Don't tell me, he's upset your neighbours already.'

'He's dead, Rebecca.'

'Dead? Oh, right. Didn't expect that. OK, thanks for letting me know. Speak to you–'

'No, hang on a minute. Is that it?'

'What do you want me to say, Mac? Gnash my teeth and wail? Compose a eulogy on the spot?'

'He was killed, Rebecca. Murdered. Some fucker came into my flat and *murdered* him.'

'Ah.'

'Yeah, exactly.'

'Did they break in?'

'No. I guess he opened the door to them.'

'Any struggle?'

'No. Everything's exactly the same as when I left.'

'Except you left behind a living man and returned to a dead one.'

'Not remotely funny, Rebecca.'

'Oh shit, was there a mouse?'

'Yes.'

'Fuck.'

'The flat's swarming with police right now, and forensics and what-have-you. I'm going to see Mum. Thought I'd better tell her in person.'

'Good call. Shit, this is too freaky for words. Why is someone plucking us off one by one? Could be you and me next, Mac.'

'That's what I thought but if it's to do with Dad's past, we were just kids.'

'Oh shit, so that's another funeral to organise. Could do without that right now. Oh, hell, that call's coming through. Gotta go.'

'No, wait a…' But she'd gone, cut him off.

A young hoodie whizzed by on an electric scooter, going at an incredible speed. Right, thought Mac, time to go to break the news to his mother.

*

The Montrose looked like any other house on this terraced street, a Victorian house with three floors. Outside, it boasted a large, teapot-shaped sign with the words 'Bed and Breakfast' written in a cursive script. A sign inside the downstairs bay window stated 'Vacancies'.

Mac walked in, setting off a small bell. The reception area was dominated by a high counter, on which stood a lamp with a tartan lampshade, and behind which sat a black girl, scrolling on her phone which she immediately put aside on seeing him. The walls were decorated with large, framed photographs of what looked like the Scottish Highlands, behind the counter, an old-fashioned map of Scotland. Opposite the counter a half-moon table featuring a Perspex rack full of leaflets advertising the best of London's many attractions and ideas for days and nights out in the capital.

He asked the young receptionist if he could see his mother, Patricia Roberts. She directed him up the stairs – room four, the only room on the second floor.

He knocked on his mother's door and went in. He found her sitting in an armchair looking at her phone. 'Your father's been murdered, hasn't he?'

'How did you know that?' He pulled up a chair and sat opposite her.

'It's already on the BBC news app.' She held up the screen for him. 'No details yet, just says an elderly man has been found strangled in his flat near Camden High Street. More to follow as they update the story.'

'How are you feeling?'

'I've not had time to process it yet but…'

'But?'

'I can't lie, Mac, but it's difficult to feel any great emotion here.'

'I understand. Honestly, after you told us about… you know, I wanted to kill him myself. I felt… I don't know, so ashamed,

I guess.'

'Oh, Mac. You were just a little boy. He had the decency at least to wait until you'd gone to school or bed before he "punished" me.' She said the word in air quotes. She leant forward and placed a hand on his knee. 'You have *nothing* to feel ashamed about.'

He looked around the room. Being the loft, it was big, cosy, a slanting ceiling. The pictures hanging from the walls all seemed to feature stags and misty hills. 'There's a lot of Scottish stuff here.'

'Aye, there is,' she said in a rather decent Scottish accent.

'Didn't know you could do accents.'

'My hidden talent.'

He smiled.

Reverting to her normal voice, she said, 'Have you told your sister?'

'Ahuh. I phoned her before coming here. Oh, sorry, I should have told you first.'

She batted away his apology. 'You two were with him a lot longer than me. It doesn't matter. Would you like a cuppa?'

'No, you're alright.'

'What will you do now?'

'Me? I might go to work.'

'Won't it be closed now?'

'Yeah, but I might do some admin quietly at the back. I don't want to go home – not yet. Then I might go have a Chinese at the place up the road. They do a rather nice prawn dish in ginger and garlic.'

'You'll have to face it at some point.'

'I know. Mum, some person unknown to us has been in my flat and *murdered* my father. I can't get that out of my head. I know he... he wasn't the best of people but the thought of someone killing a helpless old man *in my flat*, it's…'

She took his hand. 'I know, love. It's a horrible thing to deal with, I know.'

He so didn't want to cry but the tears came. 'Who would do such a thing? He had dementia for fuck's sake. What harm could he do? What danger did he pose to anyone? No one, that's who, no one.'

'They'll catch him. Whoever did this, the police will catch him and bring him to justice.'

'I hope so, Mum. I bloody hope so.'

*

Mac returned to the shop. He still couldn't face returning home quite yet. He walked down the high street, his hands in his pocket, realising that he did feel better having spoken to his mother. It was strange, he thought, how he'd grown up without her, yet she was back and they'd immediately slotted into their mother/son roles. And he was grateful for that. It was as if he had been missing a part of himself for so long that he no longer realised it was absent until it was restored. And now that it was back, he felt more *whole* somehow.

He passed the British Heart Foundation charity shop, and his eye was caught by a whole display devoted to St Valentine's Day which wasn't too far away now. He hadn't bought a girl a Valentine's card since sixth form. He couldn't even remember her name. He only liked her because she looked vaguely like Jenny Frost from Atomic Kitten. He smiled at the memory while, at the same time, his heart felt as if it'd been covered in a cloak of longing.

At that very moment, he saw the reflection of a familiar figure in the charity shop's window. He spun round, his heart soaring. He saw Marcus in his school uniform on the other side of the street. He wondered whether they'd been to the Chelsea game yet. Caroline came into view. He opened his mouth to call her name when a man appeared, a tall, good-looking white guy, the two of them laughing together. Her name died on his lips.

The three of them knew each other well, the way the man ruffled Marcus' hair. He guessed the man wasn't Marcus' dad as Marcus was of dual heritage, so even worse, this was Caroline's boyfriend. He couldn't blame the man; she was beautiful. The three of them sauntered up the street, in no hurry, and Mac watched them go. All his past romantic failures and 'if onlys' and 'should have beens' came crashing into his mind all at once, and it took all his strength not to break down there and then and sob in the street.

Chapter 36: Benedict

Monday morning. Benedict Paige woke up feeling concerned but not sure why. He made Sonia and himself a cup of tea, two sweeteners in his, and turned on the morning news on Radio 4. Lying in bed, they could hear the children getting up and getting ready for school, making an awful lot of noise about it. Invariably, the call came up the stairs… 'Mum? Mum! Where's the Cheerios?'

'Ask your sister. I think she finished them last night.'

'What? You're joking. Charlotte, you snake, have you eaten all the Cheerios…' Harry's voice trailed off as he tackled his sister.

'All's well in the Paige household,' said Sonia.

'When isn't it?'

'He was very young to have dementia.'

'Yeah, but it happens, doesn't it? A person's risk of developing dementia rises from one in fourteen over the age of sixty-five, to one in six over the age for those of eighty.'

'Crikey, how do you know that? Doctor Google, perchance?'

'Yep.'

'What did we do before Google?'

'Use a library? Anyway, I'd better get going.'

'When are you going to wear that nice new suit of yours?'

'Oh, that.' He still hadn't worn it and rather hoped that his wife had forgotten about it. He should have known better. 'Sure but no time now. Must dash. See you later, my love.'

*

DC Prowse rushed into the office, a cup of Starbucks coffee in one hand, a closed umbrella dripping water in the other. 'It's raining cats and dogs out there.'

Benedict chortled at the young man's use of such an old-fashioned expression. DC Prowse switched on his computer while taking his coat off, shaking off the excess rain.

'So, boss, I hear we have another white mouse murder on our hands.'

'Unfortunately so,' said Benedict. 'We've got Thomas McIntosh coming to see us in an hour.'

'Cool.'

DC Kelly sauntered into the office with a fresh cup of coffee. 'Oh, sorry, boss, did you want one?'

'Wouldn't say no.'

Kelly tried to suppress a sigh. 'Two ticks, boss.'

Three minutes later, he was back with his boss's coffee.

'Mine's gone cold now,' Benedict heard Kelly mutter to himself. He smiled.

'Oh, boss, we got old Marjorie McIntosh's will. She had about three thousand pounds in her savings, that was it.'

'Not much of a motivation for murder then?'

'Not on account she left it all to Battersea Dogs Home.'

'Oh dear, oh dear.'

'But she left Mac her portrait of the queen.'

202

'I'd kill for that,' said DC Prowse.

Benedict finished his coffee while slowly relishing an almond croissant. Jessica turned up, looking flustered but she offered no reason for it. The office hummed with quiet and feverish activity. Come half nine, Benedict rang Sunny Grove and had a short but enlightening conversation with Mrs Hale, the manager.

*

Thomas McIntosh looked decidedly relaxed for a man who'd just lost his father and grandmother within a space of days, both at the hands of a cold-blooded killer. He looked clean-shaven, fresh and his hair immaculate, as always. His sleeves rolled up, exposing part of his tattoo, a swirl of reds and blues. He sat opposite Benedict and Jessica, his hands clasped together on the table, ignoring the glass of water put there for him.

'So,' said Benedict, 'could you start off by telling us again where you were on both the nights of your grandmother and father's deaths?'

'Oh, erm… Tuesday night I went straight to Granny's from work. Yesterday morning, like I said, I met Rebecca and my mum in Holloway. Loads of people can vouch for me. Then I went to the shop to see how things were going, like I told you. Eoin and Tony at the shop will vouch for me also.'

'You found your grandmother on Tuesday night but her time of death was some twenty-four hours before, so what were you doing Monday night?'

'Monday night? I was at home.'

'Can anyone corroborate this?' asked Jessica.

'No, I live alone.'

'So, in terms of a timeline,' she said, 'you had ample

203

opportunity to kill your grandmother–'

'No, no,' he shouted. 'I didn't kill her, either of them, I didn't.' Calming himself, he added, 'Why would I want to kill them?'

'OK, moving on,' said Benedict. 'Let's rewind a few years. Can you give us the timeline of your parents' lives?'

He shrugged. 'If I must. My mum and dad lived in this house in Stoke Newington with me grandmother, but she'd moved out by the time I'd come around. Got herself her council flat in Camden.'

'How? Camden is a different council.'

'I think it was because she went on their list when she lived in Camden with my granddad. But after they split up, she moved in with my parents. I think it was only meant to be a temporary thing, but she ended up being there for a good year or two.'

'What happened to your parents' house in Stoke Newington?'

'Dad had to sell it after Mum ran off. We moved into this three-bed flat up the road, my flat now. Rebecca moved in with a friend as soon as she turned sixteen.'

'You rent?'

'Yeah.'

'How old was your father when he was diagnosed with dementia?'

'About sixty.'

'Very young,' said Jessica.

'Well, yeah, he'd not looked after himself. He ate poorly and drank too much and got fat. He developed diabetes, had high blood pressure. And he had bouts of depression.'

'All classic preconditions for developing dementia,' said Benedict.

'Yeah. Unfortunately.'

'What did your father mean the other day when he said his mother did what he told her to about the bloody police?'

'Those bastard cops,' said Jessica. 'Those were his exact words: those bastard cops.'

'Well, Mr McIntosh?'

'I don't know. I honestly don't know. But I have thought about it. My dad got into gambling after Mum left. I think he may have had some bad debts, and perhaps he did something slightly illegal to pay them off.'

'What?' asked Jessica. 'Did he rob a bank?'

Mac almost laughed. 'He wouldn't have gone that far. And also, he's got that old-fashioned working man's aversion to cops. Never trusted them, you know?'

Jessica produced the CCTV printout of the mysterious nurse. 'Recognise this woman?'

Mac's brow furrowed in concentration. 'Nope.' He pushed the photos back.

'How did your mother contact you? A phone call, a letter?'

'I got this email out of the blue asking to meet up with us.'

'A nice surprise or…?' asked Jessica.

'I wasn't sure. I'm still not sure, to be honest.'

'How was she?' asked Jessica.

'Alright. She's got her life in order, she seemed sound. She's just moved back to London. She'd been living in Spain, but it became too difficult what with Brexit and all that.'

'How long had she been in Spain?' asked Jessica.

'Almost since the day she walked out on us.'

'Thirty years or so.'

'Yes.'

'And, just to confirm, she's only recently moved back to England?'

'Oh yes, very recently.'

'Will you meet her again?'

Mac shrugged. 'Yeah. Don't see why not.'

'Did you or your sister tell your father?' asked Benedict.

'God no.'

'How did your father take it when his wife walked out on him and her kids?' asked Jessica.

'Not well. He got angry, he got sad. He started gambling. Money was short, like I said. It wasn't easy.'

'I bet,' said Benedict. 'Moving on, how long was your father in Sunny Grove?'

'Three, three and a half years.'

'And then, all of a sudden, you decide to move him out? Did you consult your sister?'

'No, I told you before, either of us can make decisions on his behalf.'

'Why did you, of your own volition, decide that it was best to move your father out of Sunny Grove with its professional care?'

'Why? Erm, because, well, because I wanted him to enjoy his twilight years in a proper home, not an institution.'

'But being only sixty-five, he could've lived for another twenty, even thirty years. Was that wise?'

'It was also the money. Rebecca and I were struggling a little. And to be honest, he didn't really like it there.'

'But you work, Mr McIntosh,' said Benedict. 'That would mean leaving your father by himself for hours at a time. Surely, he needed round-the-clock care?'

'My job is mainly administrative and marketing and stuff. I've got a lot to do, and I can do that from home.'

'So,' said Benedict. 'You withdrew your father from the care home for his own good?'

Mac shrugged. 'In a nutshell, yes.'

'No other reason?'

'No.'

'Right. You see, I had a conversation with the home's manager this morning. Mrs Hale. She's saying your father was about to be evicted for bullying.'

'Ah, yes,' said Mac, shifting in his seat. 'I suppose there was that.'

'Your father seemed to have taken against a fellow resident called Mrs Hunt to the point the woman was terrified of him.'

'Maxine's grandmother. I suppose–'

Benedict put his hand up. 'Wait a minute. Who did you say?'

'Maxine Hunt, she's–'

'This Mrs Hunt has a granddaughter called Maxine?' Benedict felt Jessica's gaze.

'Yes. Why, is there something wrong?'

Benedict leant forward again. 'How well do you know this Maxine Hunt?'

Mac puffed out his cheeks as if trying to remember. 'I've only met her a few times. She comes to me for her haircuts and I've seen her in the home. She's nice. Pleasant enough. She's not…'

'She's not what?' asked Jessica.

'Erm, I'm not sure how to put this without sounding rude. She's perfectly capable and all that but she's… a tad on the simple side.' He grimaced at his own choice of words.

'Would vulnerable be a–'

'Yes, yes, vulnerable. She's rather vulnerable. That's it.'

'In what way?'

'I don't know. But when you speak to her, you can tell straight away. I mean, she's lovely and all but… yeah, vulnerable.'

'OK. Fine,' said Benedict. 'So, you decided, quite unilaterally, to move your father into your flat, what you described as a proper home, not an institution, an institution that looked after him so well for some three years or more. Yet, within twenty-four hours of him moving into your proper home, he ends up dead.'

'Yeah, alright, alright,' said Mac, wringing his hands. 'Don't you think I've beaten myself enough over that already?'

'It's just that I'm rather struck by the coincidence here.'

'I didn't do it, I'm telling you, I had no reason to do it.'

'You haven't seen your sister since?' asked Jessica.

'No.'

'Did you speak to her?'

'Of course. I had to tell her dad had died. What do you take me for?'

'You tell me, Mr McIntosh.'

'Did you plan it together, Rebecca and you?' asked Benedict.

'God no. No!'

'We'll need to speak to her, of course. Right then, I think we're done here. Unless, Jessica, you have–'

'No, no. I'm good.'

'Great. OK, thank you for your time, Mr McIntosh.'

Mac leant back. 'You mean I'm free to go?'

'Unless you particularly want to stay.'

'Ha-ha. No, thanks. Right. Great. Good.' He stood and scooped up his jacket from the back of the chair.

'Don't go too far though, Mr McIntosh. We may need to speak to you again. Understood?'

He nodded while wrestling with a jacket sleeve.

'I'll see you out,' said Jessica,

'Oh,' said Benedict. 'One more thing, Mr McIntosh. Are you concerned for your own safety in any way?'

'Me? No. Why? Should I be?'

'Two close family members murdered in a space of days…'

'Yeah, two *frail* family members. But don't worry – if anyone approaches me bearing a white mouse–'

'I'm being serious, Mr McIntosh. All I'm saying is be careful.'

'Yeah. OK. Thanks.'

Chapter 37: Derek

December 1982

The Christmas party at the Mulberry Duck Inn on Oxford Street, London, was in full swing. The booze was flowing, the music was loud, and, joy of joys, no more work until the day after Boxing Day. Derek was in a great mood. He'd had three pints and smoked through half a pack of ten Benson and Hedges. He and his colleagues from various branches had nabbed a large, round table and claimed it as their own for the night. The pub was rammed full, full of workers like themselves, enjoying the Christmas spirit and letting their hair down.

Lots of young women, wearing far too much make-up and showing far too much flesh for Derek's liking, screeched and shouted and made a show of themselves. God, he hated them, the little flirts. Did they not have any sense of self-pride; would their parents approve of them flaunting themselves like this? He doubted it. No daughter of his would ever behave like this.

About three hours earlier, soon after they arrived and were still sober and the pub was still relatively quiet, Mr Smith made a short speech and toasted the memory of Miss Jones. 'Life at work without Ruth just isn't the same,' he said. 'We, at Tottenham Court Road especially, miss her terribly, and I know my colleagues from across town who had the pleasure of meeting Ruth over the years will feel the same. She was such a fine woman, a lady whose life was cut tragically short by some monster who, for reasons we may never know, carried out this terrible deed. Our prayers are with her family, and her boyfriend, Paul. We just hope and pray that come the New Year, the police will catch the man who did this and put him in jail where he belongs. Friends, colleagues, please raise your glasses to Ruth.'

'To Ruth,' they all echoed, raising their glasses.

Four days earlier, Mr Smith, Richard and Derek had joined Ruth's family at her funeral, which took place in the Kent town of Sevenoaks. Derek had been desperate not to go and had volunteered to stay behind and man the shop. But no, Head Office, insisting all Ruth's direct colleagues, past and present, should attend, sent cover for the morning. Derek stood next to his colleagues throughout the ceremony and the wake and spoke to no one else. He kept his eyes down the whole time, not wanting to engage with anyone. While Mr Smith and Richard, at various points, approached Miss Jones' parents to offer their condolences, Derek had hung back, desperate not to speak to them, not to see the anguish in their eyes. At one point during the wake at Ruth's parent's grand house, he saw Richard talking and laughing with the man Derek now knew was Paul. Richard even called Derek over to introduce him, but Derek, pretending not to hear, escaped to the bathroom where he sat on the toilet almost hyperventilating with the stress of it all. He only came out when he heard a knock on the door. That in itself gave him a dreadful shock, reminding him of Paul knocking on Ruth's flat door on that fateful night. He'd never been so pleased to return to London and work.

It'd only been ten days since that night, but already it felt as if it belonged to another lifetime, as if it'd happened not recently but months, even years ago. There were times that Derek couldn't believe he'd killed her. It just didn't seem possible; surely, he must've imagined it.

He hadn't heard from the police since. They'd been to the shop a couple of times, but Mr Smith, as manager, had dealt with them and answered their questions as best as he could.

Pat, his mother and his brother had indeed confirmed that Derek had returned from work early that day, about twenty-to-four, and had spent the whole evening together, during which they had dinner and watched *Jaws* on ITV. And no, he hadn't gone out at all.

Today, at work, Mr Smith had popped out, saying he had to go to buy some Christmas stamps from the post office. Derek took today's post and, entering Mr Smith's office, saw a large pile of envelopes on his desk – Christmas cards, about thirty of them, Derek reckoned, all sealed and addressed but without stamps. He took one from near the bottom, perhaps the smallest one, being careful only to hold it by its edges. It was addressed to a woman in Winchester. He stepped out of Mr Smith's office, directly into the kitchenette and dropped the Christmas card into his briefcase. He heard Mr Smith's voice in the shop; he was back.

'God, it's cold out there, Derek,' he said, rubbing his hands. 'If you've got time, make me a cup of tea, would you?'

'Yes, Mr Smith.'

'You know, I still can't work out what happened to my Arsenal mug. It's been missing for days. You haven't seen it, have you?'

'No. Sorry, Mr Smith.'

During his lunch break, Derek returned to the pet shop he'd recently discovered and bought a couple more frozen mice.

Derek had almost finished his pack of ten cigarettes and was halfway through his third pint of lager. Or was it his fourth? He'd been speaking to a man from the Westminster branch, an older man called Ronald, with long sideburns, as if his fashion sense had frozen in about 1973, who was predicting the advent of computers for the masses, a computer in every home. Derek mentioned he'd been campaigning for a Sinclair computer. 'Those ZX Spectrums they make look brilliant.'

Later, as Derek made his way back from the bar, one of the young women bumped into him, spilling some of his drink. 'Hey, look where you're going, will you?' he shouted at her.

'Shut up, don't shout at me.' She was wearing a plunging dress that didn't leave much to the imagination with the word 'Relax' blazoned over her large bosom and an array of black and silver necklaces.

'You spilt my drink, you silly cow. You'll have to buy me another.'

'You what?' she said in a hard northern accent, her dangling earrings shaking. 'Sod off, I'm not buying you anything, you twat.'

Another girl appeared, similarly attired. 'You alright, Lizzie? Anything wrong?' She had the same accent, Derek reckoned Mancunian.

'Apart from this sad twat, no.'

The two girls linked arms and laughing, disappeared into the throng.

Derek, fuming, meandered his way back to his table. 'How are you, Derek?' asked Richard, a large grin on his face.

'Little tarts.'

'You what, mate?'

Ronald, with the long sideburns, caught him again, keen to talk about a computerised database he'd seen somewhere. Derek wanted to leave, it was too loud and too raucous for him now. Luckily, Richard had seen a similar database, and the two men got talking. Derek drank his drink as quickly as possible. Slade's *Merry Xmas Everybody* was now playing on the jukebox which got everyone in the pub singing: So, here it is… With a satisfying belch, Derek finished his drink and placed the glass on the table. Hoping no one would notice, he retrieved his coat and briefcase and slipped away.

He stepped out onto Oxford Street and gulped down the cold air, happy to have escaped the claustrophobia of the pub. And that's when he first heard them – the two Mancunian accents shouting and laughing a hundred yards or so further down the street waiting at the 73 bus stop – his bus stop. He saw a 73 bus approaching. Quickly, he walked down the street and hopped on the back of the bus just as it was about to pull away. The girls had gone upstairs so Derek sat behind the driver downstairs. The Perspex glass behind the driver gave him a perfect reflection by which he could see people getting on and off the bus.

Even from here, you could hear them screeching upstairs and having zero regard for their fellow passengers. Disgraceful behaviour.

The bus wound its way through Euston, Kings Cross, into Islington, and from there Newington Green. Here, finally, one of the girls alighted, not the one called Lizzy, but her friend. Even as she got off the bus, the two girls managed to keep their conversation going, shouting at each other across the two decks. The girl stood on the pavement, looking up at her friend, waving goodbye and blowing kisses.

The bus now passed his house but Derek remained in his seat, picking at his cuticles. Finally, at the end of Church Street in Stoke Newington, the second girl, Lizzy, came clattering down the steps and almost fell off the bus. Gathering his briefcase, Derek rushed off the bus, jumping off just as it started picking up speed. He stepped into the doorway of the Three Crowns pub and watched as the girl struggled to light a cigarette. Finally lit, she staggered up Church Street, positively zigzagging across the width of the pavement. Derek followed from a distance, his heart thumping with adrenalin. To his horror, the girl got into a conversation with some black kid. They laughed as if they'd always known each other. He feared they were going off to have sex there and then; he wouldn't put it past her. He knew her type.

Finally, the boy wished her goodnight and, crossing the road, disappeared.

Lizzie, was that her name?, turned right down a quieter residential street, passing a park, Clissold Park, on her right. She was walking fast, considering how drunk she appeared. Derek, meanwhile, felt so alive, his nerve endings twitching with nervous anticipation and pure excitement. She turned into a narrow cut-through called Spensley Walk. The only noise now was the click-clack of her shoes and Derek's laboured breathing. He fingered the white mouse in his pocket, and, checking in his inside pocket, he still had Mr Smith's Christmas card to his friend in Winchester.

Halfway down Spensley Walk, she stopped as if aware, for the first time, that someone was following her.

She turned just as Derek's gloved hand squeezed tightly over her mouth, stifling her scream.

Chapter 38: Benedict

Benedict returned to the office having had a meeting with DCI Lincoln to update him on the progress of his cases when he received a phone call from Diana Pettigrew in Forensics. Yes, Derek McIntosh was killed at some point during Saturday morning, around midday-ish. Benedict thanked her.

DC Kelly skipped into the office like an overbearing puppy and almost jumped on him. 'Boss, forensics have said that Volkswagen Polo did have blue paint fragments from a Dacia Sandero on its side. So, in other words, they match up. The Polo scraped the Sandero which was parked on Hatherley Avenue.'

'Marvellous!'

'And this, boss,' said Kelly, handing Benedict a purple Post-It note, 'is the Polo owner's name, address and number.'

'Antonio Cassese. Excellent. Well done, Kelly, good work.'

'Thanks, boss.'

'Jessica? Where's Jessica?'

'Here, boss, sorry, just nipped out.'

'Come, we've got someone we need to talk to.'

*

Antonio Cassese lived in a flat on a housing estate in Kentish Town. But, according to his wife, as the manager of a Spanish café nearby, he was at work. Benedict and Jessica walked down the high street until they found Cassese Café. An appealing place, thought Benedict, lots of lovely-looking pastries and paninis, but almost empty, just two young women feeding two toddlers in high chairs. The song *Mandy* by Barry Manilow played quietly on the speakers. Jessica approached the dark-haired waitress behind the bar, wearing a black apron with the words 'Cassese's Café' emblazoned in white. The girl's smile disappeared in an instant even before Jessica opened her mouth to speak. 'Hi, is Mr Cassese available, please?'

'Er, yes, sure. Who shall I say is calling, please?'

'Police.' She showed the woman her ID.

'Oh, right, er, hang on, please.'

'We won't be going anywhere.'

Antonio Cassese appeared from the back; the concern written all over him. 'Do you want to come through?' He was dressed head to toe in black and had a neatly trimmed black beard and, visible beneath his unbuttoned shirt, a tattoo of a crucifix. It reminded Benedict of the wooden cross hanging above the fireplace in Mac's grandmother's flat.

Nodding a thanks to the waitress, Benedict followed Jessica through to a small office at the back.

'So, Mr Cassese, thank you for your time,' said Jessica. 'Nice place you've got here.'

'Thank you.'

'Now, is there anything you'd like to tell us?'

'I'm sorry?' His eyes darted from one to the other; he knew he'd been rumbled. 'I – I'm not s-sure what you are meaning?' His Spanish accent was strong.

'In your own words, Mr Cassese, tell us exactly what

217

happened on Hatherley Avenue on Monday night at about ten in the evening.'

'Oh, that.'

'Yes, that.'

'Is the girl OK?'

'Ah, so you are concerned for her welfare, after all?'

'But, yes, of course…'

'But not so concerned that you stopped to check on her, or call an ambulance perhaps? Something a decent human being would do?'

'I'm sorry. I'm s-so sorry. I-I c-couldn't stop. It was not possible for me. I see another woman. I think she help.'

'OK, OK,' said Jessica. 'Let's start at the beginning, shall we? Tell us exactly what happened. Where you were going, where had you been?'

They were interrupted by a gentle knock on the door. The young waitress popped her head around the door. 'Sorry to interrupt, Ant, but someone wants to speak to you.'

'A customer?'

'Yes.'

Mr Cassese stood. 'Sorry, you'll have to–'

'Sit down, Mr Cassese,' barked Jessica.

'But–'

'They'll have to wait.'

The waitress slipped away.

The three of them sat in silence for a while. 'Would you like a coffee and a slice of cake, maybe? On the house, of course.'

'Are you trying to bribe us, Mr Cassese?'

The man almost fell out of his chair denying it.

'Well, sir,' said Benedict. 'In your own time, what exactly happened Monday night on Hatherley Avenue?'

'Oh, yes. Well…' He rubbed his hands over his face and

looked skywards. 'Right. So, yes, I'd been at a friend's house–
'

'Does this friend have a name?'

'No.'

Jessica pulled a face.

'Well, yes, of course, but I cannot tell you this.'

'Mr Cassese… please,' said Benedict. 'Don't waste our time.'

The man sighed. 'It was a friend, a lady friend.'

'Oh, I see,' said Jessica. 'And does your wife know about this lady friend?'

He looked down and muttered a 'no'.

'OK.'

'My wife mustn't know, she–'

'Mr Cassese,' said Benedict, 'everyone will know if this comes to court. Unless of course you plead guilty beforehand but let's not get ahead of ourselves here. Pray, continue.'

'I was running late. I think my wife will think something's wrong, so, yes, I'm sorry, I was driving a little bit too fast maybe. And I was on that street–'

'Hatherley Avenue.'

'That is the one, when this woman just ran across the road right in front of me.'

'This would've been the young woman you hit,' said Jessica. 'Zoe Wright.'

'No, not her. Not her.'

'Oh?'

'An old woman, older. A nurse, I think–'

'A nurse?' said Benedict, almost shouting the word, such was his surprise.

'Yes, I think so, perhaps. She was wearing that nurse dress.'

'What colour was her hair?'

'Oh. Her hair? I don't know. Long. Long hair. Maybe, yes, I

think she have ginger hair.'

Benedict and Jessica exchanged glances.

'I had to brake, and I swerved to miss her and I…'

'Hit the teenage girl instead.'

He picked at his fingernail. 'Yes. But listen, I stop and, in my mirror, I see the nurse lady running to the girl. So, I thought…' He paused, rubbing his beard.

'You thought, oh good, she's being attended to by a nurse, so I needn't bother myself.'

'Yes. No! Not like that but yes, I see the nurse will look after her, and I was worried about being late home and my wife, see.'

'Not a very Christian thing to do,' said Jessica.

'I'm not Christian.'

'Oh? Sorry, I rather assumed by that massive cross on your chest…'

He looked down as if he'd forgotten about his tattoo. 'No, this doesn't mean… It's just…'

'You like the design perhaps. Was that it?'

'Yes, yes. It's a nice design.'

'So, no obligation to act the Good Samaritan and stand up to your responsibilities and go to that poor girl's assistance.'

'But the nurse, I told you.'

'Did you hit another car?' asked Benedict.

He nodded. 'So, I drive but I am shaky still and I hit another car, a parked car. But not heavy, just a…'

'Scrape?'

'Yes, a scrape, that is all.'

'Had you been drinking, Mr Cassese?'

'Drinking? No! Honest to God, no. Not a drop.'

'What type of car do you drive?' asked Benedict.

'A Volkswagen Polo.'

'Colour and year?'

'Grey, well, silver really. The year? Erm, 2017, no, 2016.'

'We found paint fragments from your car on a Dacia Sandero that was, at the time, parked on Hatherley Avenue. Equally, we found paint fragments from that blue Sandero found on your Polo, Mr Cassese.'

The man rubbed his eyes again, he looked close to tears. 'How is the girl?'

'Ah,' said Jessica. 'I was wondering when you might ask. Zoe is out of critical now but, from what we understand, she's still in hospital. You were going more than just "a little bit too fast". You were doing almost forty in a twenty zone, almost double the speed limit there.'

No response.

'Mr Cassese, did you hear what I just said?'

'Yes, yes, sorry.'

'Did you get a good look at this nurse?' asked Benedict.

'Yes, for sure. It was like, erm, a horror movie. I saw her clearly in the headlights, yes? The look of fear on her face, but, honestly, she just ran out of nowhere.'

'Would you recognise the nurse if you saw her again?'

'*Pft*, yes, for sure.'

'OK, Mr Cassese, we're going to arrest you now–'

'No. No, please, my wife, she mustn't–'

'Mr Cassese, you hit a person and almost killed them, it really was touch and go for a while. She will live, thank God, but you have caused her serious injury. Secondly, failing to stop after an accident is a criminal offence, one that could result in imprisonment–'

'No, please, no. That nurse, she ran out in front of me, I try to miss her, I…'

'You'll have plenty of chances to explain yourself, sir.'

'*Dios me salve*,' he muttered in Spanish, crossing himself. God save me.

Chapter 39: Benedict

Tuesday morning. Benedict entered the office to find DC Kelly almost hopping with glee. 'Boss, boss—'

'Heck, DC Kelly, can't a man take his coat off before being pounced on? What's the matter? Do calm down, man.'

'Sorry, boss. You're going to like this. It's the CCTV from the high street at the end of Richmond Avenue where Mr McIntosh lives, or rather lived'

'OK, now I'm interested.'

Benedict joined Kelly at his desk and peered down at his computer screen. Kelly clicked play. The clip played for only four seconds when she came into view – the nurse with the red hair but this time without the brimmed hat. 'Well, I'll be damned.' She remained in shot for less than three seconds but it was definitely the same woman. 'Maxine Hunt.'

Jessica chose that moment to make her appearance. 'What's up?' she asked, sensing the charged atmosphere.

'Don't bother taking your coat off; we've got someone of interest to speak to, DS Gardiner.'

'Oh wow, OK. Exciting.'

Thanks to Mrs Idowu in St Cuthbert's Hospital's HR department, they already had Maxine Hunt's address. It wasn't too far from the station, Ferndale House, sixth floor, not far off the high street, a seven-minute drive according to the Waze app.

Benedict parked up in front of Ferndale House.

'Remember what Thomas McIntosh said about Maxine Hunt, boss.'

'That she's rather simple?'

'Vulnerable, boss. Vulnerable.'

'Yes, sorry. You're quite right, Jessica. Vulnerable. So, in other words, we need to proceed with caution here. Do you think she'll have a carer?'

'I doubt it. You can have special needs and still lead a totally normal existence; she probably has no need for a carer.'

'Let's go and see.'

They knocked on Maxine Hunt's door on the sixth floor and waited. And waited. Finally, a neighbour popped her head out, a black woman with large earrings and a turquoise turban. 'Hello, can I help?'

'We're looking for Maxine Hunt?'

'And who are you? Oh,' she said. Peering at Jessica's card. 'You're police.' She looked immediately worried. 'She won't be here. She'll either be at work or with her grandmother.'

'That's fine. We'll try to catch her. Thank you.'

'I haven't told you where she works yet, or where her mum lives.'

'Don't worry,' said Jessica. 'We know.'

The woman looked even more concerned now.

'Actually,' said Benedict. 'While we're here, can I ask, does Maxine live alone?'

'Yes, she does.'

'Does she have any parents or siblings?'

'No.'

'Any friends?'

The woman shook her head. 'Not that I know of. She doesn't get visitors. I keep an eye on her, make sure she's alright. The Lord too keeps her safe.'

'That's good of you.'

'She's a good girl. I knows it. The Good Lord knows it too.'

'Thank you for your time, madam.'

'When did the ward staff say she'd be back at work?' asked Benedict, as they got back into the car.

'Sunday at nine.'

'I knew you'd remember.'

'Sunny Grove it is, then.'

'Yep, Sunny Grove it is.'

Seven minutes later, the detectives pulled up outside the care home.

A member of staff escorted them through to the manager's office.

Mrs Hale rose from her chair and shook their hands. Benedict complimented her on her home.

'Thank you; that's very kind of you to say. We try our best to provide our residents with a home-from-home. You say you're here to see Maxine Hunt.'

'Yes,' said Benedict. 'Is she here?'

'She is.'

'We understand her grandmother is one of your p–' He stopped himself from saying *patients*. 'One of your residents.'

'Yes, that's right. She's not been here long, four months, I think. Can I… can I ask you what this is about?'

'I'm sorry but no,' said Jessica.

'I understand.' The woman clasped her hands and leaned

forward a little. 'This is all a little awkward. Because of course Maxine is not one of our residents, so I have no duty of care over her; put simply, she is not my responsibility. But, having said that, as a concerned citizen and as someone who, over the months, has grown fond of Maxine, I feel a certain… obligation. Maxine is a lovely young woman. I don't know if you know this but–'

'We do, Mrs Hale,' said Jessica. 'We appreciate that Maxine is vulnerable.' That word again.

'She's fine within her orbit, the world she knows and feels comfortable in, but… I know she gets easily upset if there are things beyond her control. For example, when Mr McIntosh's father was being aggressive towards her grandmother. Maxine found that most upsetting. She is very protective of her grandmother.'

'Mr McIntosh died yesterday,' said Benedict. 'That's why we're here. We can't tell you more than that. We're looking into the circumstances of his death.'

'Why? Was it suspicious?'

'We can't say at this stage. But we would like to speak to Maxine if that's possible.'

'I can't stop you.'

'But this is your gaff, so to speak.'

'This room will afford you the most privacy.'

'Actually, Mrs Hale, do you mind if DS Gardiner and I step outside for a moment?'

'Be my guest.'

Standing in the foyer, the sound of a television reached Benedict's ears and someone, an older person, laughing, another coughing. The smell of something cooking drifted up, beef perhaps. 'Why don't we ask Mrs Hale to sit in as Maxine's representative? Then, we're all covered.'

'Yeah, don't see why not. She obviously cares for the girl. And it's not as if we can ask anyone else, is there?'

'OK.'

Returning to the manager's office, they sat. Clearing his throat, Benedict made his request. 'Like you say, Mrs Hale, you're not responsible for Maxine, you're under no obligation, even if we do talk to her in your premises. I just feel she might feel intimidated by the two of us and having a familiar presence in the room might help.'

Mrs Hale shook her head slowly.

Jessica interjected. 'It could be somewhat uncomfortable for Maxine. I don't know her but… there is a chance she might get upset.'

'Oh dear. In that case, yes, OK, I'll do it.'

'You'll have to bear in mind, Mrs Hale, that it is not our intention to upset anyone, but we do have some questions we have to ask which could prove difficult.'

'You're only doing your job.'

'Exactly.'

'The only thing is,' said Benedict, 'what we discuss here will be highly confidential, so we'd have to ask–'

Mrs Hale put her hand up. 'Nothing you say will leave this room, detective. You have my word.'

'Excellent. Thank you. OK, DS Gardiner?'

'Yep.'

'Would you mind, Mrs Hale, fetching Maxine for us?'

'I'd better fetch another chair first.'

Chapter 40: Benedict

Mrs Hale returned to the office with a nervous-looking Maxine Hunt in tow. 'So, this is the lady and gentleman just here, Maxine. Come in, come in.' She closed the door behind her and closed the door blind.

Maxine sat down and the first thing Benedict noticed was her shoulder-length red hair. He tried to smile. 'Do take a seat, Ms Hunt.'

Maxine sat perched on the edge of the chair, her knees together, her hands clasped on her lap.

As agreed, Jessica led the way. She began by introducing the two of them and confirming that Maxine was indeed Maxine Hunt of Ferndale House. 'Maxine, tell us about your grandmother if you will.'

'Granny? Oh, erm, I don't know what to say. She's granny.'

'Where was she living before she moved here?'

'She was living with me. I suppose, really, I was living with her. But the council kept paying us visits and, in the end, they said that Granny couldn't live at home any more, that she had to live here.'

'Were you OK about that, or a bit sad?'

'I…' She looked at Mrs Hale. It was clear she was trying to find the answer she thought they *wanted* to hear, the 'right' answer. In the end, all she said was: 'She likes it here.'

'You must miss her?'

'Yes, but she likes it here.'

'Do you have any siblings, Maxine? Any brothers or sisters anywhere?'

'No.'

'Your parents.'

She shook her head. 'They both died. My dad last year.'

'I'm sorry. So, your granny is all you have left.'

'Yes.'

'She must be very precious to you?'

'Oh, yes. She means… everything in the world to me.'

'What did you think of Mr McIntosh?'

'You mean Mac? Or his dad?'

'His dad.'

'Oh. He was… I don't know.'

'Don't worry, Maxine, you can tell us.'

She looked down at her hands. 'Granny and I don't like him very much.'

'And why's that?'

She glanced again at Mrs Hale.

'It's OK, Maxine, you can tell them.'

She took comfort from this. 'He was horrible to Granny. But it's OK now because he's gone. Mac moved him away.'

'Do you know where he's gone to?'

'To his place.'

'In what way was Mr McIntosh horrible to your granny?'

'He… he shouted at her, called her rude names. He tried to hit her once.'

229

'That's not very nice, is it?'

'No.'

'Maxine, I'm going to show you a couple of photos now. They're screenshots taken from a couple of CCTV cameras in the area.' Jessica slid an envelope from her buff folder and from the envelope, withdrew the first photograph. 'This shot is of a woman entering a block of flats in Camden, Holbrook House. Take a look at it, please.' She handed the A5-sized photocopy to Maxine.

Maxine studied it, her eyes narrowing. 'Do you recognise that woman, Maxine?'

'No.' She laughed a little. 'She looks a little like me what with her red hair and all that.'

'Can I see?' asked Mrs Hale.

'Sure.'

Mrs Hale could also see the similarity, that much was obvious, although she said nothing. She handed the photo back to Jessica. 'You can hardly see anything of her face.'

'Is it you though, Maxine?'

'Me?'

'The woman in the photo – is it you?'

Maxine glanced from Jessica to Mrs Hale and back again. 'No, that's not me. It's not me.'

'Can you tell me where you were on Monday night, please?'

Maxine shrugged. 'I don't know. At home, I guess.'

'You weren't working.'

'What time?'

'Mid to late evening, about ten o'clock.'

'No, I don't work that late on Mondays. I was at home by then.'

'What time did you get home?'

'Monday? I work to six on Mondays, so probably about half

past.'

'Once you got home, what did you do?'

'I don't know. I can't remember. Had some tea and watched telly.'

'What was on telly that night?'

'Er, I c-can't remember. Sorry.'

'Were you by yourself?'

'Yes.' The implication sunk in at that moment. Her eyes reddened. 'But… but I didn't go anywhere. Honest.'

'And what about this one?' Jessica passed Maxine the second photograph. 'This one was taken just Saturday morning on the high street near the end of Richmond Avenue. Again, it looks a little like you, don't you think?'

'Oh my, that *is* me.'

'OK, so what were you doing walking along Richmond Avenue on Saturday morning, Maxine?'

'I…'

'Yes?'

She glanced nervously at Mrs Hale. 'I d-don't know.'

Jessica took a deep breath. 'I think you do know.'

Maxine wiped her eyes with the back of her fingers.

'Saturday morning, Maxine. At eleven seventeen, according to this CCTV image. Why were you on Richmond Avenue?'

'I don't know. I c-can't remember.'

'It was only a few days ago, Maxine,' said Jessica, her voice rising. As if checking herself, she added quietly, 'You need to tell us.'

'Is this really necessary?' asked Mrs Hale.

'Yes,' snapped Jessica. 'Very much so. Maxine, I ask again, where—'

'I went to this house there.'

'What number house was that? Can you remember?'

'Erm, I don't know. No, wait, it was sixty-two, number sixty-two. Flat three, first floor.'

Benedict's heart almost jumped through his chest – that was Thomas McIntosh's address.

'Number sixty-two, Richmond Avenue. Flat three, first floor?'

She nodded while finding a tissue in her skirt pocket and using it to blow her nose.

'Why did you go to that flat?'

'I – I had to meet someone there.'

'Who? Who were you meeting?'

'Erm, I don't know.'

'You don't know who you were meeting at this flat? Is that what you're saying?'

'Detective, please–'

Jessica put her hand up, cutting Mrs Hale off. 'Almost done. Maxine?'

'She said I couldn't tell anyone.'

'I understand, Maxine, but we're the police, you have to tell us.'

'It's OK, Maxine,' said Mrs Hale. 'You can tell them.'

'It was… it was Mac's sister.'

'Thomas McIntosh's sister? Thomas' sister asked you to come to her father's house Saturday morning?'

'Yes, yes.'

'Why?'

'Because… because she said her dad wanted to say sorry.'

'Sorry for what?'

'For being horrible to Gran, I think.'

'She didn't say exactly?'

'Yes, she did. That's what he wanted to say.'

'I see. And you went?'

'Yes.'

'And?'

She shrugged her shoulders. 'No one was there. I knocked and knocked, and no one answered.'

'So, then what did you do?'

'I went home.'

'You went home?'

'Yes.'

'So, to recap, you went to Mr McIntosh's flat Saturday morning because Thomas McIntosh's sister asked you to, but when you got there, she wasn't there and no one answered the door, so you went home?'

'Yes. Yes, that's right.' Benedict noticed the gleam of sweat on Maxine's brow.

'How did she ask you? Did you meet Mr McIntosh's sister?'

'No, I've never met her. She phoned me.'

'She phoned you? How did she know your number if you've never met?'

'She said Mac gave it to her. She had a funny phone.'

'How do you know that?'

'Well, when I picked up, I just heard all these beeps and then she spoke.'

'Beeps?'

'Mr McIntosh's sister phoned you from a public payphone,' said Benedict, speaking for the first time since the interview began.

Maxine shrugged.

'That explains the beeps, the pips, as we used to call them back in the day.'

'Christ,' said Jessica. 'I've never used a payphone; I wouldn't know how to.'

'Only…,' said Maxine.

'Only what?'

'I d-don't remember giving Mac my number. But I suppose I must have.'

Jessica puffed out her cheeks. 'Wow, OK, I think we've done enough for now. Thank you, Maxine. You've been incredibly helpful.'

'Yes,' said Benedict. 'Thank you, Maxine. Actually, one more thing. Here, take my card. Now listen, this is important, OK?'

Maxine nodded solemnly.

'If Thomas' sister ever phones you again, for whatever reason, you ring any of the numbers on my card and let me know straight away. In fact, if you're worried about *anything*, ring me. You understand? Day or night, Maxine, you must phone me.'

'Will do, sir.' She tried to smile.

'Excellent.'

'Thank you also, Mrs Hale,' said Jessica. 'No need to disturb yourself, we'll see ourselves out.'

Chapter 41: Derek

January 1983

Being a Friday night, the Three Crowns pub on Stoke Newington's Church Street was predictably busy, heaving with, not so much youngsters, but people in their thirties, an older crowd, a dense fog of cigarette smoke floating. Derek and his brother were onto their second pint, although Derek had thrown in a couple of whisky chasers for good measure. It helped him relax, and he needed the help because, frankly, he'd rather be anywhere and doing anything than sitting in a pub with his older brother droning on about how shit his life was.

Geoff had come all the way over from Dagenham which must have taken ages, so Derek knew he had an agenda, that he wanted something, and it didn't take much working out exactly what that was. He hadn't seen Geoff for... years although, of course, he'd spoken to him on the phone. To give the man his due, he lied to the police about watching *Jaws* on TV that night and probably did a convincing job of it.

His wife, Debbie, had recently left him and he wasn't coping too well but his tale of woe was beginning to grate on Derek's nerves; the man talked about nothing else and now, after an hour of Geoff's bleating, Derek was mightily sick of hearing about it.

'Look, let's be honest, you're better off without her,' he said, finishing off his second packet of cheese and onion crisps. 'I know you've always fancied my Pat.'

'You what? Fuck off, Derek, that's not what I want to hear right now.'

'Oh come on, I mean, I know it sounds harsh but, be honest, she wasn't much of a catch, was she? Debbie Does Dagenham; she'd shagged half the local population by all accounts before you got on the scene.'

'I loved her. I still love her.' He lit a cigarette, adding to the fug. 'Anyway,' his brother continued. 'How is Pat?'

'She does as I say, she knows better than to nag me, she has me dinner ready when I get in from work and she keeps Mum off my back. Could do a lot worse.'

They sat and drank their drinks for a while. Geoff, wiping his mouth with the back of his hand, said, 'You've seen that they've arrested Klaus Barbie.'

'Who?'

'Klaus Barbie, you know, the Nazi, the "Butcher of Lyon". Haven't you seen the news? It's front-page news everywhere. To think he'd got away with it all this time.'

Culture Club's *Do You Really Want to Hurt Me* played on the pub's speakers. 'Can't stand that Boy George,' said Derek. 'He looks like a fucking girl, bloody poof.'

'I'd do him.'

'You what?' asked Derek, spluttering on his drink.

'If he was a girl. I mean, if I met a girl that looked like him, I'd do him, her.'

236

'Yeah, right, as if you'd ever get a look in with any girl.'

'What about Debbie? She liked me, didn't she?' He blew out a plume of smoke. 'She bloody married me.'

The pub was getting busier, people fighting over tables, people queuing for ages at the bar. 'Yeah, exactly, and look where that's got you. So, she's fucked off then?'

'She moved out a fortnight ago. Came back yesterday to collect the rest of her stuff. She had this bloke with her who looked like bloody Muhammad Ali, a fucking brute of a man with a neck this thick,' he said, making a circle from his hands. 'She's gone and left me right up shit creek without a paddle because now I've got to pay the rent by myself.'

'Move out to somewhere cheaper then.'

'You're joking, right?' He stubbed out his cigarette with much vigour. 'Have you seen the cost of rent these days? I'd be paying just as much for half the space.'

'Work more overtime then, I don't know.'

'Can't. Work have cut back on overtime. They reckon they can't afford to pay us any more than our basic–'

'Your round, Geoff,' said Derek, slamming his now empty beer glass on the table.

'Oh right. Will a half do?'

'You tight wad, no, a pint.'

Geoff, checking his pockets, sloped off to do battle at the bar. 'And a pack of cheese and onion while you're at it,' he shouted, hoping his brother had heard him above the sound of Olivia Newton-John singing about wanting to get 'physical'.

Meanwhile, Derek clocked a group of four young women that had come in and taken a table nearby. You couldn't ignore them, they were so bloody loud in their tarty, suggestive clothes and huge hair do's. They fascinated him and repulsed him in equal measure. He'd never let a daughter of his come

237

out looking like that; would never allow her to behave in public like that. They all smoked furiously, one fag after another. Christ, they were so brazen and so sure of themselves, and so damn loud. None of them drew breath, they all spoke at the same time and never listened and they laughed so much and so loudly; they were drawing attention to themselves.

After an aeon queuing at the bar, Geoff returned with a pint and a half and one packet of crisps. Sitting down, he carried on where he'd left off, basically complaining about his shit life. Derek sipped his pint and zoned out.

'So I'm stuck.'

'Sorry? I missed that; those damn girls, I didn't hear.'

'Which bit? All of it?'

'You can't move out of your flat and you're not earning enough so basically you're fucked.'

Geoff glared at him, furious perhaps that Derek had summarised his situation so harshly, without a hint of sympathy. But that's because Derek *had* no sympathy, not an ounce when it came to his brother. Geoff was talking again, lifting his voice to try and be heard over *Eye of the Tiger* on the stereo and the cackling girls at the table behind him.

Four years apart, they'd grown up in Essex with their mother whom they'd both hated and their tyrannical father whom they hated even more, but that was as much as they ever had in common. As brothers, they'd never got on, never experienced any affection for the other. Once Geoff left home, aged fifteen, they hadn't kept in touch, not even a Christmas card. Although, they did attend each other's marriages. Derek could have told Geoff that his marriage to Debbie was doomed from the start. In fact, he probably had several times. But Geoff just wanted a wife, anyone would have done, especially as Pat had told him where to get off.

The bar staff had wracked up the volume on their cassette player and girls were now singing along to the chorus of *Eye of the Tiger*, slapping their bejewelled fingers on the tabletop, keeping time. Derek could feel the rage rising within. He wanted to stand up and shout, 'Shut the fuck up, you little, worthless tarts.'

'Just to tide me over…'

'What?'

'Two hundred quid, Derek.'

Oh, so this was it, this was why his brother had schlepped all the way over from Dagenham to Stoke Newington, wanting to 'meet for a catch up'. He'd expected it, knew it was coming, but still felt incredulous that Geoff had the nerve to ask. '*Two hundred quid*? You're asking me for two hundred quid?'

'I reckon you owe me, Derek, don't you? I mean, why exactly did you want me to cover for you last month?'

'I told you. Because I was worried the coppers would hang that murder on me. You know what they're like. They don't care who gets banged up as long as someone does – so it looks like they've done their job. I couldn't risk it.'

'I believe you but you asked me to lie to the cops. That's worth more than a hundred.'

Derek gulped down his drink. 'OK, another two hundred. But it's got to be the last time. It's a lot of money. I'm not exactly the Sultan of Brunei.'

Geoff put his hands up. 'The last time. Scouts' honour.'

The girls shrieked and the simmering rage within Derek threatened to erupt. He had to get out of here, away from his brother, from all these people, this noise and these bloody girls with their shrieking and laughter and singing. Shit, what was happening to him?

'Look, I've gotta go.'

'What's up?'

'I'm not feeling too good. It's too loud in here.'

'We'll find somewhere quieter.'

'No.' He finished his pint, gulping down the last of it. He placed the glass neatly on a beer mat and burped. 'Look, I'm not just saying it; but I feel like shit all of a sudden.'

'Actually, you do look a bit green around the gills.'

'Yeah, exactly.' He stood and reached for his coat. 'I'll send you a cheque in the post. See you soon.' Although he knew full well it'd be months, hopefully years, before they met again. And, frankly, that was fine by him.

The Human League's *Don't You Want Me* boomed across the pub, the four girls singing along at the top of their voices as Derek lurched out of the pub, relieved to get out and into the cold night air.

Chapter 42: Benedict

'Well done, Jessica,' said Benedict as they drove back from Sunny Grove to the station. 'I thought you treated Maxine with great sensitivity.'

'Do you think so? I thought…'

'What?' He took a left onto a smaller residential street, known by the locals as a commuters' rat run despite the sleeping policemen at regular intervals.

'I don't know; I think I was too rough with her. I'm not feeling too good about myself right now.'

'No, don't say that. It was a difficult job, and you did it admirably. But much better than I would have. You noticed that I hardly said a word? I'm sorry about that.'

'No, it's fine. It was probably for the better, to be honest. The poor girl had enough to contend with, with just me. I think if both of us laid into her…'

'I know. She'd have collapsed entirely, and we'd never got anything out of her. In your opinion, do you think she was being honest with us?'

'I do, boss. I reckon she's incapable of uttering a false word.'

'I thought so too. So…' He turned right onto the high street, pausing at a pedestrian crossing. He flicked on the windscreen wipers. 'What did we gather from that? One, Maxine Hunt is very protective of her grandmother, her last living relative, possibly enough to kill. I don't reckon she'd have it in her, frankly.'

'No, nor do I.'

'Two, she did not like Thomas' father.'

'Understandably.'

'Three, coincidental or not, some woman, looking remarkably like Maxine, or at least dressed like her, is caught on CCTV at the first murder scene.'

'But that's the thing, boss. A nurse's outfit and long ginger hair, and that's it, it's just peripheral stuff. We don't know what this woman *actually* looks like; they may look entirely different from each other.'

'That's why we need to find her so that our Spanish boy racer can identify her.'

'But how are we going to find her?'

'Go back to St Cuthbert's and other hospitals in the area and show staff the photo. After all, last time we stopped as soon as we got the first whiff of an identification.'

'But, boss, with respect, there'd be no point. There's nothing of her on those CCTV shots apart from her chin. You can't even see her mouth.'

'OK. So, moving on, point three, no, point four, Maxine admits to going to Richmond Avenue at the very time Mr McIntosh senior was killed because, she said, she was asked or told to by Thomas McIntosh's sister.'

'Someone else we need to speak to pronto.'

'Indeed.' Benedict turned into the small car park behind the station, drawing to a stop. 'And finally, point five – or is it six?

242

We need to ask whether Mr McIntosh junior ever gave Rebecca's number to Maxine.'

'No, the other way around.'

'Yes, sorry, you're quite right.' He opened his car door. 'I think that'll be enough to keep us busy for a while.'

*

Rather than drive, Benedict and Jessica caught an Uber all the way from Camden to Blackheath, one of the most salubrious parts of south London. It took the best part of an hour to get there. Jessica had rung beforehand and arranged a meeting with Rebecca O'Sullivan, Thomas McIntosh's older sister. She wasn't keen, she was a very busy woman, she said; she was working from home with a 'fuck-load of work to catch up on'.

Benedict didn't know Blackheath at all, but he was impressed, full of Georgian houses and, for a London suburb, had a village-like charm about it, centred around a pretty park. 'Bet the houses cost a pretty penny around here,' he said, more to himself than Jessica, who was ensconced on her phone.

To one side of the park, stood a fine-looking church. 'According to Wikipedia, it's All Saints Church, opened in 1858,' said Jessica. 'Says here this was Terry Waite's church. Who was he?'

'Terry Waite? Oh, some churchman who got himself kidnapped in Lebanon for several years during the late eighties.'

'Eighty-seven to ninety-one to be precise. Apparently, the vicar at the time kept a candle lit in the church during the whole time of his mate's detention.'

'Detention? You make it sound like a prison sentence.'

'Here we are,' said the driver.

'Thanks, mate. Can you wait? We won't be long.'

243

'No one said nothing about waiting, mate.'

'We're telling you now. We'll add it to the bill.'

'We don't work like that—'

But Benedict and Jessica had exited the car.

Rebecca O'Sullivan answered the door in a pair of blue jogging bottoms and a baggy grey jumper. 'I've not got long.'

'Nice to meet you too, Mrs O'Sullivan. Can we come in?'

Rebecca led them through to a huge living room full of large armchairs, standard lamps, framed old-fashioned paintings and a framed map of the world which, according to its legend, dated from 1554. Two cats lazed around, neither of them taking any interest in the newcomers. Another darted in front of Benedict, causing him to trip over and almost fall.

'Mind how you go, inspector,' said Rebecca with a faint grin. She sat on the edge of an armchair in front of a low table that had her laptop, mobile, her vape and a couple of bulging buff folders. 'I'd offer you a cup of tea, but the milk's rank and I've not had time to pop out. My maid's got the day off.'

'You've got a maid?'

She pulled a face and Benedict cursed himself for falling for it.

'So, what is it you want to know?'

'First off,' said Jessica. 'Please accept our condolences on the deaths of your grandmother and your father.'

'Now we've got her body back, we've got her funeral tomorrow. Come if you want. We need to paper the house.'

'Paper the house?' asked Jessica.

'It means getting more people in, putting bums on seats,' said Benedict.

'We really won't take too much of your time, Mrs O'Sullivan,' said Jessica. 'We've got a taxi with a ticking clock waiting for us.'

'How quaint.'

'Do you know a woman by the name of Maxine Hunt?'

The answer was immediate: 'No.'

'You don't?' said Benedict. 'Are you sure? Shoulder-length red hair, she lives near your brother, she—'

'Look, you can describe her as many ways as you want, I've still never heard of Maxie Hunt.'

'Maxine.'

'Whatever.'

'That's rather puzzling,' said Benedict.

'And why would that be?'

'Because Ms Hunt told us, not more than two hours ago, that you rang her on Saturday morning and told her to meet you at your father's flat.'

'Bollocks she did.'

'I can assure you, Mrs O—'

'No, what I mean is that I made no such phone call. Why would I when I've absolutely no idea who you're talking about.'

'You phoned her from a public payphone, apparently,' said Jessica.

'You what? I've not stepped into one of those piss houses for years, if ever.'

'If you've never stepped into one, how do you know they smell like piss?' asked Benedict.

'Oh no, you've caught me out, Inspector Clouseau, well done.'

One of the cats, a black one, came to say hello to Jessica, rubbing itself against her leg.

'Push her away if she's annoying you.'

'She's fine,' said Jessica, tickling the cat's ears.

'Why do you think your brother took your father out of

Sunny Grove?' asked Jessica.

'Because he was being an arse and Dad was about to be kicked out anyway?'

'Was it anything to do with the cost of it? After all, these homes aren't cheap.'

'It was fine. I paid for it. Poor Mac; he's got his own business, of sorts, but he pays his staff more than he pays himself. But me and Gabriel, that's my husband, well, we do OK, so I pay for it, or rather paid.'

'So, to be clear, it was nothing to do with the cost?'

'Hm-mm.'

'We understand you've just met your mother for the first time in years on Saturday morning, Mrs O'Sullivan,' said Benedict.

'Yes.'

'And how was that?'

'A bit weird, to be honest, but, you know, families are weird.'

'We understand your mother left the family in the early nineties and your father never had any contact with her.'

'That's right. It was the first time Mac and me had seen her in… exactly thirty years.'

'Must've felt strange.'

'Weird, I told you.'

'Have you spoken to your mother since your father's death?' asked Jessica, as the black cat slinked away.

'No, I couldn't face it last night. I was planning on phoning her tonight. Mac's spoken to her though.'

'Oh? You know that?'

'He told me.'

'Mrs O'Sullivan,' said Benedict. 'I know your father had been ill for a long time, but do you remember him falling out with anyone? Perhaps even years ago when you were still a child?

Perhaps he owed someone a lot of money or…'

'You're asking me if anyone bore enough of a grudge against Dad to kill him. The answer is, no, I don't. Sorry,' she added, sounding anything but sorry, thought Benedict.

'OK. Thank you.'

'Although, just on Saturday morning my brother said he'd happily kill Dad. You see, Mum told us that Dad had been violent against her. Mac flew off the handle and said he wanted to kill him. In fact, his exact words were, "I want to kill the fucker".'

'Just a turn of phrase, surely?' said Benedict, rather aghast at the woman's lack of loyalty towards her brother.

'You're the copper, you work it out.'

'This violence you say your mother suffered?' asked Jessica. 'Was it… I mean, all domestic violence is awful, but was it sustained or a one-off? Would you know?'

'She sort of implied it was a lot, which is why she ran off.'

'She didn't take you or your brother?'

'No. I think she'd planned to but somehow Dad got a whiff of it and threatened her if she even tried taking us. She didn't say anything else about it.'

'Do you recognise the woman in these CCTV shots?' asked Benedict. 'They were taken at the entrance of your grandmother's block of flats.'

She glanced at them and answered, 'No.'

'You didn't look at them.'

'What's to see? A nurse? Can't see her face.'

'Can you tell us where you were Monday night?' asked Benedict.

'The night some bastard killed my grandmother? Yes, I was home all evening.'

'With your husband?'

'Ah, no. He was away Monday night at some conference. Does that make me your number one suspect?'

'And Saturday, after you got back from meeting your mother?'

'Here, doing the housework like the good wife that I am. Again, no one to substantiate that. Apart from Ralph, Rufus and Ruby.'

'And who are they?'

She grinned. 'The cats.'

'I see.'

She touched her mobile, bringing up the time. 'Look, is there anything else? Because I've still got a shit load of work to get through.'

Benedict and Jessica looked at each other. 'Jessica?'

'No, I can't think of anything else.'

'In that case, Mrs O'Sullivan, we'll leave you to get on. Here's my card should you think of anything else. Ring me, anytime. Thank you so much for your precious time.'

'*Precious* time? Yeah, right. I'll let you see yourselves out. The door's that way.' She took a puff of her vape. 'Try not to trip over any cats on your way out, inspector. There's a good man.'

Chapter 43: Derek

January 1983

Derek was pleased to have escaped the claustrophobic atmosphere of the Three Crowns pub. He'd known his brother would go on endlessly about his sorry excuse for a life, and he knew he'd end up asking him for money. Yet, Derek had made the effort to meet him and he wasn't sure why. Perhaps because he'd hoped Geoff would prove him wrong for once, that it was a genuine attempt to heal the chasm between them. But no, no such luck. Geoff was still the sad, annoying, self-pitying idiot he'd always been. The longer Derek went without seeing him again, the better.

Jesus, it was bloody cold. It was still mid-January after all. He wrapped his scarf that much tighter. One could see the shine of ice on the pavement. He had to be careful not to slip. He was starving. Hopefully, Pat had made something nice for dinner, something she could quickly heat up. He couldn't wait to get home from this bloody cold.

Turning left off Church Street, he strode down a long residential street. A sheet of today's *Daily Mail* littered the street. 'Klaus Barbie arrested at last!' announced its headline.

Up ahead, he could hear the thud, thud, thud of music, a party probably, a very loud one by the sounds of it. As he approached, he saw a girl appear on the pavement ahead. She'd come out of the party. 'I'll be fine,' he heard her say to someone unseen. 'I'll give you a ring tomorrow, yeah?' She was black, wore a rainbow-coloured beanie hat and a red scarf and mittens. 'Stop worrying, Seb; go, have fun… Yeah, speak to you tomorrow. See ya!' Something glinted on her nose, yes, she had one of those little nose studs that girls liked these days. Derek wondered whether Seb was her boyfriend and whether Seb was short for Sebastian.

As she was about to leave, he heard this Seb call to her: 'Carol, wait a minute…' Derek stepped to his left behind some bushes next to a garden gate three houses down.

Peering around the bush, Derek saw this Seb guy appear and the two of them embraced, a big, cosy hug. They kissed – there on the street in public. Shameless. Enjoy your kiss, sweet girl. You'll never kiss again. The girl giggled and said something. Derek was too far back to hear. Seb wished her goodnight and returned inside. She closed the gate and walked away with her hands in her pockets. She didn't look back.

Derek, walking about twenty yards behind her, slowed down a little in order to maintain the distance. He decided there and then that if she turned left at the end of this street, he'd leave her alone and go home; if she turned right, he'd follow her.

The fact she had no idea that her fate lay in which way she turned, left or right, excited him to no end. His heart was pumping with adrenaline now, the cold had disappeared. He just hoped she turned right. Was she even aware that someone was behind her? He didn't think so. He fumbled in his case. He was sure he had one in the side pocket, one he kept there for emergencies. Was it there, was it there? Yes! He felt its silky touch, perfect, it was there, one defrosted white mouse, now beginning to smell rank.

A car drove past, its headlights momentarily illuminating her. She wore a long, dark grey trench coat with a thick belt around its middle. Hell, the anticipation was killing him. He willed her to turn right. A cyclist whizzed by, its backlight bright in the dark. She stopped suddenly. Derek dashed onto someone's front path. Gingerly peering back, he saw her crouched on the pavement, doing up a shoelace. Straightening up, she put something over her ears. Earmuffs?

What was her name, what did Seb call her? Carol. Yes, that was it – Carol. She'd started walking again. Someone walked by her, saying good evening. Derek looked down. The man said good evening to him as well but with his head down, Derek merely grunted back.

Carol had reached the end of the road now. Which way, Carol, which way? It's your choice now, sweet girl, your destiny. Life or death? Which way, love? Which way?

She turned right.

Chapter 44: Benedict

Benedict and Jessica decided it was time to pay another visit to Antonio Cassese in his café. Before leaving, however, Benedict rang Thomas McIntosh.

'Quick question, Mr McIntosh. Did you give your sister Maxine Hunt's mobile number?'

'Maxine's number? No, why would I? They don't even know each other.'

'So, you definitely didn't.'

'In fact, thinking about it, I don't even know it myself, so definitely not, no.'

'That's fine. Thanks for your time.'

Benedict hung up. Turning to Jessica, he said, 'So, how did this woman have Maxine Hunt's number? We find her, I think we've got our murderer.'

*

This time, being late afternoon, Casseses' Café was full of customers, mainly secondary school children congregating around tables, making a lot of noise. A couple of waitresses wearing the required black apron splattered with various stains rushed around trying to keep up. A group of three young women in the corner laughed raucously at something one of them had displayed on her mobile. 'Be with you in a minute,' one of the waitresses said, carrying a tray bearing a large pot of tea and two chocolate éclairs.

'We're here to see Antonio,' said Jessica to the retreating figure.

'He's out at the back where he always is when we get super busy.'

'We know the way.'

Benedict was about to knock on his office door when the door opened, and he appeared. 'Oh my!' he said. Mr Cassese's apron, in contrast, still looked pristine. 'I was about to... What's up now?'

'A quick word, Mr Cassese?' said Jessica, obliging him to reverse back into his office.

'Look, I told you already, I will plead guilty. I'm just waiting for a letter from the magistrates' court with a date.'

'As part of your punishment, you'll probably be sent on one of those speed awareness courses.'

'I don't mind. I sent flowers to Zoe in the hospital.'

They all sat around Mr Cassese's desk. 'That's nice,' said Jessica. 'I'm sure that will help reduce your sentence. Of course, coming forward within that first twenty-four hours would've been better, and, better still, stopping to assist Zoe in the first place. But we cannot put the clock back, can we? More's the pity. How is your dear wife?'

'My wife?' His eyes shot to the window. 'My wife is fine. I won't be if she ever finds out about... you know. She'll grind my balls through the meat grinder, I'm telling you.'

'Not for us to comment, sir.'

'And how's your lady friend?'

He blushed. 'Why are you here then? We're very busy.'

'So we see,' said Jessica. She slid the photograph of Maxine Hunt across his desk towards him. 'Was this the woman you swerved to avoid that night, Mr Cassese?'

He took a pair of spectacles from his apron pocket and, without touching the photo, peered down. 'No, not her. Same uniform but her hair is a little different, I think.'

'Different?' asked Benedict. 'In what way?'

'Different colour maybe. I don't know but this is not that woman. The shape of her. This lady here,' he said, tapping the photo, 'is straight up and down. My lady is more…'

'Buxom?' asked Jessica.

'No! Bigger, I think.'

'But how can you be sure? You only saw her for… what? A split second.'

'I told you already. A split second but the image, it's like, erm… how do you say, like a freeze frame in a movie, yes, a freeze frame. I remember her clearly, and it is not this lady in these pictures.'

'What about this woman?' asked Jessica, passing him the CCTV shots of the mysterious nurse.

'Oh wow,' he said, his eyes popping out of his head. 'I think this is her. It's… you can't see her face but yes, I think maybe.'

'Really? Please take another look. It's important we get this right.'

He held both photos up in front of his face, his eyes flicking from one to the other. 'Yes, yes. The shape of her, I remember it, the way her hat is on her head. Yes, I am sure now. I'd swear on my wife's life.'

'Could you swear on your mother's life, perhaps?' asked Jessica. 'You know, under the circumstances, it might be better.' She flashed him a smile.

'Hmm? Oh yes, ha ha, I see what you mean, yes, my mother's life.' He crossed himself. *'Que su alma descanse en paz.'* May her soul rest in peace.

'Interesting, most interesting,' said Benedict. 'Thank you, Mr Cassese, that's incredibly helpful.'

'Can you speak to my judge, tell him how helpful I've been?'

'It doesn't really work like that, I'm afraid.'

'Do you know your judge is a man?' asked Jessica.

'Buen Señor, dame fuerzas hoy.' Sweet Lord, give me strength.

'I'm sorry?'

'Him, her, it could be a goat for all I care; what does it matter?'

'The other thing we wanted to ask,' said Benedict. 'Did this woman in her nurse's uniform, did she touch your car in any way, perhaps she put her hands on your bonnet?'

He shook his head. 'No. I am sure of this, she never touch the car.' He looked from one detective to the other. 'You're looking for fingerprints, yes?'

'Yes.'

'I can't help you with that. I'm sorry.'

*

Benedict and Jessica returned to the station to find Diana Pettigrew waiting for them. 'I have a feeling you've got something to tell us, Diana.'

'I have indeed, Ben. Concerning the death of Mr McIntosh. Once again, our killer was meticulous. But we did find a set of very clear fingerprints on the flat's door handle, the outside handle.'

'Oh? Now that is good. Any matches?'

'I thought you'd be pleased. You'll have to wait until

tomorrow morning to see if there're any matches. But it gets better: Derek McIntosh was strangled to death. But you knew that already. He did manage to put up some resistance albeit a futile one. And, in doing so, we found a minuscule dot of flesh under one of his fingernails. The good news is, we've got the killer's DNA.'

'And?' he asked, trying to contain his excitement.

'Again, we should know tomorrow.'

'Well, it's a step in the right direction, at last. Talking of which, any footprints?'

She shook her head. 'Nothing.'

'Pity. Still good news on that DNA. Thanks, Diana.'

'A pleasure as always, Ben.'

Chapter 45: Mac

Mac had never been to a funeral before and he couldn't imagine a more poorly attended one than his grandmother's. Waiting in the crematorium's anteroom were just him, his sister, his mother and an older gentleman he vaguely recognised. Mum approached him, and, saying hello, greeted him with a kiss on his cheek.

The unknown man now approached him, his hand outstretched, and spoke. 'Thomas, long time no see.'

'Oh, hello, Uncle Geoff. Nice to see you.' His grey hair combed to one side looked slightly unwashed, his grey suit looked way past its best and one shoe was scuffed.

'Rebecca told me the sad news. Thought the least I could do is come down and pay my final respects.'

'Sure. Good to see you again, Uncle Geoff.'

'Sorry to hear about your father. Rotten business all this, I don't mind telling you, I'm worried. If we've got some nutter plucking off the older members of our family, I could be next. I'm keeping my doors and windows double locked, I can tell you.'

Rebecca and Mum joined them. 'Maybe you should get yourself a shotgun, Uncle,' said Rebecca.

'I'm sure it won't come to that,' said Mum.

'I'm taking no chances, Pat. I mean, Christ, what did either of them do to deserve such a fate? That's what I keep asking myself, you know? Horrible, just horrible.'

Mac asked his uncle how he was doing. Geoff still lived in Dagenham, still single, never remarried after his wife left him some forty years ago. He was surviving though, just about. Mac wanted to ask why he'd never visited his brother but he couldn't bring himself to ask. He knew their relationship had never been good; there'd never been, as far as he knew, any affection between them.

Mac remembered the time, the only time, his uncle visited during the post-Mum years. Even then, the brothers, from what he could tell, didn't particularly get on, and, if truth be told, Mac wasn't too enamoured with Uncle Geoff either.

One day, on returning from school, Mac found Dad and Uncle Geoff in the sitting room drinking tea. Mac hung around long enough to appear polite and answer various questions from his uncle about how he was getting on at school and how Arsenal were doing that season. As soon as he could, Mac ran upstairs to his room. Twenty or so minutes later, he went to the toilet. On his way back, he could hear raised voices coming from downstairs. Neither man sounded happy.

'Look, Geoff,' he heard his father say. 'You know life's tough for me right now what with the kids and all that.' Mac crept to the top of the stairs to better hear. 'I'll pay you back, you know I will. It's just that things are a bit desperate right now. A hundred quid, that's all I'm asking for. Come on, Geoff. Remember all that money I gave you back along?'

'That was different and you know it. That was hush money.'

'I still gave it to you.'

'Listen, I'm not lending you a bloody penny.'

'Great. Thanks. You might as well fuck off then.' Dad's voice was getting louder now.

'Don't you worry, I'm going.'

'Go on then, get out. Get the fuck out of my house.'

Mac never saw Uncle Geoff again.

'So, Pat, Rebecca tells me you've been hiding away in Spain these last thirty years.'

'I wouldn't say *hiding*, Geoff, but yes, I only got back last week.'

A female member of the crematorium staff came into the anteroom to quietly announce that they could go through now.

Grandmother's coffin was laid out on a catafalque under a lilac cloth in front of a pair of similarly coloured curtains. Upon it, a framed photograph of Granny, presumably supplied by Rebecca, with a card with her name: Marjorie McIntosh.

The mourners, if one could call them that, took their places side-by-side on the second pew from the front. Rebecca and Mac sat on either side of their mother. The service began with the hymn, *Abide With Me*.

Rebecca had done all the work here: she'd liaised with the police as to when Granny's body might be released, she'd talked to the funeral director and arrange the service, including providing the crematorium's officiant with the few sparse details of Granny's life that she knew. Apart from a couple of hymns, Rebecca had insisted the religious element was kept to a minimum. Mac never heard his grandmother mention religion despite having that large wooden crucifix on her living room wall.

Following the hymn, the officiant dutifully talked as best as he could about Granny's life, although most of what he said was so generic it could have applied to any human being that had ever lived beyond childhood. Mac had to give it to the man, he was an absolute professional.

A second hymn followed: *Praise My Soul the King of Heaven*. The four mourners sang along badly, barely a sound.

Mac swallowed. He still hadn't recovered from the shock. Discovering his grandmother's body was bad, discovering his father's body was worse, this… this was off the scale. Mac's thoughts were brought back to the present as Granny's coffin was committed to the flames. He stood there, watching, and a deep melancholy came over him.

The crematorium service came to an end with a final hymn – *Immortal, Invisible, God Only Wise*. It must have been, thought Mac, the shortest service in the history of crematoriums.

They each thanked the officiant and filed out.

'One down, one to go,' said Rebecca.

'When is Derek's funeral?' asked Uncle Geoff.

'Whenever the police finish with the body. Shouldn't be too long now. So,' she rubbed her hands, 'same time next week then, folks?'

'Don't be so flippant, Becky,' said Mum with a weariness in her voice.

'I do beg your pardon, Mother.'

'Fancy a pint anyone?' asked Uncle Geoff.

No one did. Mac, himself, couldn't think of anything worse right that minute. Uncle Geoff didn't hide his disappointment. 'A long way to come for fifteen minutes,' he muttered. But no one was listening.

'Listen, why don't you all come round to my lodgings this

evening?' said Pat. 'We could order a pizza or something.'

Mac and Rebecca said yes, but Uncle Geoff declined, giving no reason.

They returned to their cars. Rebecca offered to give Uncle Geoff a lift to the train station in her Hyundai. Mac said goodbye to his uncle and kissed his sister goodbye. He drove his mother back to the bed and breakfast. They didn't speak until she exited the car, thanking him for the lift. 'See you tonight then, Mac.'

'Yeah.'

'I look forward to it.'

Chapter 46: Derek

January 1983

Derek ran like he'd never run in his life. He only stopped when he was totally sure he wasn't being followed any more. In truth, he was sure the man hadn't chased him at all and had, instead, stopped in the alleyway to see whether the girl, Carol, was all right. His legs had turned to jelly, the blood pumped through his body. He swore. Doubled over, he coughed violently. His chest heaved as he tried to catch his breath, his breath billowing out of him in the cold night. A few people would have seen him running but would they recognise him if questioned? He doubted it. He spat several times and felt the slight stinging pain on the right side of his jaw. He was about to touch it but thought better of it; the blood might leave a trace on his glove. So, taking off his gloves, he touched the wound. A dab of blood, that was all, it was nothing. But still, it'd be visible for a while; he'd need to come up with an excuse.

Still breathing heavily and his legs still wobbly, he slowly made his way home, crossing the street whenever someone came towards him. He felt deflated. Geoff had annoyed him but, much worse, he'd cocked up with that girl. The first two had been relatively easy but not this one. She should be lying

262

dead in a darkened alleyway right now, and his spirit would be soaring in some form of ecstatic euphoria. Instead, his heart weighed heavily in his chest. He swore again.

Somewhere in the distance, he heard the wailing siren of, presumably, an ambulance.

Twenty minutes later, he was home. It'd been a long evening, a long day. He was utterly knackered. It was gone eleven. With any luck, Pat would be in bed by now; his mother certainly would be. He crept into the flat and, to his relief, found it empty.

Removing his shoes, he crept into the bathroom. He removed his clothes, checking for any suspicious stains. Nope, everything seemed fine. He had a wash and a shave, despite the fact he had had a shave only this morning.

Quietly, he opened the bedroom door and snuck into bed. Pat stirred. 'What time is it?'

'Late. Go back to sleep.'

'How was your night?'

'Long. Too long.'

'How was Geoff?'

'Alright. I'll tell you in the morning.'

She yawned. 'Goodnight.'

'Goodnight.'

*

Derek dreamt of his father again. Bent over the dining room table, his trousers and underpants at his feet, shaking as he watched his father slip his belt from his trousers and pull it taut. He'd have begged but he knew that would only enrage his father further. 'So, who's the worthless little shit around here then?'

'I am, Daddy,' the words said through a veil of tears.

'What? Speak up. I didn't hear you.'

'I am, Daddy.'

Saturday, seven a.m. Derek woke up, his brain immediately assaulted by images of the previous night: the girl, Carol, kissing her boyfriend at the front gate, following her as she walked up the street, her rainbow-coloured beanie acting like a moving beacon. His heartbeat became progressively faster as he scented the thrill of the kill. His gloved hand over her mouth, the way she fought, the way she tried to escape his clutches, the sharp, piercing scratch on his face. And then, the sound of that man's voice echoing down the alleyway: 'Oi, what's going on? Miss, miss, you OK?' The sound of the man's pounding footsteps. He ran, Christ, Derek ran, the sound of her whimpering fading as she lay on the cold pavement.

He felt wretched, his head pounding, every bone in his body aching. He was tempted to call in sick even if it was a Saturday, by far the busiest day of the week. But the thought of a whole weekend cooped up with the two witches in his life was enough to propel him out of bed, albeit slowly.

Slipping on his dressing gown and slippers, he padded through to the kitchen and made himself a cup of tea. He found a packet of paracetamol and sat at the Formica table, watching the clock tick by.

Pat came through, also in her dressing gown and slippers. 'Good morning, Derek – oh my, what happened to your face?'

'Oh,' he said, waving his hand as if batting away her concern. 'Stupid really. I came in drunk last night and for some mad reason decided to have a shave, and I cut myself. Lesson learned – never shave when you're pissed.'

'Oh dear, it looks bad. Have you put some Dettol on it?'

'Nah, it'll be alright.'

'Let me have a look.'

He batted her away again. 'I said it'll be alright, didn't I?' She stepped back. Had he convinced her? Yes, he reckoned so.

And so, that was the story he used every time someone mentioned his cut which was surprisingly often.

*

That Saturday evening, Derek returned from work exhausted – as he always did on a Saturday. Manically busy as always. At least it wasn't as busy as the weeks leading up to Christmas. But this time exacerbated by the heavy night before and the emotional exhaustion of his escapade with the girl called Carol. He really needed to get fit.

He walked into the flat to the delicious aroma of a stew slowly cooking in the oven. He hadn't realised how hungry he was. He said hello to Daisy and found Pat and his mother watching the early evening London news.

He almost shat himself. They were reporting on last night's attack in Stoke Newington. He should have known it would make the news; he should have prepared himself but he'd been too busy at work to think.

'"The White Mouse Killer" strikes again, said the TV news reporter, but this time, thankfully, he failed.

'The miserable bastard,' said Pat.

'He wants hanging,' said his mother. 'Whoever he is. I hope they catch him and hang him.'

'I agree, Marj,' said Pat. 'But unfortunately, they stopped hanging people twenty years ago.'

Gwynne Evans and Peter Allen, thought Derek. He once got a book on capital punishment from the library. These men were the last to be executed in the UK, August 1964.

The unnamed victim, said the reporter, a seventeen-year-old girl, was in hospital having suffered nothing more than bruising but was in shock. Her parents were at her side. Women, especially those around the area of Stoke Newington, were warned to be extra vigilant until the police caught the man responsible for this run of heinous crimes. 'And, mark my words, we will catch you,' said the leading detective, one DI Peter Grainger, staring straight at the TV camera, talking directly to Derek, his eyes piercing into him. Derek remembered the man from his police interview. His knees buckled and he needed the back of his armchair to prop himself up.

The news turned to a story about a car crash on the A406. 'I'm just going to get changed,' said Derek.

'I'll check on tea,' said Pat, shooting up from her chair.

He wasn't fast enough to escape to the bedroom. He caught her eye. 'That cut doesn't look good, Derek.'

He couldn't answer but the way she looked at him, the fire in her eyes, she knew, she bloody knew.

*

The following Saturday, Derek arrived at work ten minutes late to be greeted by Richard Prentice who now worked at the Tottenham Court Road branch on a permanent basis following the death of Ruth Jones. He apologised for his lateness, blaming it on delays on the tube. Richard was about to say something when the phone rang in the office. 'Ah, hopefully that'll be the head office about sending relief,' said Richard, running off to get the phone.

Derek hung his coat up in the kitchenette and flicked the kettle on. He always started work with a cup of milky coffee. Richard entered the kitchenette. 'Why do we need relief?' he asked. 'Where's Mr Smith?'

'Oh, Del Boy, you missed all the fun. The police came.'

'Fuck! What for?'

'Oo, your language! Wash your mouth out. They arrested him.'

'*Who?* Mr Smith.'

'Yes! Would you believe it? They arrested him for the white mice murders. Can you imagine?'

The world seemed to spin off its axis for a moment. The kitchen swayed in and out of focus. He needed to sit down. Grappling the table to prop himself up, he staggered to the chair and fell onto it.

'My God, Derek, are we feeling a little queasy all of a sudden?'

'Arrested?' he gasped. 'You sure?'

'As sure as can be. I'm telling you, it was dead exciting. They came, four of them, no five of them, and they said…' He put on a gruff voice. '*Are you Neil Smith of…* whatever address he lives at, I don't remember now. *We're arresting you on the suspicion of murdering Ruth Jones and Elizabeth Blinkhorn, and the attempted murder of Carol Russell.*'

'And they took him away?'

'No, they said he could have a day out at Alton Towers. Of course they took him away, silly.'

'Oh my God. I don't believe it.'

'You'd better believe it, Del Boy.' He shook his head with disbelief. 'Just to think, we've been working with an evil murdering bastard all this time. Just thinking about it gives one the willies, don't you think?'

Chapter 47: Benedict

Interview Room 2. The first thing that struck Benedict was how pale Thomas McIntosh's mother was. He'd have thought that after so many years living under the Spanish sun, she'd be somewhat browner. His wife had a friend who lived in Spain for two or three years, and she came back as brown as a nut. Her hair was entirely grey and cut short, in a style not too dissimilar to the actress, Judi Dench.

'Madam, the first thing we need to establish is your name. Unless you still go by McIntosh.'

She laughed. 'Good God no, I shed that name the first moment I could. I thought you'd ask me that, so here, I've brought my driving licence.' She slid it across the table to him.

'Oh, it's your Spanish one.'

'Give me a chance, inspector. I've only been back five minutes; it's hardly top of my list.'

'Patricia Roberts.'

'My maiden name.'

'And your address?'

'I'm staying in temporary accommodation at the moment, a

bed and breakfast not too far from here.'

'Could you write it down for us?' He slid a pen and paper across the table.

While writing her details, Ms Roberts said, 'I hope to find somewhere to rent soon but, frankly, I'm shocked by how expensive everything is. It's a lot cheaper in Spain. It'd almost be cheaper for me to stay in the B and B. Here…' She handed the sheet of paper back.

'Maynard Road? I know that road. Where is it again?'

'Not far from the high street. Remember, I don't know the area these days; I don't know where all the landmarks are yet.'

'So,' said Benedict. 'How did you feel when you learnt that your ex-husband had been killed?'

She looked up at the ceiling as if collecting her thoughts. 'Not much. I mean, I was sorry he met his end in such a gruesome way but you have to remember, inspector, we'd had no contact for thirty years. That part of my life feels as if it belongs to a different person now, so I'd be lying if I said I felt any great emotion.'

'I'm guessing you feel the same way about your ex-mother-in-law,' said Jessica.

'Yes.'

'Where were you the night your mother-in-law was killed?'

'Oh.' She pulled on her necklace. 'It was Tuesday night?'

'No, that's when your son found her. She'd been dead a whole twenty-four hours, more or less. So we're talking about Monday. Mid-evening-ish.'

'Monday? I was at the B and B watching TV.'

'What were you watching?'

'A David Attenborough documentary on catch-up, followed by two episodes of some crime drama with that Irish actor.'

'James Nesbitt?'

269

'That's the one. I've got so much catching up to do. British TV is so much better than what the Spaniards produce.'

'So you won't have anyone to verify this?'

'Oh, yes. The B and B keep a receptionist downstairs until about eleven at night. If I'd gone out, she'd have seen me.'

'And what about Saturday morning, the day of your ex-husband's death?' asked Benedict.

She ran her hand through what was left of her hair. 'I had coffee with my children. It was the first time I'd seen them in thirty years. We went to a café in Holloway, Berties, I think. We were there for a long time.'

'And afterwards?'

'Afterwards, as you can imagine, I was emotionally drained. I returned to the B and B with a raging headache and had to have a shuteye.'

'What time did you get back?

'Let me see, about one-ish.'

'And you slept?'

'Yes, until I felt better, then I spent some time on my iPad looking for somewhere to rent. You can check my search history if you like.'

'Any luck?'

'Not yet.'

'So, moving on,' said Benedict. 'Tell us about your relationship with Derek McIntosh.'

'How long have you got?'

'Maybe the edited highlights then,' he said with a trace of a smile.

'Derek was my casual boyfriend. We'd met in eighty-one, the very day Prince Charles and Princess Di got married. It wasn't serious and I was gearing up to dump him, as we said in those days. But then I got pregnant. We both came from

270

conservative backgrounds and I think we were both frightened of our parents, so we did the decent thing and got married, found somewhere to live in Stoke Newington and pretended everything was OK. But then, I lost the baby anyway. I wanted to leave him but I had no money. I was stuck. Then his foul mother came to live for us for a while until she moved into this council flat in Camden. I wanted to leave again and had even made plans but then I got pregnant a second time and Becky was born. A year later, Thomas arrived.'

'Thomas was born in eighty-four?'

'That's right. When Thomas was about seven or eight, Derek hit me for the first time. He apologised and it didn't happen again – until, of course, it did. And then it became frequent. It got to the point I began fearing for my life and the safety of my children. So, one night, I did a moonlight flit. This would have been 1993.'

'So Thomas would've been nine?'

'Nine. Yes.'

'You didn't take your children?' asked Jessica.

'No. Derek knew I'd leave one day and said if I took the children, he'd hunt me down and kill me.'

'You believed him?'

This time she took a while to think. After a while, she said, 'I did, yes.' She took a drink of her water.

'You're doing well, Ms Roberts,' said Benedict. 'This can't be easy for you.'

'It was a long time ago,' she said quietly. 'I'm OK. But thank you anyway.'

'Where did you go once you'd left your husband?'

'I ended up in a women's refuge in Cornwall. I stayed there, oh I don't know, a month or two, when a friend of a friend of someone I met in the refuge said she needed a waitress in

271

Barcelona. I jumped at the chance.'

'And you stayed there for the best part of thirty years?'

'Yes.'

'Always Barcelona?'

'For the first five years or so, yes, but then I moved in with a man in the town of Cádiz in Andalusia. The relationship fizzled out; he moved on but I stayed.'

'You must've missed your children.'

'It hurt every moment of every day. I wrote to them twice a month. They never wrote back and I understood why. But it was on seeing Becky and Thomas the other day, I found out the real reason – Derek kept all the letters, the cards, the little presents I bought every birthday and Christmas. He never told them. Now…' She wiped her eyes with a tissue. 'That *did* hurt, to think my children must've thought I'd forgotten about them.'

'Do you need to stop, Mrs Roberts?'

She shook her head while blowing her nose.

'So, after all this time, Mrs Roberts, what made you come back?' asked Jessica. 'And why now?'

'Good question.'

Jessica waited but on hearing nothing forthcoming, said, 'And the answer is?'

'One day it hit me that Thomas was fast approaching forty, and it… Oh, this is getting difficult now. It hit me just how much I still missed them both. The pain I'd swallowed down for so long suddenly erupted and I couldn't… I couldn't bear it a moment longer. Do you understand?' she asked of Jessica.

'I don't have children but yes, I can imagine.'

Ms Roberts smiled. 'So I came back, and here I am.'

'Ms Roberts,' said Benedict, leaning forward. 'Why would anyone kill your ex?'

'Because he was a nasty piece of work?' She said it more as a question than a statement.

'Was there anyone back in the eighties or early nineties who might have borne a grudge against him?'

'For thirty, forty years? I don't think so.'

'So there's no one you can think of that might have wished him dead.'

She shook her head.

'What about your former mother-in-law?'

'Again, no idea. I mean, she was an old witch but otherwise…'

Something sparked in Benedict's brain on hearing those words but, whatever it was, eluded him. He clasped his hands. 'Is there anything you'd like to tell us before you go, Mrs Roberts?'

'No, I can't think of anything else.'

'Well, get in contact if you do. Here's my card. Anytime, OK? Day or night.'

'Thank you.'

'Jessica, anything else you want to ask?'

'Not at this stage.'

'In that case, thank you for coming to see us, Mrs Roberts. It's been most enlightening.'

Chapter 48: Benedict

'What time are you finishing tonight, honey?' asked Sonia, as she stepped out of the shower, a towel wrapped around her.

'Erm…' Benedict was knotting his tie.

'Why don't we go out straight after you finish? Try that new Italian on Greenleaf Street. Everyone's raving about it.'

'Yeah, sure. Love to. Friday night is date night.'

'Yeah, a date night.' She sat at her dresser and looked at him in the mirror. 'So, honey, as it's a date night, why don't you put on your new suit today?' asked Sonia.

'Yeah, guess so.' But he'd just got dressed; did he really have to start all over again? But he knew he couldn't put it off any longer. 'Absolutely. Good idea, my love.'

'Make an effort. Be handsome for me. You know you want to.'

'Yes, my love.'

'And then…'

'And then?'

'Well, we could have an early night. Hmm?'

'Ah, now you're talking. I like the sound of this.'

'Yes. I thought you might.' She smiled at her reflection.

*

Benedict walked into the office, removing his coat.

'Oo,' said DC Kelly. 'Are you going to a funeral?'

'Very nice,' said Jessica. 'Have you got an interview today, boss?'

'Nice cut,' said Prowse. 'I like it, boss. I'm sure the bank manager will be impressed.'

'When you've all finished! No, I'm not going to a funeral, I don't have an interview and I'm not seeing my bank manager. Kelly, a coffee, please. And make it strong.'

Having gathered his thoughts, Benedict called for everyone's attention. He stood in front of two whiteboards, his team sitting in a sort of semi-circle before him. 'Time for a review, I think,' he said, pointing at the whiteboard with all the details of the Marjorie and Derek McIntosh murders. 'Not that we have much to go on. Certainly no firm suspects. I've just learnt that there is no match for the DNA found under Derek McIntosh's fingernail.'

This new piece of information was met with obvious disappointment from the ensembled.

'Now, the first thing to say is that our double killer is a smooth operator. Two murders, a mother and her son, and only one case of DNA. But without a match, frankly, that's of no use to us. It means that our killer has never been in trouble with the police before. So, either these are his first crimes or he's been very lucky thus far. Then we have the single fingerprint on Mr McIntosh's door handle, the outside one. The chances are it belongs to Maxine Hunt. Ms Hunt was sent to Mr McIntosh's flat on what appears to be a fool's errand. DC Prowse, could you ask Maxine for her fingerprints and, while you're at it, take a swab kit and take her DNA, would you?'

'Sure, boss. What about asking Mac and Rebecca for their DNA too?'

'Good idea. Now, if we are to believe Maxine and Rebecca O'Sullivan, it seems that someone, pretending to be Rebecca, told Maxine to go to Mr McIntosh's flat because Mr McIntosh senior wanted to apologise for his behaviour towards Maxine's grandmother while he lived in Sunny Grove care home. The question is why?'

'Because,' said DC Prowse. 'To frame her. She has the motivation and the real killer hoped she'd leave her fingerprints and someone would see her.'

'Exactly! Well done, DC Prowse. It'd also explain the first CCTV of the woman in the nurse's uniform with what I believe now to be a wig – another attempt to frame young Maxine. That woman I believe is our killer. Unless it's Thomas McIntosh but he couldn't have killed his father.'

'Yes, it could be a man dressed up as a woman in those CCTV images,' said Jessica. 'They're fairly grainy, after all.'

'It could be a man, yes. But not Mac; he has a beard after all.'

'But shouldn't we check Thomas McIntosh for his fingerprints anyway, boss?' asked Kelly.

'No. Think about it, Kelly… he lived there. It's his flat. His fingerprints will be everywhere.' Kelly looked suitably chastised and Benedict regretted his flippant response. 'Also, Mac was with his mother and sister all of Saturday morning, the time Derek McIntosh was killed. So, basically that rules all three of them out.

'So, moving on to our hit and run case,' said Benedict, pointing at the second whiteboard. 'It rather appears now that the two are connected. Our Spanish café owner positively identified our mysterious nurse as the woman he swerved to miss and, in the process, ended up hitting the unfortunate Zoe Wright instead. We also showed him a photo of Maxine, and he was sure that the woman he almost hit was *not* her.'

'He was sure of this?' asked DC Prowse.

'Yes, he seemed very sure, wouldn't you say, Jessica?'

'He did, yes, boss.'

DC Kelly gingerly put his hand up, obviously wanting to say something but worried in case his boss put him down again. Benedict smiled encouragingly at him. 'DC Kelly?'

'It might seem a stupid question, boss, but…'

'Go on, what is it?'

'What happened to Zoe Wright's mobile?'

'I wouldn't know.'

'Has she used it since?'

Benedict wasn't impressed but, for the sake of Kelly's ego, decided to play along. 'I doubt it; she's still in intensive care. Out of the woods, thankfully, but still very sick. Why do you ask?'

'Well, bear with me, boss, but you said the Spanish guy reckoned the nurse or the fake nurse, whoever she is, ran over to Zoe. And we know someone texted 999 but it couldn't be Zoe because… you know, she was out of it.'

'OK…' Was this going somewhere? 'Go on.'

'Well, there's a chance, a small chance maybe, that the nurse used that phone and, unless she was wearing gloves, she might have left her fingerprints on it.'

Benedict stared at DC Kelly in disbelief. 'Oh my god, DC Kelly. That is bloody genius. I mean…' He thought it through. Yes, what the young detective constable said made total sense. 'Hell, DC Kelly, I could kiss you right now.'

DC Kelly blushed. 'No disrespect, boss, as much as I like

your suit, I'd rather you didn't.'

*

Benedict tasked DC Kelly and DC Prowse to visit Zoe Wright's parents. Zoe was still in St Cuthbert's but expected home within three or four days. Yes, her parents had her mobile. They were worried that someone might nick it if they left it in the hospital. Her mother, Tracey, kept it charged up but her father hadn't touched it, not once. 'More than my life's worth,' he'd told the detectives. No one had used it since the night of the accident and only Tracey had touched it – but she hadn't pressed any of the digits on the keypad, of that she was certain. So, they took Zoe's mother's fingerprints, dusted the keyboard and lid on Zoe's laptop, so they could discount her prints, and dusted Zoe's mobile thoroughly for fingerprints, front and back, paying particular attention to the digit nine, where the unknown caller had texted 999. Kelly and Prowse returned to the office satisfied with their afternoon's work.

'You were a long time,' said Benedict as Kelly and Prowse traipsed back into the office.

'Yeah,' said DC Kelly, removing his coat. 'We got called to a fight on the next street.'

'Well, more of an altercation,' said Prowse.

'Over what?' asked Jessica, without looking up from her screen.

'A motorist and a bloke walking his dog. Apparently, the motorist almost ran the bloke over on a zebra crossing. We sorted it.'

Chapter 49: Mac

'The way DI Paige looks at you,' said Mac. 'He makes you feel guilty. I mean, Christ, I almost confessed there and then.'

'And that woman,' said Rebecca. 'The Watson to his Holmes, the Hastings to his Poirot, she's the quiet one with the brains.'

'A formidable duo in other words,' said their mother.

They laughed.

Mac and Rebecca had come over to their mother's loft room in her bed and breakfast after the funeral for an Indian takeaway and several cans of lager. The time was approaching half past nine, their stomachs full, their heads light, their mood jolly. They'd all been interviewed, or interrogated, by Paige and Gardiner and had lived to tell the tale.

'*Where were you on the night of your grandmother's death? Hey? Ve 'ave ways of making you talk*,' said Mac in his Nazi accent.

Rebecca giggled. 'Don't, it's not funny.'

'It must be awful being a copper,' said Pat. 'The things you must see.'

'They get paid well for it,' said Mac. 'And it must be good

thinking you're making a difference, locking up all the bad guys.'

'Tell that to Timothy Evans,' said Rebecca, with her can of Stella lager at her lips.

'Who?'

'The guy they hanged for several murders in the fifties. Turns out they got the wrong man and Evans was totally innocent. The police even got him to confess.'

'Why would he do that if he was innocent?' asked Pat.

'Because he was pressured into it, and he was a bit... simple.'

'Did they get the guilty one in the end?' asked Pat.

'John Christie, yeah. And they hanged him too.'

'Good.'

'Well, here's to our erstwhile detectives,' said Rebecca, holding up her can. 'Here's hoping they find the guy that murdered our grandmother and father and hang the bastard.'

'Cheers.' Mac hiccupped and realised he hadn't felt this drunk in a long time. 'So, what's it like being back in grey, wet England, Mum? Are you missing Spain yet?'

'I am and I'm not. I never truly relaxed in Spain. I missed you both too much.'

'And we missed you, Mum,' said Mac.

'Thank you, Thomas. You know, I thought about you every day, both of you, wondering how you were, how you were getting on. Anyway... I don't want to bring the atmosphere down; we're having such fun. We should do this more often. In answer to your question, Thomas, I rather like the cold and the wet, to be honest. It's a novelty. But of course, the best bit is seeing you guys.' Her eyes drifted into the distance. 'It was *hard* at times.'

Mac didn't want his mother to go all moribund, so changing the subject, he asked, 'How's your Spanish, Mum? It must be good after thirty years out there.'

'Yeah, go on, Mum,' said Rebecca. 'Say something in Spanish.'

'Oh, actually, no. I never… never really got the hang of it.'

'What? Come on, Mum, you were out there for thirty bloody years. You *must* have picked something up.'

'The odd word or two, of course,' she said with a flicker of a nervous smile. 'But–'

'Like what? Say, God save the king in Spanish.'

'No,' she said firmly. 'I'd rather not right now, if it's all the same.'

'All right, Mum,' said Rebecca, her hands up.

'Is there any more lager?' asked Mac.

'Steady on, tiger,' sniggered his sister. 'You can't cut hair tomorrow if you're still half pissed.' She giggled at the thought. 'We don't want the trendy young men of Camden all coming out of Mac the Knife with mullets!'

'Mac the Clipper,' said Mac, slightly frostily.

'And how's Mac the *Clipper* going, eh, Mac?' asked Rebecca. 'How's business?'

He knew a loaded question when he heard one. His sister had always been dismissive of his occupation and business. 'It's doing fine, thank you.'

'Still paying your staff more than yourself?'

He'd told her that months ago and had rued the day ever since. The answer was, yes, he was. 'No, not any more.'

'Do you shave your customers too?'

'Yeah, of course. I used to shave Dad once he couldn't be trusted to do it himself. He had that little scar near the jawbone, do you remember? Nothing grew there.'

'Oh yeah. His scar,' said Rebecca. 'How did he get that? Do you know, Mum?'

281

'He told me he cut himself shaving. I didn't believe him.'

'What then?'

'I… I don't know. Maybe he got into a fight or something.'

'Dad? In a fight?' She laughed. 'Hardly likely, is it, Mum?'

'Anyway, I think it's a grand thing you're doing, Mac,' said Pat. 'Your own business in London; that's very impressive in this economic climate.'

Mac was taken aback by how pleased he was to hear such a compliment, something Dad had never said. 'Thank you, Mum.'

'As long as it pays the bills,' said Rebecca. 'When are you opening your second branch then?'

'No plans as yet.'

'No? There's a surprise.'

'Oh, fuck off, Rebecca.'

'Now, now,' said Pat. 'Stop it, both of you.' She laughed. 'Otherwise, I'll have to knock your heads together.'

'What's so funny?' asked Rebecca.

'Oh, it's been years since I've said that. You two were always bickering as kids; I was always having to say it. Ah dear me.' She sighed at the memory.

Mac and Rebecca exchanged a smile.

'Mum?' said Mac. 'Did Dad ever hit us? I mean, I don't remember–'

'No, no, honestly, he never hit you guys. I promise you that.'

'I think you would've remembered, Mac.' said Rebecca.

'I don't know, suppressed memories and all that.'

After a moment of silence, Rebecca looked around the room and said, 'You don't have much stuff here, Mum.'

'Most of it is in storage.'

'What about your clothes?'

'I've got a few old things in the wardrobe but not much.'

'Are you alright for money?'

'Oh yes, fine, thanks, love. No, honestly, Becky, it's nice of you to ask but I'm fine, really.'

They sat in a satisfied silence for a few moments sipping their lagers when Pat stood. 'Excuse me a minute. Nature calls.' She made her way, slightly unsteadily, to the en suite.

As soon as she closed the bathroom door, Rebecca sprung up from the settee. She scooted over to the wardrobe and opened it.

'What are you doing?' asked Mac, in a whisper.

'Just seeing exactly how many clothes she has.'

'You can't do that,' he said, also getting up, intrigued, despite himself.

'I could help if she's short. See, she's hardly got anything. Look at it. Hell, what's this?'

Mac's mouth fell open – there, hanging from a clothes hanger in his mother's wardrobe, was a nurse's uniform and, hanging from a hook on the inside of the wardrobe door, was a black, wide-brimmed hat and, hanging beneath it, a wig of red hair.

He turned to stone. Rebecca too had turned white.

'Oh my God,' she whispered. 'What the fuck?'

Suddenly, he couldn't wait to get out.

As soon as Pat returned from the bathroom, they both said about having to go. Mum sounded surprised, as well as she might, and disappointed. She said words like, 'So soon?' 'But we're having such fun.' 'Can't you stay a little longer?' But nothing could induce Mac to remain in that room, knowing that something was off, something was very wrong indeed.

As soon as they'd stepped outside onto Montrose Road, Rebecca screamed, 'What the actual fuck did we just see, Mac?'

'Did you see the CCTV photos too? Did the inspector show

you?'

'Yep – and it was all there, in Mum's bloody wardrobe – the uniform, the big hat and that wig. Christ, Mac, what are we dealing with here?'

'I don't know. I don't bloody know, Rebecca.'

They walked to their cars lost in their own thoughts. Why, thought Mac, would his mother dress up as a nurse and come to Granny's flat? It didn't make sense, no sense at all, unless…

Having kissed his sister goodbye, Mac drove home. He parked up but remained in the car, his eyes clenched, his mobile in his hand, his finger stroking its side. 'Damn it,' he shouted, hitting the steering wheel. He wanted to make the call but should he speak to Rebecca first? No, damn it, he would not. This was his decision, if he wanted to make the call, he damn well would.

He retrieved the inspector's business card from his wallet. But the call went unanswered. Damn. No matter, he'd try again later.

Chapter 50: Derek

Tottenham Court Road, Central London, December 1983

It was a year to the day since the tragic killing of Ruth Jones. Richard put up a photograph of her on display in the shop together with a vase of flowers. Head office had sanctioned it. And so Derek felt as if he was being watched all day by her knowing eyes. The small shrine to Miss Jones seemed rather incongruous next to all the tinsel and the large, fake Christmas tree decorating the shop.

'Such a waste,' said Richard, soon after opening the shop and during a rare quiet moment. 'Taken from us too young.' He shook his head. 'Not yet thirty. Tragic, just tragic.' He ran his finger along the glass. 'You poor girl. You didn't deserve that.'

'No, Mr Prentice,' said Derek, trying to think of something profound to say but failing.

'At least, Smith is in jail now and can't harm any more young women.'

'Thirty-one years and six months.'

'Hmm? Yes, I believe so.'

'No chance of parole before the first twenty-three years.'

'My, Derek, aren't we the informed one?'

He tried to laugh. 'My wife told me.'

'I still can't get my head around the fact that we were actually working alongside a monster. A wolf in sheep's clothing here with us. You worked with him for a while, Derek. Did you ever suspect?'

'Me?' He shook his head mournfully. 'No. Not at all.'

'He seemed such a decent sort of bloke. Just shows you never can tell. He was so kind to me after my mother died, God rest her soul. And all the time, he was murdering and attacking these poor girls. Evil, Derek. That's what it is, pure evil. Well, I hope he rots in hell.'

The door opened, a customer, bringing the winter cold in with them. 'Madam,' said Richard. 'A merry Christmas to you. How can I help you today?'

Derek almost ran to the toilet. Locking the door behind him, he sat on the toilet and put his head in his hands. 'Evil,' he muttered. 'Pure evil.'

He knew Pat knew. He was convinced of that. He still, after all these months, couldn't shake off the memory of the expression on her face when it hit her, the day after he attacked Carol Russell. Carol had lived. She was lucky. But Pat wouldn't squeal, not in a million years. She was too frightened of him. On a practical level, how could she live without him? Where would she get the money from? She'd never get a better job than her current role as a dinner lady in a primary school. She had no discernible skills and didn't have the brains to get another job. No, she *needed* him.

Had it really been a year already?

It'd been Ruth Jones' diary in her flat, mentioning Mr Smith, that had given him the idea. Then, planting all those clues proved child's play: stealing his tea mug with his fresh fingerprints on it and leaving it in Miss Jones' kitchen sink, and the Christmas card Derek swiped from Smith's desk, and leaving it at the scene of the second attack. The fact that Smith lived alone and was never able to provide any form of concrete alibi certainly helped. Poor man.

His plan had a drawback, though. It had effectively brought his killing spree to an end. Mr Smith had the *perfect* alibi now – he was in jail for at least the next twenty-three years. If Derek claimed another victim now, Smith would be freed and he'd run the risk of being caught. He knew he'd never experience that sense of ecstasy of taking another human's life, seeing them breathe their last, the sense of fulfilment it gave him. He took a life in order to feel *alive* himself, truly alive. But not now; he couldn't chance it. Yes, he could kill without leaving the mice but it wouldn't be the same. It'd be like Picasso painting a fantastic painting without adding his signature. What was the fun in that?

He heard his name being called. Richard was looking for him. 'Oh, Derek, where are you?' he called in a singsong voice. 'Are you hiding out here, Del Boy? Come on now, we've got customers.'

'Coming, Mr Prentice. Just coming.'

He flushed the toilet for effect and washed his hands.

He returned to the shop, a wide, fixed smile on his face.

'Good morning, sir; good morning, madam. Merry Christmas to you both. How can I help?'

Chapter 51: Benedict

While his team beavered away at their desks in silence, Benedict remained on his feet, staring at the various photos, Post-It notes and scribblings on the whiteboards, mulling things over, trying to work things out. Something someone said was bugging him, but whatever it was remained elusive, that little bit out of reach.

Right now, Thomas McIntosh dominated his thoughts. He had ample opportunity to kill his grandmother. But to what gain? Certainly not money but why had he lied about the cost of the care home? But, of course, he had a cast-iron alibi for the time of his father's death.

If only they could identify the mysterious nurse. *She* was the key to this; he was sure of it.

Benedict jumped on hearing DC Prowse's sudden shouting. 'Bloody Nora! I've got something.'

'Heck, Prowse, break to us gently, why can't you? So, what is it?'

Prowse looked up from his computer screen. 'You're gonna like this, boss. You're gonna like this a lot. I've just got the results back from all our fingerprinting tests and we have a rather unexpected match.'

'Really?'

'Boss. Zoe Wright's mobile has, as we suspected, three sets of fingerprints on it – hers, her mum's and an unidentified third set.'

'Aha, good man. Thanks, DC Prowse. Well done.'

Yes, he thought, that was useful but it didn't actually shed any light except tie the two crimes together, which he knew already, and point even more at the nurse. They *had* to find this wretched nurse.

Returning his attention to the whiteboard, he stroked his chin. What about Maxine Hunt? He was convinced she was innocent so, who rang her that day and persuaded her to go to Derek McIntosh's at the very time he was murdered? Was someone really trying to frame her? Perhaps, she wasn't as simple, or vulnerable, as she made herself out to be.

And he couldn't count out the acerbic Rebecca O'Sullivan. She also had plenty of opportunity for her grandmother's murder but, like her brother and mother, had an alibi for her father's. And again, what about motive?

Behind him, he heard Jessica ask DC Prowse whether he'd filed his report yet on the altercation that he and DC Kelly had attended yesterday near Zoe Wright's house.

'Just doing it right now,' said Prowse.

'Where was it, anyway?' asked Jessica.

'Maynard Road. Know it? It's the road that runs parallel to Hatherley Avenue where Zoe Wright got hit by the Spanish guy.'

The world stopped spinning for a moment. The realisation hit Benedict right between the eyes… Maynard Road? 'Oh my God,' he muttered. That's where Patricia Roberts, Mac's mother, said she was staying. Of course, he remembered now, Maynard Road, next to Hatherley Avenue. Wasn't there a long pedestrian passageway that joined the two streets halfway down? A narrow passageway the locals called 'Dog Shit Alley'?

He pulled up the Google Maps app on his phone and searched for Maynard Road. Yes, there it was, barely registering as a line on the app but a definite cut-through between the two streets. Monday night. Where did McIntosh's grandmother live again? Holbrook House on Winslow Avenue. He searched for Winslow Avenue, then, using the app's directions feature and selecting 'by foot', traced the line of travel from the flats to Maynard Road. 'Jesus,' he said aloud.

'You alright, boss?' asked Jessica.

It was an eleven-minute walk according to Google Maps, and the quickest route from Winslow Avenue was along the high street, then turn down Hatherley Avenue, then use that cut-through onto Maynard Road.

'Jessica, have you got that sheet of paper Patricia Roberts wrote the name and address of that bed and breakfast she's staying at?'

'Yes, right here. Why?'

'Excellent. Right, stop whatever you're doing. Grab your coat. We're going to visit that B and B right this minute. What's the name of it?'

Jessica consulted the sheet of paper. 'The Montrose, boss. Number eighty-one Maynard Road.'

'DC Prowse, another fingerprint job for you. Take that sheet of paper from Jessica and get it dusted.'

'What sheet of paper?'

'The one Pat Roberts wrote her details on.'

'Can I just finish this report, boss? I'm almost done.'

'No, you cannot. Get onto it now.' Then, as an afterthought, he added a please. 'And DC Kelly, dig up whatever you can on Patricia Roberts, Derek McIntosh's ex-wife. She says she lived in Barcelona for a while in the mid-nineties, then lived until very recently in the town of Cádiz.'

'Where's that?'

'Spain, Kelly, Spain. Ms Roberts says she returned to England just a few days ago. Check flight records and see if that's true.'

'I'm ready, boss,' said Jessica.

'Good. Let's go.'

*

Benedict cruised down the high street, heading for Maynard Road. 'Heck, something's just hit me.'

'What's that, boss?' asked Jessica.

'Pat Roberts referred to Marjorie McIntosh as an old witch.'

'And?'

'Don't you remember? That was exactly the same expression that Geoffrey McIntosh used. An old witch.'

'Oh yes, so it was. Just a coincidence.'

'Yes. Probably.'

He took a right into Maynard Road and slowed down, looking for number eighty-one. 'This is it.'

Benedict and Jessica entered the B and B, setting off a quiet bell. They approached the receptionist, showing their IDs. Her name, she said, was Beatrice.

Benedict asked about all the Scottish connections. The owners, apparently, were Scottish and had lived in Montrose before moving to London and setting up the bed and breakfast in 2012. Beatrice knew her stuff. Benedict asked, 'Do you have a resident at the moment by the name of Patricia Roberts? She's not Scottish.'

'Yes, room four on the second floor,' said Beatrice, without having to look it up.

'Is she in at the moment?'

'No, she went out about half an hour ago, I guess.'

'When did she check in originally?'

'Sunday just gone.'

'Has she said when she's due to leave?'

'Not to my knowledge.'

'Were you working Monday evening?'

'No, I don't do nights; you'd have to ask Monica. She does nights. She's in tonight if you want to speak to her. Starts at four. Or I could give you her mobile if it's important?'

'That'd be helpful. Does she work all night?'

'Oh no, she clocks off at eleven. After that, if a resident comes back late, they'll have their own front door key.'

'Oh OK. Tell me, Beatrice, do you have CCTV here?'

'Yes, but it's broken at the moment.' Looking quickly to one side, she quietly added, 'It has been for months.'

'Ah, pity.'

'But we do have a photo of Ms Roberts.'

'You do?'

'We always ask residents if we can take a photocopy of their passports or driving licences. I can run you off a copy if you like.'

'Yes, that'd be really helpful. Thank you.'

Jessica asked the next question: 'Beatrice, have you ever seen Ms Roberts in a nurse's uniform.'

'A nurse's uniform? No, can't say I have.'

'Do you recognise her from these shots?'

Beatrice studied the two CCTV photos and, after a few seconds, shook her head. 'It *could* be her; hard to say.'

Benedict asked, 'Can we have a quick look around in her

room?'

'Oh? Erm, I'm not sure about that. I'd have to ask the boss. Don't you need a warrant or something for that?'

'It's just a cursory look; we'd be no more than a minute.'

'Erm…'

'Please?'

'OK but be quick. You could get me into trouble for this.' She handed them a key with a Scottish flag key ring and repeated the room number.

'We'll be quick as a flash. Perhaps you could do that photocopy for us and jot down Monica's number?'

The loft bedroom had a slanting ceiling and a dormer window that looked out over north London. It was tastefully decorated, thought Benedict, pleasant light green walls, a small double bed, neatly made, more Scottish countryside prints and, to one side, an en suite, on the bedside table, a vase of brightly coloured plastic flowers. Of Patricia Roberts there was little evidence of her being here but, hanging up in the wardrobe – the uniform of an auxiliary nurse, plus, hanging from a hook on the inside of the wardrobe door – a black, wide-brimmed hat and, best of it, a ginger-cum-red haired wig.

'Bingo,' said Jessica, taking a photograph of it on her mobile.

Benedict went through to the en suite and stole Ms Roberts' toothbrush, putting it in the inside pocket of his jacket. 'I reckon that's all we need for now.'

'Sir, isn't what you're doing count as inadmissible?'

'I'll worry about that later. I think we should scarper before Mrs Roberts returns.'

'Yes,' agreed Jessica. 'Before we get Beatrice into trouble.'

Returning to reception, they thanked Beatrice for Monica's number and the photocopy of Patricia Robert's passport. 'Oh, one more thing, Beatrice. If Ms Roberts should return, will you let me know asap? Here's my card.'

'Sure thing,' she said with a wink.

Sitting in the car, Benedict smiled. 'I reckon we're almost there, don't you?'

Jessica smiled. 'Sure thing, boss.'

'You're not going to wink at me, are you?'

Chapter 52: Benedict

From the Montrose bed and breakfast on Maynard Road, Benedict and Jessica drove straight to St Cuthbert's hospital, a thirteen-minute drive through Camden's afternoon traffic.

'I don't understand, boss,' said Jessica as Benedict waited at a red traffic light halfway up the high street. 'Why are we going back to the hospital? If Patricia Roberts has only been back in England for five minutes, she won't have a job yet.'

'I think she's lying.'

'Based on what?'

'A hunch.'

'Oh, a hunch, eh? My old boss in Manchester wasn't a believer in hunches, reckoned it always led detectives on pointless wild goose chases.'

'He may be right but, look, it's not too much of a detour, is it?'

'She.'

'What?'

'My old boss – she.'

'I beg your pardon.'

They headed straight for the Fraser Booth ward. Last time they were here, the staff they spoke to all knew Maxine Hunt.

Maybe, Patricia Roberts worked there too. The first person they saw was the nurse Benedict remembered, Nigella, pushing a trolley that had a blood pressure kit. She too recognised him. 'Can't keep away?' she asked with a wry smile.

'Love a hospital, me,' said Benedict.

'So I see. Still looking for Maxine?'

'Actually, no. This time, we're looking for a woman who we think you might know called Patricia Roberts.'

She pulled a face. 'Who?'

'Patricia Roberts. But obviously you don't know her. Still, while we are here, can you take a look at this photo of her?' He showed her the photocopy of Patricia Roberts' passport.

Nigella laughed loudly. 'That's Jean, not… whoever you said.'

'Jean? Are you sure?'

'Of course I'm sure. I've worked with her long enough. That's Jean Mulholland.'

'Really? Are you sure?' he repeated.

'One hundred per cent. That woman there is Jean Mulholland. She's been here the best part of… six months. Maybe more.'

'Six months? Good god. Is she working today?'

'She's due in later.'

Jessica looked at her boss, clearly impressed, or so Benedict hoped.

'Is Jean friends with Maxine?'

Nigella thought about this for a moment. 'Yeah, I'd say so. They seem to get on.'

'And what about Mrs Idowu? Is she working today?'

'Hannah? I don't know but unless she's on leave or something, I guess so. She's full-time.'

'Shall we go see?' he asked Jessica. 'Hannah, thank you for

your time. You've been most helpful.'

'Sure, although the name's Nigella.'

'Nigella, of course. I do apologise.'

'No probs.'

Benedict and Jessica found Mrs Idowu in her office on her phone. She signalled for them to sit down while she finished her conversation, something about agreeing to someone's leave request.

She finished her call, replacing the receiver, and shook her head. 'It's all I ever do, deal with holidays and sickness. Anyone would think staff here are entitled to holidays.'

'Erm…'

'A joke, Inspector, a joke.'

'Oh, I see. Very funny.'

'Anyway, what brings you back so soon?'

'Yes, sorry to bother you again but we need to ask you about another of your employees here. She works on the Fraser Booth ward, Jean Mulholland.'

'Oh yes, Jean.' Her eyes narrowed. 'Are we speaking in confidence here?' she asked in a whisper.

'Totally.'

Mrs Idowu sighed. 'Jean is a funny one. She has an attitude, a bad one, you know what I'm saying? And she has a terrible sick record. Always off sick for this, for that, for something else. I was on her interview panel, and I rue the day. You sure this is just between–'

'Fret not, Mrs Idowu,' said Benedict, his hand raised. 'Confidentially is my middle name.'

'Is it indeed?'

'So, presumably,' said Jessica, 'you checked out her references.'

'Of course. It's procedure.'

'Can we see them?'

'Jean's references? Sure, but I'd need to retrieve them. Could take a while.'

'Could you fax them over to us?' asked Benedict.

'I didn't know we had a fax, boss,' said Jessica.

'Actually, you're right; we don't any more.'

'I'll scan them over to your email. I still have your card, inspector.'

'Perfect. And perhaps any other information, her CV perhaps.'

'I can do that.'

'In that case, Mrs Idowu, we need take up no more of your time. Thank you.'

'Anytime, inspector. Anytime.'

*

Benedict and Jessica returned to the office. Benedict's blood was up; the excitement bubbling within him, the way he always felt when he knew he was closing in for the kill. 'Kelly? Prowse? Any updates?'

'There most certainly is, boss,' said Prowse. 'The fingerprints on that sheet of paper that Patricia Roberts wrote her details on, match the fingerprints we found on Zoe Wright's mobile.'

'Bingo! That's it; we've got our woman.' He sat at his desk, swinging around on his chair, his arms folded. 'But, to be sure, we need a DNA match from that dot of flesh under Derek McIntosh's fingernail.'

'And how we are going to do that, boss? We haven't any matches on the database and it's unlikely…' He saw his boss holding up a toothbrush. 'Is that actually a toothbrush I see, boss?'

'And who said you'd never make a great detective, DC

Prowse? If the DNA from this matches the other, then it's game, set and match, goodnight Vienna. Oh, what was that other thing?'

'Oh yes. Do you remember you asked me to look into who Neil Smith's pen pal was while he was in prison?'

'Yes; I'd quite forgotten about that. Well?'

'Yes, well, boss,' said Prowse, looking like a magician about to perform his last trick. 'The woman was called Jenny, we don't know any more than that, but the letters were all postmarked Spain, sir. More precisely… Cádiz.'

'You're joking? Cádiz? Oh my word.' He let that sink in for a moment. Patricia Roberts was writing to Neil Smith from Spain. Wow. Sitting down at his desk, he shouted, 'And what about you, Kelly? Any luck?'

'Yeah, but it's all rather puzzling.'

'In what way?'

'Well, I checked flights into Heathrow, that's where Cadiz planes fly to in London, and it seems she returned in July last year.'

'*July*? That's seven months ago. I thought she looked rather pale for someone who'd just returned from Spain. Are you sure, Kelly?'

'Yes, boss. I've got the details here,' he said, pointing at his computer screen. 'Landed London Heathrow July fifth at nineteen twenty hours.'

'What colour was her suitcase?'

'It doesn't tell me that.'

He heard Jessica snigger behind him.

'What happened to her after that?'

'Well, that's where it gets really puzzling. She disappears.'

'*Disappears*? What do you mean she disappears?'

'I checked her national insurance details with the HMRC and

299

there's nothing. As far they're concerned, she's not in the country.'

'Financial records? You got her mobile number – have you checked on that?'

'I've asked for both of them. Later today if we're lucky. If not, tomorrow.'

'What about any prior convictions?'

'I did check that. Nothing.'

'Missing persons database?'

'Oh, I hadn't thought of that. I'll get on it right away, boss. But I did think to check whether she has any social media presence. But nothing. Not a single social media account. Not a single squeak in cyberspace.'

'Good man for checking.'

'The other thing I think you should know, boss, is that uniforms asked all the house residents if they saw a woman entering or leaving Thomas McIntosh's house on Saturday.'

'And?'

'A mother of twins identified Maxine Hunt from the photo they showed her. She held the front door to her.'

'Interesting. Thanks, Kelly.' But all that did, as far as Benedict's thinking went, was to confirm that Maxine Hunt had been set up.

'OK, this is what we've found out… Patricia Roberts has been going by the alias – Jean Mulholland.' He told his team about the results of their visits to the bed and breakfast and the hospital. 'This woman is our murderer. Not entirely sure why – but I reckon we're looking at revenge. After all, Derek McIntosh had abused her for a sustained period, and, because of him, she lost all contact with her children for three whole decades. We just need a bit more firm evidence before we arrest her. So, team, well done for your good work so far; now, let's finish the job. Let's get to it.'

*

Three fifteen, Benedict received Hannah Idowu's email featuring three scans – Jean Mulholland's CV and two references. The CV stated that Miss Mulholland had worked the last twenty years as a part-time bookkeeper for a small design company that had recently gone bust – hence her looking for a new job. How convenient the firm no longer existed. Still, they could check on Companies' House and see if it ever existed. But if she's making this up, she probably would have been looking for such a firm herself, a small firm that had been in existence for these twenty years and recently gone bust. it wouldn't have been difficult. Before that, according to this CV, Mulholland had been a full-time mother and carer for her autistic son. What bollocks! The references were glowing. He didn't expect anything less. He emailed Mrs Idowu back, thanking her.

Three thirty. Benedict's mobile rang – unknown number, but nothing unusual in that, not the way he handed out his card like confetti. But he would never have expected Thomas McIntosh to call. He listened as a very flustered Mac related his concerns about what he and his sister found hanging in his mother's bed and breakfast wardrobe. He didn't like to tell Mac that he'd been there himself and seen the same items. Instead, he thanked Thomas for his time and recognised how difficult it must have been to have made this call. He appreciated it.

Chapter 53: Maxine

'Maxine, can you take Mrs Woods' blood pressure, please?'

'Yes, sister.'

Maxine Hunt was halfway through a six-hour shift at St Cuthbert's, working to seven at night, as she always did every other Friday. She'd come to work via Sunny Grove. Her grandmother was still pleased as punch with her green, starry fingernails. 'Everyone wants them now, Maxie,' she'd said.

Mrs Woods had recently been operated on: a partial nephrectomy where the diseased portion of her kidney was removed. The doctors were keeping a careful eye on her. She'd woken up from her anaesthetic but was still feeling groggy. 'Hello, Mrs Woods, how are you feeling today?' asked Maxine.

Mrs Woods was too groggy to answer. That was fine. 'I'm just going to take your blood pressure, is that OK?' On receiving no reply, Maxine carried on. Four minutes later and the job was done. She noted the results on Mrs Woods' chart. 'Thank you, Mrs Woods.'

Maxine saw an envelope on the floor next to Mrs Woods' bed. It was an internal communication addressed to Jean

Mulholland. She scooped the envelope up. Maxine liked Jean, Jean was her friend, they were 'besties' as Jean often said. They'd even swapped mobile numbers because 'that's what besties do'. She got on well with all the staff in the Fraser Booth ward but Jean was the only one who took an active interest in her. Over the months, their friendship had blossomed, auxiliary nurses together. She'd told Jean things she hadn't ever told anyone else, not because she was being secretive but because, frankly, Maxine didn't have any friends. Jean knew all about her granny, how long she'd worked at St Cuthbert's and where she lived. Why, yesterday, she'd painted Jean's fingernails, a pale-yellow colour with one daisy on each hand. Jean, like Granny, had been delighted. Every time she saw Jean, Jean waved her hands: 'See, still looking great!'

Maxine found Jean alone in the staff room, making herself a cup of tea. 'Oh, hi, Maxine. Fancy a brew.'

'I'm alright, thanks. Look, I found this under Mrs Woods' bed. It's yours.'

She handed Jean the envelope. 'Oh, Christ on a bike, what am I like?'

Maxine stopped short. That expression, the way she said it. 'It *was* you, wasn't it?' She laughed nervously.

Jean, about to pick up the boiling kettle, paused. 'What do you mean?'

'You, Jean. You phoned me last week pretending to be Mac's sister. You said that thing… Christ on a bike. I *thought* it sounded like you, remember I said?'

Jean replaced the kettle on the counter without pouring. 'I don't know what you mean.'

'Yes, you do, you told me to go to Mac's flat. I *knew* it was you.' She laughed again but had the nasty feeling that there wasn't anything remotely funny about any of this. 'I don't

303

understand though. Why would you do that, pretend to be someone else?'

'Sorry, Maxine, but I have no idea what you're talking about. Are you on the happy pills again?'

'Ha ha, no!'

'I don't even know who this Thomas is.'

'Thomas? I never said the name Thomas. I said Mac.'

'Mac. Whatever. Anyway, you sure you won't have a tea? Kettle's just boiled. One sugar, isn't it?'

'No, I'm fine, I'm not on break yet. I'd better get back.'

'Oh, OK. See you in a bit, Maxine.'

Maxine continued with her work but she found it hard to concentrate. Jean was her friend; Jean wouldn't lie to her. Would she? It was all too puzzling for words. Jean didn't even know Mac or Mac's father. So she wouldn't know Mac's sister, would she? She shook her head, as if trying to free up space in there. She must be mistaken. Maybe Jean was right, perhaps she should go back on those pills. She'd ask her doctor. Meanwhile, she had to forget about it; no harm done, nothing to worry about.

Maxine remembered what the policeman said to her, about phoning him day or night if she was worried about *anything*. She remembered how he emphasised that last word. Did this count as 'anything'? Would he think her silly if she phoned him about this? Would he say she was wasting police time like they always did on those police dramas on the telly? She decided it could wait until she finished work; it'd be too difficult to make a phone call now during work time, especially as she wasn't even sure what she wanted to tell the policeman. Yes, she'd wait until after work and if she still felt the same, she'd phone the policeman and if she didn't, well, that'd be good.

Six o'clock, an hour of work to go. Maxine was emptying a

commode when Nigella approached her with her coat on, about to go home. 'Hey, Maxie, have you seen my scarf by any chance? It's got swallows on it.'

'Scarf? No. Why?'

'I've lost it. Not to worry.'

'Have you tried looking in the cloakroom?'

'I have. I only bought it last weekend. Got it at Brick Lane market. And now, some fuckwit's nicked it. Well, if you should see it, let me know, will you?'

'I will.' Maxine didn't like it when people used the f-word.

Seven o'clock. Home time. The intervening hours had not calmed Maxine; indeed, if anything, she felt a whole lot worse. Jean had lied to her, Maxine was sure of it now, she couldn't be trusted. She didn't like Jean any more.

Jean always started work before Maxine on Fridays but they finished at the same time. Usually, they walked out of the hospital together and walked up the road until they reached the high street and then parted ways. But today, Maxine didn't want to walk with Jean; she didn't want to see her at all. She'd decided that yes, she still wanted to phone that nice policeman and for that she needed to be alone. So, having gathered her bulky coat and shoulder bag, she rushed out of the ward and trotted down the back stairs to the ground floor, safer than waiting for the lift.

She got to the ground floor, wished the reception and security staff a good night and, exiting via the revolving doors, stepped into the cold air outside.

A light fog was forming. Ahead of her, in the gloom, the pathway towards the high street, and to the right, a small car park, reserved for staff only, and even then, only for the most senior of staff. The likes of ordinary, auxiliary staff wouldn't be allowed to park there, not that Maxine had a car or even knew how to drive. She hovered near one of the posh cars and retrieved her phone. No messages, no missed calls, no notifications, but, to be fair, she hadn't expected any. She found the policeman's business card. DI Benedict Paige it read in bold and italic lettering. Should she phone his mobile number or his office one? She'd start with his office number.

'Maxine, wait up!'

Damn. 'Oh, Jean, hi.'

'What are you doing?' asked Jean, approaching her quickly. She was wearing a black hat with a rather wide brim that Maxine hadn't seen before although it looked vaguely familiar. 'Who are you phoning?'

'Me? No one.'

'Go on,' said Jean, jovially. 'You can tell me. We tell each other everything, don't we, us besties.'

Maxine hesitated but she realised she could never say no to people like Jean. As much as she wanted to, in the end, it was just easier to give in. 'Just this nice policeman who came to speak to me in the care home.'

'A *policeman*? He wanted to speak to you?'

'Yes.'

'Why?' She laughed although, thought Maxine, it sounded a little false. 'What have you been up to then, hey, Maxine? Mugging old ladies?'

'I wouldn't do that!'

'It was a joke, Maxine, just a joke. Seriously though, what did this policeman want with you?'

'They wanted to know if Granny was alright but I told them Mac's dad has left so she's alright now.'

'They?'

'Two of them, a man and a woman.'

'Right. I see.' Various people walked by behind them, a

woman helping a man on crutches, a man pushing an old woman in a wheelchair. A man in a dressing gown paced nearby smoking a cigarette. Jean seemed lost in thought, and Maxine wasn't sure how to get away from her. She still liked Jean but she was tired now; she just wanted to go home, have dinner and watch telly.

'Look,' said Jean. 'Let me explain everything. You were right, Maxine. It *was* me that phoned you the other day. It's a long story and I owe you an explanation – and an apology.'

'It's OK.'

'No, I do. Really I do. I know! Why don't we go out for a drink? We could nip into the Red Lion, it's nice in there and at this time of night, it won't be too busy. Go on, what do you say? My treat.'

'Erm…'

'I'll even pay for your Uber home. Come on now, Maxine, I can't say fairer than that.'

Every fibre of Maxine's being wanted to say no, go away, leave me alone. But she knew she'd never say it in a thousand years. Instead, meekly, she said, 'OK then.'

'Good girl.'

'Can I make a call first?'

'You're not phoning any policemen, are you?

Maxine forced a laugh. 'No, Gran. I said I'd pop by after work, so–'

'Fair enough, no probs. Hurry up though. I'm dying for a drink.'

Turning her back, Maxine edged away from Jean. Luckily, the woman didn't follow. Instead, she remained next to the posh car, checking her phone. Maxine retrieved the policeman's card and quickly rang his office number. Engaged. Blast! The answerphone came on and she left a quick message,

307

hoping she was far enough away for Jean not to hear. She'd wanted to try Mr Paige's mobile number but what if Jean asked whom she was phoning again? She couldn't think of a second person that sounded plausible. Mac? No, that'd look weird. Oh dear, what if Mr Paige rang back? What would she say to Jean if that happened? It was too risky. She switched her phone off.

With her phone switched off and tucked into her coat pocket, Maxine returned to Jean. She saw what looked like a different phone in Jean's hand, a tiny old-fashioned model with one of those old flip-tops.

'Ready?' asked Jean. 'Shall we go?

Maxine nodded.

'Look, I've got a better idea. I don't know about you but I'm starving! How about we go back to mine and I'll order us a takeaway and a bottle of wine? It's not too far from here.'

'I don't like wine.'

'OK, scratch the wine. So, what do you fancy? Chinese, Indian or pizza? My treat still.'

'Don't mind.'

'Well, let's get back to mine and then we'll decide.'

'But it's foggy.'

'So what? A bit of fog's not going to kill you. Here...' Jean offered her arm and it took Maxine a moment to understand.

Arm-in-arm, the two women walked away from the St Cuthbert's hospital towards the high street.

Chapter 54: Benedict

Five past seven, Benedict phoned Monica, the woman who worked the evening shift at the bed and breakfast. He didn't know her surname. Beatrice hadn't mentioned it and he'd forgotten to ask. Having introduced himself and stressed the importance of his call, he asked her the only question he needed to ask – had she seen Patricia Roberts leave the B and B on Monday evening? He knew that if Monica clocked off at eleven pm, Roberts, or Mulholland, would have let herself in.

'Monday night. Well, erm, no, I didn't see her.' She spoke in a strong East End accent. 'No, definitely not, no, no, I don't think so, darling.'

'You don't *think* so? Surely, if you were on duty, the answer's either a yes or a no.'

'I might have popped to the loo.'

'And did you?'

'I don't bloody remember,' she shouted down the phone.

'No. No, of course not. I do apologise. The thing is though, Monica, I detect a hint of hesitancy on your part. Why would that be?'

'I don't know what you're talking about.'

His mobile pinged with a text. He ignored it; this was more important, probably Sonia asking whether he was home for dinner tonight. 'Monica, you're talking to a police detective here and I'm investigating a possible crime, a serious one. You need to be honest with me, otherwise, if, further down the line, I find out something you don't want me to know, I could have you for perjury.'

'Could you repeat that in English, please?'

'What I'm saying, Monica, is tell me the truth.'

'I… look, if I tell you, d-don't tell the boss, OK? I can't afford to lose this job and if he knows, he'll have me guts for garters.'

'I promise that whatever you tell me, will not reach the ears of your boss.'

'Right, OK. Good, See, the thing is, Monday nights at eight o'clock, the boss and his missus go out for a curry, regular as clockwork, every Monday night. They always come back around ten stinking of Jalfrezi. So, anyways, I pop out the back a couple of times for a quickie.'

'A quickie? A quickie *what*?' The mind boggled.

'A fag, darling.'

'Oh, a cigarette, right. That's a… how many times, Monica?'

'I don't remember, do I? Two, three times maybe.'

'Is there a garden at the back, a yard?'

'Yeah, both.'

'Tell me, can you be seen at the back from the loft window?'

'Erm, I suppose. Thinking about it, yeah, as it happens, yes.'

'Thank you, thank you so much; you've been most helpful.'

'You won't tell, will you?'

'Your secret's safe with me.'

'Mrs Roberts ain't happy, by the way.'

'No? Why's that then?'

'She's accused me of nicking her toothbrush.'

'Oh?'

'I mean, for fuck's sake, who'd ever want to nick someone else's *used* toothbrush?'

'People are strange, Monica.'

'Telling me, darling.'

He finished the call. He was about to update Jessica when he remembered the text. But it wasn't a text; he'd received a voicemail.

'Hello, Inspector,' said a whispering voice. 'It's Maxine here. Maxine Hunt. You remember you said I should call you if I was worried about anything? Well, I'm going to the pub tonight with a woman from work called Jean. We're going to the Red Lion. Thing is, I'm sure it was *her* who phoned me telling me to go see Mac's dad, not Mac's sister. Erm, I'm sorry to bother you. I'd better go; she's waiting for me. I hope you get this message. Bye.'

Benedict stared at his phone for a few seconds before letting out an anguished cry of 'Oh, blast!' She sounded genuinely worried. Quickly, he dialled Maxine back. Her number rang... and rang. 'Come on, Maxine, pick up, pick up.' The phone connected. 'Maxine, it's DI Benedict–'

'Hi, Maxine here. Please leave a message and I'll get back to you.'

'Maxine, DI Paige here. Listen, do not go out with this woman, Jean. Repeat, do not go anywhere with her. Make up an excuse, say you're feeling ill. Anything, Maxine, say anything, just don't... Please phone back or text me as soon as you hear this message. OK, thanks.'

He dialled again – for good measure, but, again, it went straight through to voicemail.

'OK, team, we've got an issue here…'

*

Benedict drove speedily through the dark streets of Camden, but being in an unmarked, pool car, kept to the speed limit. Jessica sat beside him. In a squad car behind were DCs Kelly and Prowse with PC Stevens in the back. All uniforms had been alerted to keep an eye for two women walking together, possibly both in nurse's uniforms, one middle-aged, the other in her early twenties, and to approach with caution.

'How did Maxine sound?' asked Jessica.

'Not good. She sounded strained, as if worried. And now her mobile's off.'

'But if they're going to the pub, she'll be safe enough unless…'

'Exactly, unless it's a ruse. Come on!' Benedict shouted at a couple leisurely crossing at a green man crossing. 'For flip's sake. Right, let's go.'

Benedict brought the car to a screeching halt outside the Red Lion pub, parking illegally on a double yellow line, the squad car arriving only seconds later. Benedict and Jessica rushed into the pub. It was a Friday night, the place was busy, a Bruce Springsteen track playing in the background. Kelly and Prowse joined them. Jessica circled the tables.

'Can't see them,' said Benedict. 'Kelly, Prowse, go check the beer garden if they have one.'

'Boss.'

Benedict, taking the opposite direction from Jessica, checked the tables. Every table was taken with rowdy drinkers. A dog barked at him from beneath one of the tables, its owners, a sullen-looking couple, shushing the mutt. Still no sign of them. He approached the bar which was packed with people waiting

312

their turn. Benedict tried squeezing through. 'Excuse me, sorry.'

'You can't push in, mate. Wait your bloody turn.'

Ignoring him, Benedict called for a member of staff, any of them, but not one of them took any notice of him. He had no choice but to identify himself, drawing attention to himself. Holding up his ID card, he barked at a passing barmaid. 'Miss, a moment of your time, please. Miss, here now, don't ignore me.'

The young, white barmaid sighed. 'Yeah, what is it? I'm busy.'

'Have you seen this woman come in tonight?' He showed her the photocopy of Patricia Roberts' passport.

'No.'

'You haven't even looked at it. Try again.'

This time, she deigned to look. She shook her head. 'Nah, never seen her.'

'Here, take it, ask your colleagues. Hurry up, this is important.'

Without any great urgency, the woman asked each of her colleagues in turn. Benedict drummed his fingers on the sticky bar, aware of everyone watching him, intrigued. Finally, the barmaid returned. 'Nope, no one's seen her,' she said, handing him back the photocopy.

'Cheers.'

The four of them reconvened near the door. 'Not here, boss,' said Kelly. Jessica shook her head.

'Right, let me make a phone call.'

The couple with the dog pushed past him.

'Monica? It's DI Paige here. Listen, has Patricia Roberts returned to the B and B yet?'

'No.'

'Are you sure? Have you been out for a… quickie?'

Her answer was too quiet to hear. He stepped outside and asked her to repeat herself.

'I said, no, can't tonight. The boss is in.'

'Listen, Monica, if she returns, you ring this number immediately and let me know.'

'No worries, darling.'

He rang off. His three colleagues joined him outside, returning to their cars.

'Where now, boss?' asked Prowse.

Benedict ran his hand through his hair. 'I don't know. I don't bloody know,' he yelled.

'What about Maxine's flat?' asked Kelly.

'Yes. No. If Patricia Roberts does intend to harm Maxine, she wouldn't suggest going back to Maxine's place, too risky that she'd be seen. She'd need somewhere quiet, no one around. The park or the cemetery. Anywhere else we can think of? Quickly. Anywhere within walking distance of Maynard Road?'

'The Tesco car park?' suggested Prowse. 'That's underground.'

'No, she'll know that every inch is covered by CCTV. Come on, we're wasting time. Kelly, Prowse, you head for the park. DS Gardiner and I will head for the cemetery.'

Benedict hadn't reached the end of the street when he suddenly braked. A car behind screeched to a halt. 'The hospital. Shit, they could still be at the hospital.'

'But you said–'

'I know but perhaps Roberts persuaded Maxine to go back in. At this time of night, there'd be plenty of empty spaces.'

'Surely, too risky, boss.'

'Damn it, you're right.' He hit his forehead with his fist. He drove forward, indicating left. 'Think, think, for God's sake, think.'

'Dog Shit Alley, boss!'

'The cut-through?' he braked again, this time earning a honk from behind. 'No, that'd be too risky too. Anyone could turn up.'

'But it's a quiet area, boss, it's late, it's foggy.'

Benedict tried to think, would he take someone he intended to kill to the passageway? It was certainly long and yes, it curved round in the middle, so one couldn't see from one end to the other. It only takes a few seconds to kill a person when you're prepared and got evil in your soul. 'Jesus, Jessica, you might be right. Radio the others, tell them to go to Hatherley Avenue immediately. Ask for backup. We'll head for Maynard Road.' Another honk from behind and a faint voice, shouting, 'Get a bloody move on, will you?'

Now, with a determined idea of where to go, Benedict indicated right and put his foot down.

*

'It's not too far,' said Jean as she escorted Maxine back to her place. They were on the high street now, lots of traffic, lots of people. 'I'm on Maynard Road. Once we get to Hatherley Avenue, there's an alleyway. That'll save a couple of minutes. You have to mind where you walk though – people call it Dog Shit Alley.' She laughed. 'People are funny, aren't they? You OK, Maxine?'

'I don't feel so well, to be honest. I think maybe I should go home.'

'Nonsense; we're almost there now. You'll feel better with a bit of food inside you. I promise. You can trust me, Maxine. We're besties, after all. You do trust me, don't you, Maxine?'

'Mm.'

'Here, we go down this street. This takes us to Hatherley Avenue and then we'll be at the cut-through. Almost there now.'

'Do you have a new phone now?' Maxine asked.

'No. Why do you ask?'

'I thought I saw you earlier with one of those really old flip-top ones.'

'Oh that! Yes, sorry. My phone's broken so I'm just using an old one while I get it repaired.'

They walked in silence for a while. Maxine was sure the fog was getting thicker. Jean stepped up the pace and Maxine had no choice but to keep up. She glanced behind her. No one was around. She so wanted to be back in her cosy flat with Charlie, her lovely Charlie.

'You and I, we're quite similar,' said Jean.

'Are we?'

'I'd say so. We're outsiders. Do you know what I mean? People tend to avoid us, but that's only because they don't understand us. Maybe because we're cleverer than most people and they don't like it, they feel threatened by us. Who knows?'

Maxine couldn't imagine anyone ever feeling threatened by her.

'So, it's even more important that people like us stick together. Besties together and forever! Fuck the rest of them.'

'I don't know.' She didn't like it when people used the f-word.

'Not far now.'

She kept saying that but according to Maxine's watch, they'd been walking for over half an hour and she ached from tiredness after her long day at work. It was seven forty now and a fine drizzle had begun to fall.

'It's getting colder, isn't it?' said Jean. With that, she pulled a scarf out of her handbag, a chiffon scarf with swallows on it. Maxine watched goggled-eye as Jean wrapped it around her neck.

'Your scarf.'

'Yes? What about it?'

'It's got swallows on it.'

'Aren't you the observant one? Christ on a bike. So what, it's got swallows on it?'

'It's nice.'

'Thanks.'

'Where did you get it from?'

'Oh, I don't know, I can't remember now. No, wait a minute. I bought it in a market, you know, one of those trendy street markets.'

'Brick Lane?'

'That's the one.'

'Nigella's got one.'

'Has she? Can't say I've noticed. This is Hatherley Avenue. Hurry up, there's a takeaway back at mine with our names on it. The cut-through's just up here on the left.'

'It's very quiet here.'

'Middle class, isn't it? Middle-class people know how to behave.'

Maxine looked around, desperate now to see another person emerging from the gloom. She'd call out to them and ask them for help. She'd beg them to get her away from this crazy woman whom she thought was her friend. Friends don't lie to you, though. They don't ring you up and pretend to be someone else nor do they steal other people's things.

Some primal instinct told her she had to get away from Jean but however deep that instinct, it still couldn't compete with

317

her sense of wanting to appear normal, of not wanting to look 'weird', something that a lifetime of convention had drilled into her. She couldn't get away from that.

Jean adjusted her hat.

'I like your hat,' said Maxine, trying to remember again where she'd seen it before.

Jean laughed. 'What is this? Compliment Jean's accessories hour? Ah, here's the alleyway.'

Maxine peered through the mist down the narrow, paved alleyway with its high, brick walls on either side, the bend halfway down that prevented one from seeing the other end. 'It's very dark down there. Is it safe?'

'Safe? Of course it's safe, Maxie. It's a middle-class neighbourhood, like I said.'

Jean had never called her 'Maxie' before.

'Look, if anyone jumps out at us…' She removed her swallow-patterned scarf. 'I'll strangle them with this.' She laughed a hollow laugh, stretching the scarf tight between her hands. 'Come on, the B and B is only two minutes from here and I'm bloody starving.'

'I'm not sure about this, Jean. Look, if you d-don't mind, I think I'll just head h-home. I need to feed Charlie.'

'Who?'

'My cat.'

'But it's raining. Don't be silly. Here, give me your hand.' She held out her hand.

'No, it's alright.'

'Walk, Maxie.'

'I'd rather–'

'Just fucking walk.'

She stepped into the dark alleyway.

'Mind where you step,' said Jean, behind her. 'Remember –

Dog Shit Alley.'

They were almost halfway down the alleyway, approaching the bend. Maxine was desperate to get to the other end where, she hoped, she'd see another human being. And yes, squinting, she could see a blue and white tape stretched across the far end of the cut-through. A police tape? Were the police here? Oh, the relief.

It was at that point, she stopped dead in her tracks. Thinking of the police reminded her of where she'd seen that hat. That nice policewoman had shown her a photograph of a woman in a nurse's uniform like hers and she, whoever she was, was wearing it. Her heart beating mercilessly fast, she spun around. 'Jean? What...'

Jean's hair had changed; she was wearing a long red wig beneath that hat.

Maxine opened her mouth to scream when, quick as a flash, she felt something around her neck. 'No, no...' The scarf, the swallow scarf, tightening, tightening, getting tighter still, biting into her flesh. She couldn't breathe, she couldn't breathe. She tried to prise it off but no, Jean's grip was too hard. She could feel herself weakening by the second. Her hands dropped to her sides, her eyes lost focus, her knees buckled. The sudden sensation of heat cascaded between her legs as her knees gave way beneath her...

A shout, a scream. 'Stop! Police, stop!' Distant but loud. Urgent. Panicked. Oh God, help me, help me...

Then, as if God answered, the pressure on her windpipe slacked, slacked some more. Maxine fell to her knees, choking, fighting for air. Footsteps. She could hear lots and lots of footsteps pounding towards her, more shouting, getting louder, so deafeningly loud. Where was Jean? Where, where? Please take her away from me.

From somewhere deep inside her, she found the strength to loosen the scarf a tiny fraction.

Footsteps rushed by her. Another set stopped. The scarf was untied in circles, every circle diminished the pain, the unbearable pressure. She heard a man's panicked voice urging someone to call an ambulance. Another voice, a lovely soothing voice in her ear, a woman's voice. 'It's OK, Maxine, you're safe now, darling, you're safe.'

The scarf was off but she couldn't breathe with her mouth so full of phlegm. Her hands went immediately to her neck, soothing the raw skin. She still couldn't see. A force erupted from deep, deep inside her and she puked, a huge, painful ejection of vomit, bile and panic.

She wanted to know where Jean was, to make sure she was safe from her, that she wouldn't come back but the words wouldn't come.

A warm hand rubbed her back. 'I'm DS Gardiner, Maxine. We met last week, remember? Jessica Gardiner. And I want you to know, Maxine, that I'm not going anywhere. I'm staying here with you, so you're totally safe now. Totally safe, my darling; my poor, poor darling.'

The tears came, huge fat, baby-like tears. Jessica's arms wrapped themselves around her, lovely, caring arms. 'It's OK, darling; you're safe now. You're totally safe.'

And still she cried. She cried for herself, she cried for her mother who died so long ago, she cried for her father taken just last year by pneumonia, she cried for her grandmother. But it was OK; for once in her life she let go of her inhibitions and let it all out while this lovely woman held onto her, telling her everything was OK, that she was safe, safer, thought Maxine, than she'd ever been; safer than a babe in its mother's arms.

*

Benedict reached the end of the passageway on the Maynard Road side, parking his car directly in front of its entrance. He and Jessica jumped out of the car, slamming the doors behind them. A squad car screeched to a halt behind him, presumably Kelly and Prowse on the wrong side of the cut-through. A fine drizzle had started falling, adding to the Victorian-esque atmosphere. He ran down the alley, Jessica behind him. Kelly and Prowse, being much younger, catching up.

He could see around the bend. Someone there, two silhouettes, something wrong, terribly wrong. One of them, the one pressed against the brick wall, slumped. Benedict shouted. 'Stop! Police, stop!' The other immediately started running away. They gave chase, four sets of shoes pounding on the pavement.

'You look after Maxine,' shouted Benedict, jumping over her.

He could see Roberts ahead of him. But why was no one waiting at the other end to cut her off? He was gaining on her. Beyond her, at the end of the cut-through, he glimpsed a police tape. Who'd put it there?

She swung right out of the alleyway, pushing the tape to one side. He lost his footing on the wet ground, cursed, and righted himself. He reached Hatherley Avenue. Where was she? Where the hell was she? He could hear the sirens of the squad cars coming now. He caught his breath. 'Patricia, come out now. It's finished, Pat. There's nowhere to escape to now.'

A blurred movement, dashing out from between two parked cars.

'Patricia! Stop.' He gave chase again, quickly gaining on her, conscious that DC Prowse wasn't far behind him.

She shouted, 'Run, run, run…'

Who was she shouting at? A second figure running further ahead. He caught up with Roberts. She spun around and he crashed into her, sending her tumbling to the ground, landing awkwardly. 'Prowse, arrest her,' he screamed.

He kept going, his eyes fixed on the shadowy figure ahead. The man could barely run, he'd soon have him. But the man got into a car facing in Benedict's direction, slamming the door shut.

His lungs burning, Benedict pushed himself forward as the car revved up and swung quickly out of its parking space. Shit, it was coming straight at him, its headlamps blinding him. He leapt to his right just as the car whizzed by. He skidded across the wet asphalt, the grit tearing into his right side. He screeched in pain at the same moment he heard an almighty bang.

Lifting his head, Benedict saw that the car had smashed straight into a parked car only a few yards ahead beneath the glare of a streetlamp. The stationary car's alarm went off, so incredibly loud.

Hauling himself up, he half ran, half limped over.

Reaching the car, he saw the smashed windscreen and the driver with his head arched back against the headrest, a circle of blood on his forehead. It was Geoffrey McIntosh. The car door was locked.

'Can you hear me in there?' he shouted, trying to make himself heard over the incessant rhythm of the car alarm.

Slowly, McIntosh lifted his hand and unlocked the door.

'Are you OK?'

'I've been better,' came the croaked reply.

So, this was McIntosh's old Vauxhall Viva he'd mentioned. And the car he'd crashed into, a blue-coloured Dacia Sandero.

Doors were opening, residents coming out to see what the hell was happening. A man in a dressing gown switched off the car alarm with his key and promptly began crying.

McIntosh groaned.

'You were right about your car,' said Benedict, grimacing with pain. 'It is a shitty colour.'

DC Prowse finally arrived, hardly out of breath. 'Are you OK, sir?'

'This is Mr Geoffrey McIntosh, DC Prowse. Kindly read him his rights and arrest him.'

'A pleasure, boss.'

Holding his grazed arm and with his right sleeve and trouser leg flapping loose, Benedict limped back down the road to see DC Kelly and a couple of uniformed officers, one of them holding Pat Roberts up as she escorted her towards a squad car. They all stopped on seeing him, her chest heaving, her face filthy.

'He deserved it,' she said, the tears coursing down her smeared face.

'Who deserved it, Patricia?' He stepped slowly towards her.

She didn't answer, didn't elaborate.

'Is Maxine alright?' he asked.

'I shouldn't have hurt her.'

Benedict made his way back down Dog Shit Alley, his new suit ruined beyond repair. So much for the long-awaited date night and an early night. He checked his phone and, sure enough, he had numerous missed calls from Sonia and progressively irritated texts asking him where he was; had he forgotten?

He reached Hatherley Avenue on the other side. An ambulance had arrived, its blue light flashing. He caught Jessica's eye through the melange of paramedics, her arm around a sobbing Maxine. 'Is she OK?' he mouthed.

With her free arm, Jessica gave him the thumbs up.

He smiled to himself.

Chapter 55: Benedict

First thing on returning to work on Monday morning, Benedict had a meeting with the chief to update him on the progress of the case. DCI Lincoln listened with interest as Benedict related last night's events.

'Excellent work, Ben,' said the chief. 'You seem to have everything tied up – except why exactly did Pat Roberts and Geoffrey McIntosh kill her ex-husband and mother-in-law? I mean, husbands and wives kill each other all the time, it's fair enough. I know Mrs Lincoln has often looked at me in a peculiar way while holding a kitchen knife but after a gap of thirty years? I mean, that's some time to be holding onto a grudge. See what you can find out from her. Turn the screws, whatever it takes.'

'Yes, sir. Will do.'

DC Kelly looked delighted to see Benedict again. Benedict had seen dogs looking less excited. Jessica, sitting at her desk, smiled at him. 'What is it, DC Kelly? Have you won the lottery or something?'

'Geoffrey McIntosh's DNA matches, boss.'

'Really? Remind me again.'

'The DNA we found under Derek McIntosh's fingernail is a fifty per cent match for his own.'

'Are you sure of this?'

'Totally, boss.'

'And now we've caught them red-handed trying to kill Maxine Hunt,' said Jessica.

'As if I could overlook that not insignificant detail.'

Prowse walked into the office. 'Oh, good morning, boss. Just been on the phone to St Cuthbert's. Apparently, Maxine Hunt is doing fine. She's in shock, of course, and it's a shame she doesn't have anyone with her, like a family member or a friend or someone, but essentially, she's fine as can be expected, you know, considering…'

'Of course. So then–'

'Oh, and, sorry to interrupt, boss, but Mrs Roberts' solicitor is here.'

'Her own or duty?'

'Duty.'

'OK.'

Benedict took his mobile and stepped into an empty office. He rang Thomas McIntosh who answered on the first ring.

'Has something happened?' asked Mac, breathlessly.

'You could say that. Are you *a*, alone, and *b*, sitting down? And preferably, *c*, not too far away from a stiff drink, Mr McIntosh?'

It's not the easiest thing in the world to tell a man that you've arrested his mother and uncle for two murders. But, of course, he was expecting the former and took it comparatively well. Less so when Benedict informed him that his mother and uncle had also been arrested for attempted murder.

'My God. Who?'

'Maxine Hunt.'

The sharp intake of air, and the quick firing of questions, asking mainly if Maxine was alright, told of Thomas McIntosh's shock. He was also about to tell Mr McIntosh that his mother had been back in England since July, not last week as he believed, but Mac had enough to absorb for now. He'd find out soon enough; the truth always came out in the end. He was about to end the call when he remembered the main reason why he'd wanted to speak to Mac.

'Can I ask you a favour? Can you go visit Maxine in St Cuthbert's?'

'Oh yeah, of course I will.'

'I forgot to ask which ward but ask at reception.'

'Poor Maxine. It's kind of hard getting my head around the fact that my own mother, my own flesh and blood, almost killed such a lovely person as Maxine. It actually makes me feel physically sick, inspector.'

'I'm about to speak to your mother now.'

'Are you? Oh, good luck. Please… *don't* send her my love.'

Breezing back into the office, Benedict said, 'Kelly, what are you working on right this minute?'

'Right this minute, boss? Erm, I was–'

'Good. Go make me a coffee, there's a good man. And make it strong, I have a feeling I'm going to need it. Jessica, shall we?'

Jessica, rising from her chair, smiled. 'It'd be a pleasure, boss.'

Together, they made their way to interview room number one.

Chapter 56: Benedict

'Ms Roberts. Or perhaps we should call you Ms Mulholland, or, if you prefer, Mrs McIntosh. Any preferences?'

Pat Roberts shook her head. Mr Newman, her solicitor, looked across at her.

'I think we'll stick to Ms Roberts then. So, just to be clear for the record, we are questioning you with regard to two murders, the murder of your former mother-in-law and as an accessory in the murder of your ex-husband, plus the attempted murder of Maxine Hunt. Is there anything you wish to say at this point?'

'No comment.'

'No? That's fine, it's your prerogative, of course. So, I'll do the talking and you can listen but, if at any point, you wish to say anything, please don't hesitate to interrupt.' He stretched his arms, interlocking his fingers. 'Sorry, it was a long night. First of all, how are you feeling?'

She didn't respond.

'I do apologise for knocking you over. I really didn't mean to. Geoffrey McIntosh, you might be interested, is still in hospital. They should be letting him out today but they wanted to keep him overnight. He had concussion. We're very keen

328

to speak to him, get his side of the story. But first, you, Ms Roberts.

'When I talked to you last night, you said, and I quote: *He deserved it*. Who deserved it, Ms Roberts? And what did they do to deserve it?'

'No comment.'

'But, hey, we're jumping ahead of ourselves here. Let's step back a little. Now, you've told your children and us that you returned from Spain for good last week. But we all know that's not true, don't we? You actually returned from Cádiz on July fifth last year. I believe your reason for returning to England was to kill your former husband, Derek McIntosh. But first, I reckon you held back because you were worried – after all, if Mr McIntosh was killed straight after your return from Spain, naturally, you're going to be the prime suspect.

'Secondly, you had to see to the practical demands of life, i.e. earning some money. So, what did you do? You saw a job going at the hospital and you applied, but not under your name, but under the name Jean Mulholland. You had a CV and two excellent references which unfortunately no one could check because the firm you worked for as a part-time bookkeeper had gone bust. You know, it's amazing what one can buy now – that is if one's prepared to enter the murky world of the dark web. And I believe you did. What is the going rate these days for a completely new identity, a DBS and driving licence included? We will charge you for fraud, Ms Roberts, a contravention of the Forgery Act of 1981.

'So, you got the job at St Cuthbert's and behold! You meet Maxine Hunt whose grandmother is a resident at the same care home as your former husband, although I appreciate you probably didn't realise that at first. I don't know when you knew Derek was in a care home and Sunny Grove in particular.

329

But, whatever, first you needed time to befriend Maxine. She's lonely and trusting, and it was easy to manipulate her. You got her mobile number, as a friend, of course. I do like your fingernails, by the way, I love those little daisies, most decorative, aren't they? Did Maxine do them for you?

'And also at some point, you recruited your former brother-in-law, Geoffrey McIntosh. How did you persuade him to be part of your nefarious plans, Ms Roberts?

'Now, let's go back another step and ask, why did you decide to kill your ex-husband? Was it because he hit you? Was it because he denied you access to your children? That might have helped motivate you but the main reason, I believe, is because you *knew* that Derek McIntosh was the White Mouse Killer–'

'Yes, he was.'

Mr Newman almost jumped out of his chair. 'Hang on, Pat, don't say that.'

'But I just have…'

The silence stretched, she'd said it and in the ensuing silence, her words echoed, *Yes, he was. He was The White Mouse Killer.* She had said something that could never be unsaid. Yes, Benedict had known it, but to hear it coming out of her mouth, and said with such certainty, had shocked him. Pat Roberts' eyes glistened in the poor light. He could see her mind stretching back to those days, being married to a killer, living in the same confined space as him, the damage that must have done to her. No wonder she ran away. Two minutes of silence passed.

'So, you agree? Your husband murdered those women back in the winter of eighty-two, eighty-three. But what I don't understand, is that you and your mother and brother-in-law gave him an alibi; you both said–'

'I know what I said. She forced me into it.'

'She?'

'His cow of a mother. She suspected also but she forced me into providing him with the alibi. Living with her was hell. It was alright for Derek, disappearing to work all day. I worked as a dinner lady a few hours a week, but otherwise I was stuck with the venomous cow. The woman had poison in her veins.'

'The old witch?'

'Hm.'

'How did you know your husband was the killer, and not the man that a jury convicted, Neil Smith? After all, the evidence against Smith was compelling enough to convince the jury of his guilt. They sent him down in good faith. So, how did you know that it was your husband, Ms Roberts?'

Ms Roberts' eyes drifted away, gazing at a space above Benedict's head. 'Once the police released the information about the white mice. I used to buy him his mice from a pet shop near where I worked. Frozen mice. He fed them to his awful snake. He called it Daisy. Daisy the snake. Can you imagine? We always had a Tupperware box of dead mice in the freezer. It used to turn my stomach.'

'I see.'

'And he changed, almost overnight. Became paranoid, aggressive, just horrible. And the more horrible he became, the more his mother matched it. The words she called me when we were alone. That woman reduced me to tears, and I mean, every day, every bloody day.'

'Pat,' said Mr Newman. 'Think carefully before you answer. We can always demand a recess.'

Benedict waited for the solicitor to finish. 'That last girl he attacked—'

'She cut him somehow.'

'Yes, she did. How did you know? It wasn't in the news, the police didn't even know because she cut Derek, she didn't cut Neil Smith.'

'He came back the night she was attacked; he'd been out until quite late. I think he'd been drinking with Geoff and he had this cut across his chin, his jaw. He said he'd cut himself shaving and at first I didn't think much of it. But when I heard of the attack, just a mile or so from our flat, then I knew, I knew how he'd got it.'

'You were right. The girl he attacked caught him with her key.'

'They jailed the wrong man.'

'Yet, you never came forward?'

'I'd lied to the police.'

'Pat, please, we should—'

'Providing a false alibi is a serious offence. They would have sent me down for that—'

'They might not have.'

'I know but it was too much of a risk; I couldn't face it. And as the wife of a woman killer, I'd have been a target in prison. I was frightened, inspector. So, I sank my head in the sand and pretended it'd all gone away. Spain helped.'

'Did you not want to see your children? It must have been hard for you over there, so far away from them?'

'I thought they hated me. They never responded to any of my letters or cards or gifts I sent. I was too frightened to face their anger. It was easier to stay away.'

'So, you killed your husband to avenge the deaths of Ruth Jones and Elizabeth Blinkhorn, and the attack on the third victim, whom we're not naming here as she's still, thankfully, with us. But why now? That's what I kept asking myself. I mean, why not a year ago, ten years, twenty years? Why *now*?

This puzzled me for a while until we found out that it was *you* who wrote to Neil Smith in prison for all those years. You used the name of Jenny, your middle name, Jennifer. You see, the prison kept photocopies of all your correspondence and our handwriting whizzes identified the handwriting on those letters as the same as the address you wrote for us, plus your letters were postmarked Cádiz.' He watched for her expression. And yes, something flickered across her eyes, a realisation, perhaps, that she should have been more careful.

He continued, 'Neil Smith and you got to know each other well, didn't you? You became the best of pen pals. The tragedy is that had Mr Smith admitted his guilt, the parole board would have sanctioned his release years ago. But he maintained his innocence, understandably as he *was* innocent, so the board basically said, until you admit your guilt, we're not letting you out. His appeals fell on deaf ears because no new evidence had come to light, and you need new evidence to reopen a case. And then, sadly, he died in prison, and I believe that's what sent you over the edge. He died only two weeks before your return to London last year. Smith's death was the trigger, was it not, Pat?'

Ms Roberts said nothing but she didn't need to, her tears, now flowing, were enough. Mr Newman handed her a tissue. She thanked him.

Benedict thought of Neil Smith's sister in Winchester who went to her grave thinking her brother was a monster, his name never mentioned again. The repercussions of this were going to be huge.

He continued. 'We've got our financial forensics team to look into Jean Mulholland so I know that, once back in London, you lived in a rented flat in Kentish Town while working at St Cuthbert's until you moved out, or maybe you got evicted, that we don't know. But, whatever, you moved temporarily into the bed and breakfast place, the Montrose. You had your job, and you befriended the poor woman who'd take the blame for your deeds. But, I ask again, why did you wait so long once you were back in London – seven whole months before you struck?

'Tell me if I'm wrong, Ms Roberts. But I think you needed time to persuade Geoffrey.'

'Geoff has always loved me. Still does. I started writing to him from Spain as well. Told him I loved him too.'

'Did you? Do you?'

She shook her head. 'I said whatever I had to say to get him onside. Told him we had a moral duty to kill Derek to avenge those poor girls.'

'So, once you got him onside, as you say, you killed Marjorie McIntosh. You waited until you saw the receptionist from the Montrose B and B having a crafty cigarette out the back, then you slipped out and went to Holbrook House on Winslow Avenue. Returning back to the Montrose, your adrenaline pumping, you almost got hit by a car going too fast down Maynard Road, a Volkswagen Polo who, on swerving to miss you, hit a teenage girl returning from the pub.'

'How is she?'

'Kind of you to ask, Ms Roberts. She'll be OK. It'll take a while but yes, she'll live. You were, at least, good enough to stop and use the girl's phone to text for an ambulance, not wanting to use your voice but, in your panic, you did so without gloves. We found your fingerprints on her mobile, Ms Roberts.'

Her eyes widened upon hearing that.

'Then, five days later, Geoffrey killed his brother. Quite the Faustian pact you had there, one murder each. What did you say, Ms Roberts after you killed Marjorie? *I've kept my side of the bargain, now it's your turn.'*

She didn't answer. Mr Newman watched her from the corner of his eye.

'Not to worry. We've got Derek's DNA and it's a fifty per cent match for the DNA under his fingernail – in other words, a sibling, and, as we know, Derek McIntosh only has one sibling, his brother, Geoffrey.'

He paused to allow this fact to sink in. She let out a deep sigh.

'You tried to pin it on Maxine. You rang her from a public payphone, one on Camden High Street, and pretended to be your daughter. You told her to go to Mac's flat at the time, roughly, that Geoff killed Derek. It almost worked – first we found Maxine's fingerprints on the flat doorknob and secondly, we got a positive identification. You chose Maxine because you thought her an innocent. Problem is, she's too much of an innocent; that girl doesn't have a bad bone in her body. But at some point, presumably yesterday, Maxine worked it out, didn't she?

'Poor Maxine. You didn't want to kill Maxine but, once she'd worked it out, what choice did you have? You stole a colleague's scarf. I think it had some birds on it, blue tits, was it?'

'Swallows, boss.'

'Ah yes, thank you, DS Gardiner. Swallows. And you tried to entice Maxine to a quiet spot in order to kill her. You got Geoffrey to keep a lookout at the other end of the passageway. You communicated via a couple of burner phones, old pay-as-you-go flip-tops. Just in case, Geoffrey put up a police tape to prevent people from using the cut-through. Clever idea that. I didn't know a civilian could buy police tape.'

'You can get a roll of it for a fiver on Amazon, boss.'

'Ah, there you go. Thank you again, DS Gardiner.'

'Detective Inspector Paige,' said Ms Roberts. 'Mr Newman,' she added, turning briefly to meet her solicitor's eyes. 'I haven't the strength to go through a trial. I feel as if I've been running and looking over my shoulder for thirty long years. I can't run any more. I just can't do it. I want you to know I intend to plead guilty.'

'Now, wait a minute, Pat,' said Mr Newman, his hand outstretched.

Benedict cleared his throat. 'Pat, this is a conversation you must have with Mr Newman here but I'd strongly advise against it. And I'm sure he'd agree. Your husband killed two people and almost killed a third. You also killed two people and almost killed a third. If you plead guilty, you will be labelled as no better than Derek. If you stand trial, however, your defence will be able to argue that you were morally motivated. Of course, that won't count for trying to kill Ms Hunt but at least she survived. It might make a difference.'

'He's right, you know, Pat,' said Mr Newman. 'We need to talk about this in a proper setting, not here in front of these two.'

Benedict tried not to take umbrage at the solicitor's offhand remark. 'Of course, your great tragedy, Ms Roberts,' said Benedict, 'is that having been torn away from your children for the last thirty years, I fear you will be torn apart again – this time, for the rest of your life.'

'You think I haven't thought about that, inspector?' she shouted. 'You're right, it is a great tragedy, but not the greatest. The greatest tragedy of my life happened in the summer of 1981, the day Charles and Diana got married…'

*

29 July 1981

'Hey, you're a good shot. How did you manage that?'

'Beginner's luck, I guess.'

'Nah, you're an old hand. Bet you go around all the funfairs scooping up the prizes.'

'No, I do not! This is my first.'

'Well, you've got a good eye and a steady hand. Here you are, your prize. Admit it, you've always wanted a fat blue bear.'

'Ha-ha! He's huge! I can barely get my hands around him.'

'Barely, yes. He needs a name. What are you going to call him?'

'Charles, as in Prince Charles.'

'That's good, that's topical. Did you watch the wedding today?'

'Yes, I loved it. It was so romantic. Princess Di looked so pretty.'

'Our future king and queen. One day, I'm sure you'll marry your prince.'

'Yeah, right. As long as I'm treated like a princess.'

'Not asking much, are ya? How old are you?'

'Eighteen. You?'

'A bit older than you, love.'

'Tell me.'

'Nah, better not; it might shock you.'

'I'm not easily shocked.'

'Bet you are really. Hey, listen, I clock off in half an hour. How about you come back then, and I'll buy you a shandy or something.'

'Erm...'

'Go on, you know you want to.'

'What shall I do with Charles?'

'Charles? Bring him along. He can buy the first round. Go on, just a quick drink. What's the harm in that?'

'OK.'

'OK? You mean, you'll come back?'

'I'll come back.'

'I'm counting the seconds already. Hey, you haven't told me your name?'

'You didn't ask.'

'I'm asking now.'

'Patricia. But my friends call me Pat.'

'Can I call you Pat?'

'If you want.'

'Alright then, Pat. I'll see you in thirty minutes. Don't forget now.'

'I won't. What's your name?'

'Me? I'm Derek. Derek McIntosh.'

Epilogue

Four days later

Benedict

Following his interview with Patricia Roberts, DI Benedict Paige spent the rest of the day writing up his notes and catching up on paperwork. It was a job all his colleagues disliked but he didn't; he found the process, especially typing up following the conclusion of a successful investigation, therapeutic. It helped order his thoughts. Once DCI Lincoln had added his own comments, it went up the chain until it was part of the package delivered to the Criminal Prosecution Service. From there, it was out of his hands.

It was definitely Geoffrey McIntosh's DNA under his brother's fingernail; he had a small but visible scratch on his arm. Faced with such overwhelming evidence, Mr McIntosh spilt the beans.

Benedict had been to see Carol Russell, Derek McIntosh's final victim. He remembered how she'd felt a 'tiny' bit sorry for the man in the dock, Neil Smith, and how she'd felt guilty about that. He told her that her instinct had been right – the poor man had been innocent all along.

Returning to the office, he rang Neil Smith's niece in Winchester. She cried when he told her, saying how she wished her mother had lived to see this day, the day when her poor brother was exonerated.

Four thirty, a rare chance to leave work early. He deserved it. He thought of asking for a few days off, to give him a chance to recharge his batteries. He needed the rest. Sonia wasn't impressed when she saw his new suit in tatters.

But before he could make good his escape from work, DCI Lincoln called Benedict and Jessica into his office.

'First off,' said the DCI. 'Well done on putting the McIntosh murders to bed. Of course, it's not going to look good for our predecessors – sending down the wrong man. A miscarriage of justice is never a good look, is it? This is going to be hard on Neil Smith's family. A difficult road lies ahead. Anyway, you both did what was asked of you and thank you for that.'

Benedict and Jessica, exchanging a glance, smiled.

Maxine

Maxine Hunt lay on her sofa watching a daytime quiz show on TV. Charlie lay on her lap, purring loudly. Lovely boy! She'd been back from hospital for a couple of days, and tomorrow she was due to be interviewed by the police; they wanted to know *everything*, they said, about her relationship with Jean Mulholland, who, it turned out, wasn't called Jean Mulholland at all.

She kept thinking about Jean, about how nice she'd been to her, but it'd all been a lie, one massive lie, and Maxine hated her for that, that she'd been used, and made a fool of. Her

341

father always said she was too trusting, and he was right. She found herself in floods of tears at any given moment, shaking from head to toe with the memory of that night, knowing now that Jean had fully intended to kill her. The world was a puzzling and cruel place.

She hadn't been to see her grandmother for days now, and that worried her; Granny would be wondering what had happened to her. But Maxine couldn't face stepping out of her flat. She could barely move off the sofa. She knew it'd take a gargantuan effort to go to Sunny Grove. But she would; for the sake of her grandmother, she would.

Mac had come to see her in hospital which was nice. He didn't say much, but he stayed a long while and she found his company comforting. He promised he'd keep in touch.

The lunchtime news was starting when her door buzzer rang. Her heart lurched. Who could this be? She wasn't expecting a visitor, she never had visitors. Gently depositing Charlie on the floor, she padded over to the intercom. 'Hello?' she said, aware of the shakiness in her voice. 'W-who's that, please?'

'Hey, Maxine, it's me – Nigella. Can I come up?'

Nigella? From hospital? What did she want? 'Er, yes, sure.' She pushed the button, opening the door downstairs. Why was Nigella here? She'd never been before so why now; what did she want?

She left her door ajar and stepped back, bracing herself.

Nigella knocked but on seeing the door opened, stepped in, her arms behind her back. 'Maxine!'

'Hello.'

'Can I come in? I thought you could do with a bit of company. I've brought you these…' She held out a bouquet of flowers and a large box of chocolates.

Maxine looked at them, not quite understanding. 'Are they…

are they for *me*?'

'Of course they are, silly! Who else?'

'No one's ever…' She couldn't finish the sentence.

'Oh, Maxine, love, are you alright?'

'Yes, yes.' But she wasn't; her whole body shook again and, try as she might, she couldn't prevent the tears from coming.

'Oh, lovely,' said Nigella, putting the flowers and chocolates to one side. 'Come here…' Nigella approached Maxine, her arms open, and enveloped Maxine in a huge, warm hug.

It was all that Maxine had ever wanted.

Mac

Mac was sitting at his computer in his office trying, without much success, to complete the spreadsheet detailing last month's takings, costs and tax. But his mind kept drifting; he couldn't get his mother out of his mind. To think she and his uncle as well as his own father had been capable, depraved enough, to kill in cold blood and leave a mouse in their mouths. The memory of seeing his grandmother's body violated like that still rendered him speechless at times. He could live to be a thousand years old and he wouldn't understand it. Now, with both his mother and uncle in custody, the newspapers would get to hear about it. They'd have a field day. What then? What would become of him? He risked being reviled, attacked even. He'd have to sell the shop, change his name, up roots and move somewhere far away to escape it all. The future seemed bleak as hell.

His grandmother's portrait of the queen stared down at him. He stared vaguely at his Vienna paperweight. For so long, he'd missed his mother but he learned how to survive without her, then she came back like a firework into his life and, like a firework, burned out too quickly. And now he was alone again. It was proving to be a difficult pill to swallow.

He enjoyed seeing Maxine. Lying there in that hospital bed, she looked like a small girl, lost and a little confused. They talked a little but not much, Mac sensing she hadn't the strength. But he stayed a while and he hoped his visit had cheered her up a little. He'd go see her again now that he had her address. He wanted to help her to rebuild her life, to help her regain her confidence. He imagined it would take a while but that didn't matter. There wasn't any deadline, but instead, an end goal that he knew she'd reach one day.

He puffed out his cheeks. One of his formulas wasn't adding up in the way he'd expected. Maybe, a coffee and a pastry from the bakery would help focus the mind. He was checking his pockets for his wallet when he heard a knock on his office door and in came a small boy in a Chelsea shirt.

'Oh, Marcus!'

And sure enough, Caroline followed. His heart somersaulted on seeing her. 'Come in, come in.' He immediately felt better on seeing them but he had to rein it in; he remembered the good-looking bloke he saw Caroline with that day near the charity shop.

'We're not disturbing you, are we?' asked Caroline.

'No, not at all. Just boring stuff, you know?'

'Marcus has got something to ask you.'

'Oh?' He looked at the boy.

But Marcus, glancing at his mother, seemed to have lost his tongue. 'You ask, Mum.'

'But, Marcus, you wanted to do it.'

The boy turned red. 'You ask.'

Caroline smiled. 'We wondered, Mac, whether you'd like to

come to the Chelsea game with us?'

'Me?'

'We have a third ticket but my brother says he can't make it now.'

'Brother?'

'Oh, but wait, it's Saturday, your busiest day, I imagine. Oh, Marcus, we can't ask Mac, not on a Saturday.'

Mac thought of Eoin and Tony who had worked so hard recently, taking up the slack he'd caused. 'You know, you're right. I'm sorry. Saturday afternoons, especially, it gets mad here.' Turning to Marcus, he added, 'I'm sorry, mate. But thanks for thinking of me, eh?'

Caroline smiled again but it was different now. He sensed Marcus' disappointment too. 'No worries. Sorry, I should've thought. We'd better let you get on. Come on, Marcus.'

After they left, Mac sat down at his desk, his head in his hands, and groaned loudly. How could he allow himself to get close to someone now? Caroline would find out and she'd hate him, hate him for having a mother and a father – both murderers. An uncle too. Did it run in the family? Was he capable? No, of course not. But he knew he'd never outrun his family history; it'd always be there, part of him, haunting him wherever he went.

Mustering himself, he went through to the shop and found it empty of customers for once. Eoin was sweeping up and Tony polishing a mirror.

'That woman likes you, Mac,' said Tony. 'She can't keep away.'

'They were inviting me to the Chelsea game on Saturday.'

'Result!' said Eoin. 'You lucky bastard.'

'Yeah, but I can't go, not on a Saturday.'

'What?' they said in unison, their jaws dropping.

'Well, you know, it'll be too busy. All hands on deck and that.'

'You… actually… turned her down? You said… *no*?' said Tony.

'I can't let you guys down. Not again. It's not fair on you.'

'He's mad,' said Eoin to Tony. 'He's actually gone and lost it.'

'Fuck that,' said Tony. 'In that case, I'm not working Saturday.'

'You *what*?'

'Nor am I,' said Eoin. 'We're on strike.'

'Strike? You can't–'

'If you're working Saturday,' said Tony, 'then Eoin and me are not. So, you get your ass out of this shop, Mac, chase after that woman, and you fucking tell her that you'll be there.'

'But–'

'Go!' shouted Eoin. 'Now!'

Mac had never run so fast in his life, bumping into people, almost falling over a bin, zigzagging past a skateboarder. He glimpsed Marcus' blue shirt with the number ten on the back up ahead. His heart pounding, he pushed himself on, knocking over a shop sign on the pavement. He called her name. 'Caroline! Caroline, wait.'

They both turned on hearing his voice.

'Mac?'

He stopped in front of them, conscious he looked like a madman, out of breath and sweaty on this cold February morning. 'What time's kick-off?'

'Three o'clock.' Her eyes narrowed a little. 'Why?'

'Great. I can make it.'

'Yay! Brilliant!' Marcus positively skipped on the spot.

The huge smile that transformed her face melted his heart

346

on the spot. 'Y-you s-sure?' she asked.

'Yes. One hundred per cent.'

'What about your work?'

'Stuff work. This is more important.' And he realised in that moment that yes, it *was* more important than anything right now.

'That's wonderful,' said Caroline. 'Isn't it wonderful, Marcus?'

'Yeah!'

He took a step closer to her and looked into her kind, lovely eyes. 'You know, there's nowhere I'd rather be on Saturday than be with you, Caroline.'

'Oh, Mac.' She leaned up and gave him a peck on his cheek. 'The feeling's mutual.'

THE END

Novels by Joshua Black:

The DI Benedict Paige Novels

Book 1: And Then She Came Back
Book2: The Poison In His Veins
Book 3: Requiem for a Whistleblower
Book 4: The Forget-Me-Not Killer
Book 5: The Canal Boat Killer
Book 6: A Senseless Killing

To obtain Joshua's short story, *The Death of The Listening Man*, and join his Mailing List and be the first to know of future releases, etc, please go to:

rupertcolley.com/joshua-black/

Rathbone Publishing

Printed in Great Britain
by Amazon